CARA[illegible]

D0355601

From a[illegible] the Iron Curtain—the gypsies make their annual pilgrimage to Provence. The Duc de Croytor, distinguished folklorist and gastronome, is there, and so is Englishman Neil Bowman. But something is different about this year's gathering . . .

What is the secret the gypsies are so determined to hide? Bowman comes too close to it for safety, and before long he is running for his life.

From the dizzy ramparts of Les Baux to the vast limestone caverns beneath, from fiesta in Arles to the flat, salty plains of the Camargue, from the terror of the bull-ring to collisions at sea, the pace never falters.

Available in Fontana by the same author

Puppet on a Chain
H.M.S. Ulysses
The Guns of Navarone
Force Ten from Navarone
South by Java Head
The Last Frontier
Night Without End
Fear is the Key
The Golden Rendezvous
Ice Station Zebra
When Eight Bells Toll
Where Eagles Dare
The Dark Crusader
The Satan Bug

ALISTAIR MACLEAN

Caravan to Vaccarès

FONTANA / Collins

First published by Wm. Collins 1970
First issued in Fontana Books 1972
Seventh Impression July 1973

© Alistair MacLean, 1970

Printed in Great Britain
Collins Clear-Type Press
London and Glasgow

To Jean-André and Emanuela Charial

CONDITIONS OF SALE:
This book is sold subject to the condition that it shall not, by way of trade or otherwise, be lent, re-sold, hired out or otherwise circulated without the publisher's prior consent in any form of binding or cover other than that in which it is published and without a similar condition including this condition being imposed on the subsequent purchaser

PROLOGUE

They had come a long way, those gypsies encamped for their evening meal on the dusty greensward by the winding mountain road in Provence. From Transylvania they had come, from the *pustas* of Hungary, from the High Tatra of Czechoslovakia, from the Iron Gate, even from as far away as the gleaming Rumanian beaches washed by the waters of the Black Sea. A long journey, hot and stifling and endlessly, monotonously repetitive across the already baking plains of Central Europe or slow and difficult and exasperating and occasionally dangerous in the traversing of the great ranges of mountains that had lain in their way. Above all, one would have thought, even for those nomadic travellers *par excellence*, a tiring journey.

No traces of any such tiredness could be seen in the faces of the gypsies, men, women and children all dressed in their traditional finery, who sat or squatted in a rough semi-circle round two glowing coke braziers, listening in quietly absorbed melancholy to the hauntingly soft and nostalgic *tsigane* music of the Hungarian steppes. For this apparent lack of any trace of exhaustion there could have been a number of reasons: as the very large, modern, immaculately finished and luxuriously equipped caravans indicated, the gypsies of today travel in a degree of comfort unknown to their forebears who roamed Europe in the horse-drawn, garishly-painted and fiendishly uncomfortable covered-wagon caravans of yesteryear: they were looking forward that night to the certainty of replenishing coffers sadly depleted by their long haul across Europe—in anticipation of this they had already changed from their customary drab travelling clothes: only three days remained until the end of their pilgrimage, for pilgrimage this was: or perhaps they just had remarkable powers of recuperation. Whatever the reason, their faces reflected no signs of weariness, only gentle pleasure and bitter-sweet memories of faraway homes and days gone by.

But one man there was among them whose expression—or lack of it—would have indicated to even the most obtusely unobservant that, for the moment at least, his lack of musical appreciation was total and his thoughts and intentions strictly confined to the present. His name was Czerda and he was sitting on the top of the steps of his caravan, apart from and behind the others, a half-seen shadow on the edge of darkness. Leader of the gypsies and hailing from some unpronounceable village in the delta of the Danube, Czerda was of middle years, lean, tall and powerfully built, with about him that curiously relaxed but instantly identifiable stillness of one who can immediately transform apparent inertia into explosive action. He was dressed all in black and had black hair, black eyes, black moustache and the face of a hawk. One hand, resting limply on his knee, held a long thin smouldering black cigar, the smoke wisping up to his eyes, but Czerda did not seem to notice or care.

His eyes were never still. Occasionally he glanced at his fellow-gypsies, but only briefly, casually, dismissively. Now and again he looked at the range of the Alpilles, their gaunt forbidding limestone crags sleeping palely in the brilliant moonlight under a star-dusted sky, but for the most part he glanced alternately left and right along the line of parked caravans. Then his eyes stopped roving, although no expression came to replace the habitual stillness of that face. Without haste he rose, descended the steps, ground his cigar into the earth and walked soundlessly to the end of the row of caravans.

The man who stood waiting in the shadows was a youthful scaled-down replica of Czerda himself. Not quite so broad, not quite so tall, his swarthily aquiline features were cast in a mould so unmistakably similar to that of the older man that it was unthinkable that he could be anything other than his son. Czerda, clearly a man not much given to superfluous motion or speech, raised a questioning eyebrow: his son nodded, led him out on to the dusty roadway, pointed and made a downward slicing, chopping motion with his hand.

From where they stood and less than fifty yards away soared an almost vertical massive outcrop of white limestone rock, but an outcrop which has no parallel anywhere in the world, for its base was honeycombed with enormous rectangular entrances, cut by the hand of man—no feat of nature could possibly have reproduced the sharply geometrical linearity of those apertures in the cliff face: one of those entrances was quite huge, being at least forty feet in height and no less in width.

Czerda nodded, just once, turned and looked down the road to his right. A vague shape detached itself from shadow and lifted an arm. Czerda returned the salute and pointed towards the limestone bluff. There was no acknowledgment and clearly none was necessary, for the man at once disappeared, apparently into the rock face. Czerda turned to his left, located yet another man in the shadows, made a similar gesture, accepted a torch handed him by his son and began to walk quickly and quietly towards the giant entrance in the cliff face. As they went, moonlight glinted on the knives both men held in their hands, very slender knives, long-bladed and curved slightly at the ends. As they passed through the entrance of the cave they could still distinctly hear the violinists change both mood and tempo and break into the lilting cadences of a gypsy dance.

Just beyond the entrance the interior widened out and heightened until it was like the inside of a great cathedral or a giant tomb of antiquity. Both Czerda and his son switched on their torches, the powerful beams of which failed to penetrate the farthest reaches of this awesome man-made cave, and man-made it unquestionably was, for clearly visible on the towering side-walls were the thousands of vertical and horizontal scores where long-dead generations of Provençals had sawn away huge blocks of the limestone for building purposes.

The floor of this entrance cavern—for, vast though it was, it was no more than that—was pitted with rectangular holes, some of them large enough to hold a motor car, others wide and deep enough to bury a house. Scattered in a few odd corners were mounds of rounded limestone rock but, for the most part, the floor looked as if it had been swept only that day. To the right and left of the entrance cavern led off two other huge openings, the darkness lying beyond them total, impenetrable. A doom-laden place, implacable in its hostility, foreboding, menacing, redolent of death. But Czerda and his son seemed unaware of any of this, quite unmoved: they turned and walked confidently towards the entrance to the right-hand chamber.

Deep inside the heart of this vast warren, a slight figure, a barely distinguishable blur in the pale wash of moonlight filtering down through a crack in the cavern roof, stood with his back to a limestone wall, fingers splayed and pressed hard against the clammy rock behind him in the classically frozen position of the fugitive at bay. A youth, no more than twenty, he was clad in dark trousers and a white shirt. Around his neck he wore a silver crucifix on a slender silver chain. The crucifix rose and fell, rose and fell with metronomic regularity as the air rasped in and out of his throat and his heaving lungs tried vainly to satisfy the demands of a body that couldn't obtain oxygen quickly enough. White teeth showed in what could have been a smile but was no smile, although frozen lips drawn back in the rictus of terror can look like one. The nostrils were distended, the dark eyes wide and staring, his face as masked in sweat as if it had been smeared with glycerine. It was the face of a boy with two demons riding on his shoulders: almost at the end of his physical resources, the knowledge of the inevitability of death had triggered off the unreasoning and irrecoverable panic that pushes a man over the edge of the abyss into the mindless depths of madness.

Momentarily, the fugitive's breathing stopped entirely as he caught sight of two dancing pools of light on the floor of the cavern. The wavering beams, steadily strengthening, came from the left-hand entrance. For a moment the young gypsy stood as one petrified, but if reason had deserted him the instinct for survival was still operating independently, for with a harsh sobbing sound he pushed himself off the wall and ran towards the right-hand entrance to the cavern, canvas-soled shoes silent on the rocky floor. He rounded the corner, then slowed down suddenly, reached out groping hands in front of him as he waited for his eyes to become accustomed to the deeper darkness, then moved on slowly into the next cavern, his painfully gasping breathing echoing back in eerie whispers from the unseen walls around him.

Czerda and his son, their torch beams, as they advanced, ceaselessly probing through an arc of 180°, strode confidently through the archway linking the entrance cavern to the one just vacated by the fugitive. At a gesture from Czerda, both men stopped and deliberately searched out the furthermost recesses of the cavern: it was quite empty. Czerda nodded, almost as if in satisfaction, and gave a peculiar, low-pitched two-tone whistle.

In his hiding-place, which was no hiding-place at all, the gypsy appeared to shrink. His terrified eyes stared in the direction of his imagined source of the whistle. Almost at once, he heard an identical whistle, but one which emanated from another part of this subterranean labyrinth. Automatically, his eyes lined up to search out the source of this fresh menace, then he twisted his head to the right as he heard a third whistle, exactly the same in timbre and volume as the previous two. His staring eyes tried desperately to locate this third danger, but there was nothing to be seen but the all-encompassing darkness and no sound at all to break the brooding silence except the far-off keening of the gypsy violins, a far-off reminder of another safer and saner world that served only to intensify the sinister stillness inside that vaulted place of horror.

For a few moments he stood, fear-crazed now and wholly irresolute, then, within the space of as many seconds, the three double whistles came again, but this time they were all closer, much closer, and when he again saw the faint wash of light emanating from the two torches he had seen earlier, he turned and ran blindly in the only direction which seemed to afford a momentary respite, careless or oblivious of the fact that he might run into a limestone wall at any moment. Reason should have told him this but he was now bereft of reason: it was but instinct again, the age-old one that told him that a man does not die before he has to.

He had taken no more than half-a-dozen steps when a powerful torch snapped on less than ten yards ahead of him. The fugitive stopped abruptly, staggering but not falling, lowered the forearm that he had flung up in automatic reflex to protect his eyes and stared for the first time, with narrowed eyes, in a barely conscious attempt to identify the extent and immediacy of this fresh danger confronting him, but all his shrinking eyes could make out was the vaguely discernible bulk of the shapeless figure of the man behind the torch. Then slowly, very slowly, the man's other hand came forward until it was brightly lit by the beam of the torch: the hand held an evilly curved knife that glittered brilliantly in the torch-light. Knife and torch began to move slowly forward.

The fugitive whirled around, took two steps, then stopped as abruptly as he had before. Two other torches, knives again showing in their powerful beams, were scarcely further away than the man behind him. What was so terrifying, so nerve-destroying, about the measured advances of all three was the unhurriedly remorseless certainty.

'Come now, Alexandre,' Czerda said pleasantly. 'We're all old friends, aren't we? Don't you want to see us any more?'

Alexandre sobbed and flung himself to his right in the direction where the light from the three torches showed the entrance to yet another cavern. Panting as a deer does just before the hounds drag it down, he half-stumbled, half-ran through the entrance. None of his three pursuers made any attempt to cut him off or run after him: they merely followed, again walking with that same purposeful lack of haste.

Inside this third cavern, Alexandre stopped and looked wildly around. A small cavern this time, small enough to let him see that all the walls here were solid, hostilely and uncompromisingly solid, without as much as the tiniest aperture to offer any hope of further flight. The only exit was by the way he had come in and this was the end of the road.

Then the realization gradually penetrated his mind, numbed though it was, that there was something different about this particular cavern. His pursuers with their torches were not yet in sight, so how was it that he could see so well? Not clearly, there wasn't enough light for that, but well enough in contrast with the Stygian darkness of the cavern he had just left behind.

Almost at his feet there lay a huge pile of rock and rubble, clearly the result of some massive fall or cave-in in the past. Instinctively, Alexandre glanced upwards. The rubble, piled at an angle of about forty degrees from the horizontal, didn't seem to have a summit. It just stretched on and on and Alexandre's gradually lifting eyes could see that it stretched upwards for a vertical height of at least sixty feet before it ended. And where it ended it had to end—for there, at the very top, was a circular patch of star-studded sky. That was where the light came from, he dimly realized, from some roof collapse of long ago.

His body was already beyond exhaustion but now some primeval drive had taken over and the body was no longer its own master, in much the same way as his mind had lost control of it. Without a glance to see whether his pursuers were in sight or not, Alexandre flung himself at the great rock pile and began to claw his way upwards.

The rock pile was unstable and dangerous to a degree, a secure footing impossible to obtain, he slid a foot backwards for every eighteen inches of upward progress made, but for all that the momentum induced by his frenzied desperation overcame the laws of gravity and friction co-efficients and he made steady if erratic progress up that impossibly crumbling slope that no man in his normal senses would ever have attempted.

About one third of the way up, conscious of an increase in the amount of illumination beneath him, he paused briefly and looked downwards. There were three men standing at the foot of the rubble now, lit torches still in their hands. They were gazing up towards him but making no attempt to follow. Oddly enough, their torch beams were not pointing up towards him but were directed towards the floor at their feet. Even had his confused mind been able to register this oddity Alexandre had no time to consider it, for he felt his precarious hand- and foot-holds giving way beneath him and started scrabbling his way upwards again.

His knees ached abominably, his shins were flayed, his fingernails broken, the palms of his bleeding hands open almost to the bone. But still Alexandre climbed on.

About two-thirds of the way up he was forced to pause a second time not because he chose to but because, for the moment, his bleeding limbs and spent muscles could take him no farther. He glanced downwards and the three men at the foot of the rockfall were as they had been before, immobile, their torches still pointed at their feet, all three gazing upwards. There was an intensity in their stillness, a curious aura of expectancy. Vaguely, somewhere deep in the deep befogged recesses of what little was left of his mind, Alexandre wondered why. He turned his head and looked up to the starry sky above and then he understood.

A man, highlit under the bright moon, was seated on the rim of the rockfall. His face was partly in shadow but Alexandre had little difficulty in making out the bushy moustache, the gleam of white teeth. He looked as if he was smiling. Maybe he was smiling. The knife in his left hand was as easily visible as the torch in his right. The man pressed the button of his torch as he came sliding over the rim.

Alexandre's face showed no reaction for he had nothing left to react with. For a few moments he remained immobile as the man with the moustache came sliding down towards him, triggering off a small avalanche of boulders as he came, then tried to fling himself despairingly to one side to avoid the impact and the knife of his pursuer, but because of his frantic haste and the fact that he was now being severely buffeted about the body by the bounding limestone rocks he lost his footing and began to slide helplessly downwards, rolling over and over quite uncontrollably with no hope in the world of stopping himself. So treacherously loose had the surface of the rockfall become that even his pursuer was able to preserve his balance only by taking huge bounding leaps down the rockfall and the volume of the torrent of stones now crashing on to the floor of the cavern was indicated clearly enough by the alacrity with which the three men at the foot of the rockfall moved back at least ten paces. As they did so they were joined by a fourth man who had just come through the cavern entrance, then immediately afterwards by Alexandre's pursuer, whose great leaping steps had taken him past the still tumbling boy.

Alexandre landed heavily on the floor, arms instinctively clutched over his head to protect it from the cascading stones that continued to strike his body for a period of several seconds until the rain of rocks ceased. For as long again he remained dazed, uncomprehending, then he propped himself to his hands and knees before rising shakily to his feet. He looked at the semi-circle of five men, each with a knife in hand, closing in inexorably on him and now his mind was no longer uncomprehending. But he no longer had the look of a hunted animal, for he had already been through all the terrors of death and he was now beyond that. Now, unafraid, for there was nothing left of which to be afraid, he could look into the face of death. He stood there quietly and waited for it to come to him.

Czerda stooped, laid a final limestone rock on top of the mound that had now grown at the foot of the rockfall, straightened, looked at the handiwork of his men and himself, nodded in apparent satisfaction and gestured towards the others to leave the cavern. They left. Czerda took one last look at the oblong mound of stones, nodded again, and followed.

Once outside the entrance cave and into what now appeared to be the intolerably harsh glare of bright moonlight that bathed the Alpilles, Czerda beckoned to his son who slowed his pace and let the others precede them.

Czerda asked quietly: 'Any more would-be informers amongst us, do you think, Ferenc?'

'I don't know.' Ferenc shrugged his doubt. 'Josef and Pauli I do not trust. But who can be sure?'

'But you will watch them, Ferenc, won't you? As you watched poor Alexandre.' Czerda crossed himself. 'God rest his soul.'

'I will watch them, Father.' Ferenc dismissed the answer to the question as being too obvious for further elaboration. 'We'll be at the hotel inside the hour. Do you think we shall make much money tonight?'

'Who cares what pennies the idle and foolish rich throw our way? Our paymaster is not in that damned hotel, but that damned hotel we have visited for a generation and must keep on visiting.' Czerda sighed heavily. 'Appearances are all, Ferenc, my son, appearances are all. That you must never forget.'

'Yes, Father,' Ferenc said dutifully. He hastily stuck his knife out of sight.

Unobtrusively, unseen, the five gypsies made their way back to the encampment and sat down, at a discreet distance from one another, just outside the perimeter of an audience still lost in the sadly-happy rapture of nostalgia as the volume and pace of the violin music mounted to a crescendo. The braziers were burning low now, a faint red glow barely visible in the bright moonlight. Then, abruptly and with a splendid flourish, the music ceased, the violinists bowed low and the audience called out their appreciation and clapped enthusiastically, none more so than Czerda who buffeted his palms together as if he had just heard Hiefetz giving of his best in the Carnegie Hall. But even as he clapped, his eyes wandered, away from the violinists, away from the audience and the gypsy camp, until he was gazing again at the honeycombed face of the limestone cliffs where a cave had so lately become a tomb.

CHAPTER ONE

'The cliff battlements of Les Baux, cleft and rent as by a giant axe, and the shattered, gaunt and terrible remnants of the ancient fortress itself are the most awesomely desolate of all ruins in Europe.' Or so the local guide-book said. It went on: 'Centuries after its death Les Baux is still an open tomb, a dreadful and dreadfully fitting memorial to a medieval city that lived most violently and perished in agony: to look upon Les Baux is to look upon the face of death imperishably carved in stone.'

Well, it was pitching it a bit high, perhaps, guide-books do tend towards the hyperbolic, but the average uncertified reader of the guide would take the point and turn no somersaults if some wealthy uncle had left him the place in his will. It was indisputably the most inhospitable, barren and altogether uninviting collection of fractured and misshapen masonry in western Europe, a total and awesome destruction that was the work of seventeenth-century demolition squads who had taken a month and heaven alone knew how many tons of gunpowder to reduce Les Baux to its present state of utter devastation: one would have been equally prepared to believe that the same effect had been achieved in a couple of seconds that afternoon with the aid of an atom bomb: the annihilation of the old fortress was as total as that. But people still lived up there, lived and worked and died.

At the foot of the western vertical cliff face of Les Baux lay a very fittingly complementary feature of the landscape which was sombrely and justifiably called the Valley of Hell, partly because of the barren desolation of its setting between the battlements of Les Baux to the east and a spur of the Alpilles to the west, partly because in summer time this deeply-sunk gorge, which opened only to the south, could become almost unbearably hot.

But there was one area, right at the northern extremity of this grim cul-de-sac, that was in complete and unbelievably startling contrast to the bleakly forlorn wastes that surrounded it, a green and lovely and luxurious oasis that, in the context, could have been taken straight out of the pages of a fairy-tale book.

It was, in brief, an hotel, an hotel with gratefully tree-lined precincts, exotically designed gardens and a gleamingly blue swimming pool. The gardens lay to the south, the immaculate pool was in the centre, beyond that a large tree-shaded patio and finally the hotel itself with its architectural ancestry apparently stemming from a cross between a Trappist monastery and a Spanish *hacienda*. It was, in point of fact, one of the best and—almost by definition—one of the most exclusive and expensive hotel-restaurants in Southern Europe: the Hotel Baumanière.

To the right of the patio, approached by a flight of steps, was a very large forecourt and leading off from this to the south, through an archway in a magnificently sculptured hedge, was a large and rectangular parking area, all the parking places being more than adequately shaded from the hot summer sun by closely interwoven wicker-work roofing.

The patio was discreetly illuminated by all but invisible lights hung in the two large trees which dominated most of the area, overhanging the fifteen tables scattered in expensively sophisticated separation across the stone flags. Even the tables were something to behold. The cutlery gleamed. The crockery shone. The crystal glittered. And one did not have to be told that the food was superb, that the Châteauneuf had ambrosia whacked to the wide: the absorbed silence that had fallen upon the entranced diners could be matched only by the reverential hush one finds in the great cathedrals of the world. But even in this gastronomical paradise there existed a discordant note.

This discordant note weighed about 220 pounds and he talked all the time, whether his mouth was full or not. Clearly, he was distracting all the other guests, he'd have distracted them even if they had been falling en masse down the north face of the Eiger. To begin with, his voice was uncommonly loud, but not in the artificial fashion of the *nouveau riche* or the more impoverished members of the lesser aristocracy who feel it incumbent upon them to call to the attention of the lesser orders the existence of another and superior strain of *Homo sapiens*. Here was the genuine article: he didn't give a damn whether people heard him or not. He was a big man, tall, broad and heavily built: the buttons anchoring the straining folds of his double-breasted dinner-jacket must have been sewn on with piano wire. He had black hair, a black moustache, a neatly-trimmed goatee beard and a black-beribboned monocle through which he was peering closely at the large menu card in his hand. His table companion was a girl in her mid-twenties, clad in a blue mini-dress and quite extravagantly beautiful in a rather languorous fashion. At that moment she was gazing in mild astonishment at her bearded escort who was clapping his hands imperiously, an action which resulted in the almost instantaneous appearance of a dark-jacketed restaurant manager, a white-tied head waiter and a black-tied assistant waiter.

'Encore,' said the man with the beard. In retrospect, his gesture of summoning the waiting staff seemed quite superfluous: they could have heard him in the kitchen without any trouble.

'Of course.' The restaurant manager bowed. 'Another entrecôte for the Duc de Croytor. Immediately.' The head waiter and his assistant bowed in unison, turned and broke into a distreet trot while still less than twelve feet distant. The blonde girl stared at the Duc de Croytor with a bemused expression on her face.

'But, Monsieur le Duc—'

'Charles to you,' the Duc de Croytor interrupted firmly. 'Titles do not impress me even although hereabouts I'm referred to as Le Grand Duc, no doubt because of my impressive girth, my impressive appetite and my vice-regal manner of dealing with the lower orders. But Charles to you, Lila, my dear.'

The girl, clearly embarrassed, said something in a low voice which apparently her companion couldn't hear for he lost no time in letting his ducal impatience show through.

'Speak up, speak up! Bit deaf in this ear, you know.'

She spoke up. 'I mean—you've just *had* an *enormous* entrecôte steak.'

'One never knows when the years of famine will strike,' Le Grand Duc said gravely. 'Think of Egypt. Ah!'

An impressively escorted head waiter placed a huge steak before him with all the ritual solemnity of the presentation of crown jewels except that, quite clearly, both the waiter and Le Grand Duc obviously regarded the entrecôte as having the edge on such empty baubles any time. An assistant waiter set down a large ashet of creamed potatoes and another of vegetables while yet another waiter reverently placed an ice bucket containing two bottles of rosé on a serving table close by.

'Bread for Monsieur le Duc?' the restaurant manager enquired.

'You know very well I'm on a diet.' He spoke as if he meant it, too, then, clearly as an after-thought, turned to the blonde girl. 'Perhaps Mademoiselle Delafont—'

'I couldn't possibly.' As the waiters left she gazed in fascination at his plate. 'In twenty seconds—'

'They know my little ways,' Le Grand Duc mumbled. It is difficult to speak clearly when one's mouth is full of entrecôte steak.

'And I don't.' Lila Delafont looked at him speculatively. 'I don't know, for instance, why you should invite me—'

'Apart from the fact that no one ever denies Le Grand Duc anything, four reasons.' When you're a Duke you can interrupt without apology. He drained about half a pint of wine and his enunciation improved noticeably. 'As I say, one never knows when the years of famine will strike.' He eyed her appreciatively so that she shouldn't miss his point. 'I knew—I know—your father, the Count Delafont well—my credentials are impeccable. You are the most beautiful girl in sight. And you are alone.'

Lila, clearly embarrassed, lowered her voice, but it was no good. By this time the other diners clearly regarded it as *lèse-majesté* to indulge in any conversation themselves while the Duc de Croytor was holding the floor, and the silence was pretty impressive.

'I'm not alone. Nor the most beautiful girl in sight. Neither.' She smiled apologetically, as if afraid she had been overheard, and nodded in the direction of a near-by table. 'Not while my friend Cecile Dubois is here.'

'The girl you were with earlier this evening?'

'Yes.'

'My ancestors and I have always preferred blondes.' His tone left little room for doubt that brunettes were for the plebs only. Reluctantly, he laid down his knife and fork and peered sideways. 'Passable, passable, I must say.' He lowered his voice to a conspiratorial whisper that couldn't have been heard more than twenty feet away. 'Your friend, you say. Then who's that dissipated-looking layabout with her?'

Seated at a table about ten feet away and clearly well within earshot of Le Grand Duc, a man removed his horn-rimmed glasses and folded them with an air of finality: he was conservatively and expensively dressed in grey gaberdine, was tall, broad-shouldered, black-haired and just escaped being handsome because of the slightly battered irregularity of his deeply-tanned face. The girl opposite him, tall, dark, smiling and with amusement in her green eyes, put a restraining hand on his wrist.

'Please, Mr Bowman. It's not worth it, is it? Really?'

Bowman looked into the smiling face and subsided. 'I am strongly tempted, Miss Dubois, strongly tempted.' He reached for his wine but his hand stopped half-way. He heard Lila's voice, disapproving, defensive.

'He looks more like a heavy-weight boxer to me.'

Bowman smiled at Cecile Dubois and raised his glass.

'Indeed.' Le Grand Duc quaffed another half goblet of rosé. 'One about twenty years past his prime.'

Wine spilled on the table as Bowman set down his glass with a force that should have shattered the delicate crystal. He rose abruptly to his feet, only to find that Cecile, in addition to all her other obviously fine points, was possessed of a set of excellent reflexes. She was on her feet as quickly as he was, had insinuated herself between Bowman and Le Grand Duc's table, took his arm and urged him gently but firmly in the direction of the swimming pool: they looked for all the world like a couple who had just finished dinner and decided to go for a stroll for the digestion's sake. Bowman, though with obvious reluctance, went along with this. He had about him the air of a man for whom the creation of a disturbance with Le Grand Duc would have been a positive pleasure but who drew the line at having street brawls with young ladies.

'I'm sorry.' She squeezed his arm. 'But Lila *is* my friend. I didn't want her embarrased.'

'Ha! You didn't want *her* embarrassed. Doesn't matter, I suppose, how embarrassed *I* am?'

'Oh, come on. Just sticks and stones, you know. You really don't look the least little bit dissipated to me.' Bowman stared at her suspiciously, but there was no malicious amusement in her eyes: she was pursing her lips in mock but friendly seriousness. 'Mind you, I can see that not everyone would like to be called a layabout. By the way, what *do* you do? Just in case I have to defend you to the Duke—verbally, that is.'

'Hell with the Duke.'

'That's not an answer to my question.'

'And a very good question it is too.' Bowman paused reflectively, took off his glasses and polished them. 'Fact is, I don't do anything.'

They were now at the farther end of the pool. Cecile took her hand away from his arm and looked at him without any marked enthusiasm.

'Do you mean to tell me, Mr Bowman—'

'Call me Neil. All my friends do.'

'You make friends very easily, don't you?' she asked with inconsequential illogic.

'I'm like that,' Bowman said simply.

She wasn't listening or, if she was, she ignored him. 'Do you mean to tell me you never work? You never do anything?'

'Never.'

'You've no job? You've been trained for nothing? You can't do *anything*?'

'Why should I spin and toil?' Bowman said reasonably. 'My old man's made millions. Still making them, come to that. Every other generation should take it easy, don't you think—a sort of re-charging of the family batteries. Besides, I don't *need* a job. Far be it from me,' he finished piously, 'to deprive some poor fellow who really needs it.'

'Of all the specious arguments . . . How could I have misjudged a man like that?'

'People are always misjudging me,' Bowman said sadly.

'Not you. The Duke. His perception.' She shook her head, but in a way that looked curiously more like an exasperated affection than cold condemnation. 'You really are an idle layabout, Mr Bowman.'

'Neil.'

'Oh, you're incorrigible.' For the first time, irritation,

'And envious.' Bowman took her arm as they approached the patio again and because he wasn't smiling she made no attempt to remove it. 'Envious of you. Your spirit, I mean. Your year-long economy and thrift. For you two English girls to be able to struggle by here at £200 a week each on your typists' salaries or whatever—'

'Lila Delafont and I are down here to gather material for a book.' She tried to be stiff but it didn't become her.

'On what?' Bowman asked politely. 'Provençal cookery? Publishers don't pay that kind of speculative advance money. So who picks up the tab? Unesco? The British Council?' Bowman peered at her closely through his horn-rimmed glasses but clearly she wasn't the lip-biting kind. 'Let's all pay a silent truce to good old Daddy, shall we? A truce, my dear. This is too good to spoil. Beautiful night, beautiful food, beautiful girl.' Bowman adjusted his spectacles and surveyed the patio. 'Your girl-friend's not bad either. Who's the slim Jim with her?'

She didn't answer at once, probably because she was momentarily hypnotized by the spectacle of Le Grand Duc holding an enormous balloon glass of rosé in one hand while with the other he directed the activities of a waiter who appeared to be transferring the contents of the dessert trolley on to the plate before him. Lila Delafont's mouth had fallen slightly open.

'I don't know. He says he's a friend of her father.' She looked away with some difficulty, saw and beckoned the passing restaurant manager. 'Who's the gentleman with my friend?'

'The Duc de Croytor, madam. A very famous wine-grower.'

'A very famous wine-drinker, more like.' Bowman ignored Cecile's disapproving look. 'Does he come here often?'

'For the past three years at this time.'

'The food is especially good at this time?'

'The food, sir, is superb here at any time.' The Baumanière's manager wasn't amused. 'Monsieur le Duc comes for the annual gypsy festival at Saintes-Maries.'

Bowman peered at the Duc de Croytor again. He was spooning down his dessert with a relish matched only by his speed of operation.

'You can see why he has to have an ice-bucket,' Bowman observed. 'To cool down his cutlery. Don't see any signs of gypsy blood there.'

'Monsieur le Duc is one of the foremost folklorists in Europe,' the manager said severely, adding with a suave side-swipe: 'The study of ancient customs, Mr Bowman. For centuries, now, the gypsies have come from all over Europe, at the end of May, to worship and venerate the relics of Sara, their patron saint. Monsieur le Duc is writing a book about it.'

'This place,' Bowman said, 'is hotching with the most unlikely authors you ever saw.'

'I do not understand, sir.'

'I understand all right.' The green eyes, Bowman observed, could also be very cool. 'There's no need—what on earth is that?'

The at first faint then gradually swelling sound of many engines in low gear sounded like a tank regiment on the move. They glanced down towards the forecourt as the first of many gypsy caravans came grinding up the steeply winding slope towards the hotel. Once in the forecourt the leading caravans began arranging themselves in neat rows round the perimeter while others passed through the archway in the hedge towards the parking lot beyond. The racket, and the stench of diesel and petrol fumes, while not exactly indescribable or unsupportable, were in marked contrast to the peaceful luxury of the hotel and disconcerting to a degree, this borne out by the fact that Le Grand Duc had momentarily stopped eating. Bowman looked at the restaurant manager, who was gazing up at the stars and obviously communing with himself.

'Monsieur le Duc's raw material?' Bowman asked.

'Indeed, sir.'

'And now? Entertainment? Gypsy violin music? Street roulette? Shooting galleries? Candy stalls? Palm reading?'

'I'm afraid so, sir.'

'My God!'

Cecile said distinctly: 'Snob!'

'I fear, madam,' the restaurant manager said distantly, 'that my sympathies lie with Mr Bowman. But it is an ancient custom and we have no wish to offend either the gypsies or the local people.' He looked down at the forecourt again and frowned. 'Excuse me, please.'

He hurried down the steps and made his way across the forecourt to where a group of gypsies appeared to be arguing heatedly. The main protagonists appeared to be a powerfully built hawk-faced gypsy in his middle forties and a clearly distraught and very voluble gypsy woman of the same age who seemed to be very close to tears.

'Coming?' Bowman asked Cecile.

'What? Down there?'

'Snob!'

'But you said—'

'Idle layabout I may be but I'm a profound student of human nature.'

'You mean you're nosey?'

'Yes.'

Bowman took her reluctant arm and made to move off, then stepped courteously to one side to permit the passage of a bustling Le Grand Duc, if a man of his build could be said to bustle, followed by a plainly reluctant Lila. He carried a notebook and had what looked to be a folklorist's gleam in his eye. But bent though he was on the pursuit of knowledge he hadn't forgotten to fortify himself with a large red apple at which he was munching away steadily. Le Grand Duc looked like the sort of man who would always get his priorities right.

Bowman, a hesitant Cecile beside him, followed rather more leisurely. When they were half way down the steps a jeep was detached from the leading caravan, three men piled aboard and the jeep took off down the hill at speed. As Bowman and the girl approached the knot of people where the gypsy was vainly trying to calm the now sobbing woman, the restaurant manager broke away from them and hurried towards the steps. Bowman barred his way.

'What's up?'

'Woman says her son has disappeared. They've sent a search party back along the road.'

'Oh?' Bowman removed his glasses. 'But people don't disappear just like that.'

'That's what I say. That's why I'm calling the police.'

He hurried on his way. Cecile, who had followed Bowman without any great show of enthusiasm, said: 'What's all the fuss? Why is that woman crying?'

'Her son's disappeared.'

'And?'

'That's all.'

'You mean that nothing's happened to him?'

'Not that anyone seems to know.'

'There could be a dozen reasons. Surely she doesn't have to carry on like that.'

'Gypsies,' Bowman said by way of explanation. 'Very emotional. Very attached to their offspring. Do you have any children?'

She wasn't as calmly composed as she looked. Even in the lamplight it wasn't difficult to see the red touching her cheeks. She said: 'That wasn't fair.'

Bowman blinked, looked at her and said: 'No, it wasn't. Forgive me. I didn't mean it that way. If you had kids and one was missing, would you react like that?'

'I don't know.'

'I said I was sorry.'

'I'd be worried, of course.' She wasn't a person who could maintain anger or resentment for more than a fleeting moment of time. 'Maybe I'd be worried stiff. But I wouldn't be so—so violently grief-stricken, so hysterical, well not unless—'

'Unless what?'

'Oh, I don't know. I mean, if I'd reason to believe that —that—'

'Yes?'

'You know perfectly well what I mean.'

'I'll never know what women mean,' Bowman said sadly, 'but this time I can guess.'

They moved on and literally bumped into Le Grand Duc and Lila. The girls spoke and introductions, Bowman saw, were inevitable and in order. Le Grand Duc shook his hand and said, 'Charmed, charmed,' but it was plain to see that he wasn't in the least bit charmed, it was just that the aristocracy knew how to behave. He hadn't, Bowman noted, the soft flabby hand one might have expected: the hand was hard and the grip that of a strong man carefully not exerting too much pressure.

'Fascinating,' he announced. He addressed himself

exclusively to the two girls. 'Do you know that *all* those gypsies have come from the far side of the Iron Curtain? Hungarian or Rumanian, most of them. Their leader, fellow called Czerda—met him last year, that's him with that woman there—has come all the way from the Black Sea.'

'But how about frontiers?' Bowman asked. 'Especially between East and West.'

'Eh? What? Ah?' He finally became aware of Bowman's presence. 'They travel without let or hindrance, most of all when people know that they are on their annual pilgrimage. Everyone fears them, thinks that they have the evil eye, that they put spells and curses on those who offend them: the Communists believe it as much as anyone, more, for all I know. Nonsense, of course, sheer balderdash. But it's what people believe that matters. Come, Lila, come. I have the feeling that they are going to prove in a most co-operative mood tonight.'

They moved off. After a few paces the Duke stopped and glanced round. He looked in their direction for some time, then turned away, shaking his head. 'A pity,' he said to Lila in what he probably imagined to be *sotto voce*, 'about the colour of her hair.' They moved on.

'Never mind,' Bowman said kindly. 'I like you as you are.' She compressed her lips, then laughed. Grudges were not for Cecile Dubois.

'He's right, you know.' She took his arm, all was forgiven, and when Bowman was about to point out that the Duke's convictions about the intrinsic superiority of blonde hair did not carry with it the stamp of divine infallibility, she went on, gesturing around her: 'It really is quite fascinating.'

'If you like the atmosphere of circuses and fairgrounds,' Bowman said fastidiously, 'both of which I will go a long way to avoid, I suppose it is. But I admire experts.'

And that the gypsies were unquestionably experts at the particular task on hand was undeniable. The speed and coordinated skill with which they assembled their various stalls and other media of entertainment were remarkable. Within minutes and ready for operation they had assembled roulette stands, a shooting gallery, no fewer than four fortune-tellers' booths, a food stall, a candy stall, two clothing stalls selling brilliantly-hued gypsy clothes and, oddly enough, a large cage of mynah birds clearly possessed of that species' usual homicidal outlook on life. A group of four gypsies, perched on the steps of a caravan, began to play soulful mid-European music on their violins. Already the areas of the forecourt and car-park were almost uncomfortably full of scores of people circulating slowly around, guests from the hotel, guests, one supposed, from other hotels, villagers from Les Baux, a good number of gypsies themselves. As variegated a cross-section of humanity as one could hope to find, they shared, for the moment, what appeared to be a marked unanimity of outlook—all, from Le Grand Duc downwards, were clearly enjoying themselves with the notable exception of the restaurant manager who stood on the top of the forecourt steps surveying the scene with the broken-hearted despair and martyred resignation of a Bing watching the Metropolitan being taken over by a hippie festival.

A policeman appeared at the entrance to the forecourt. He was large and red and perspiring, freely and clearly regarded the pushing of ancient bicycles up precipitous roads as a poor way of spending a peacefully warm May evening. He propped his bicycle against a wall just as the sobbing gypsy woman put her hands to her face, turned and ran towards a green-and-white-painted caravan.

Bowman nudged Cecile. 'Let's just saunter over there and join them, shall we?'

'I will not. It's rude. Besides, gypsies don't like people who pry.'

'Prying? Since when is concern about a missing man prying? But suit yourself.'

As Bowman moved off the jeep returned, skidding to an unnecessary if highly dramatic stop on the gravel of the court. The young gypsy at the wheel jumped out and ran towards Czerda and the policeman. Bowman wasn't far behind, halting a discreet number of feet away.

'No luck, Ferenc?' Czerda asked.

'No sign anywhere, Father. We searched all the area.'

The policeman had a black notebook out. 'Where was he last seen?'

'Less than a kilometre back, according to his mother,' Czerda said. 'We stopped for our evening meal not far from the caves.'

The policeman asked Ferenc: 'You searched in there?'

Ferenc crossed himself and remained silent. Czerda said: 'That's no question to ask and you know it. No gypsy would ever enter those caves. They have an evil reputation. Alexandre—that's the name of the missing boy—would never have gone in there.'

The policeman put his book away. 'I wouldn't go in there myself. Not at this time of night. The local people believe it's cursed and haunted and—well—I was born here. Tomorrow, when it's daylight—'

'He'll have turned up long before then,' Czerda said confidently. 'Just a lot of fuss about nothing.'

'Then that woman who just left—she is his mother—'

'Yes.'

'Then why is she so upset?'

'He's only a boy and you know what mothers are.' Czerda half-shrugged in resignation. 'I suppose I'd better go and tell her.'

He left. So did the policeman. So did Ferenc. Bowman didn't hesitate. He could see where Czerda was going, he could guess where the policeman was heading for—the nearest estaminet—so was momentarily interested in the movements of neither. But in Ferenc he was interested, for there was something in the alacrity and purposefulness with which he walked quickly through the archway into the parking lot that bespoke some fixed intent. Bowman followed more leisurely and stopped in the archway.

On the right-hand side of the lot was a row of four fortune-tellers' booths, got up in the usual garishly-coloured canvas. The first in the row was occupied, a notice said, by a certain Madame Marie-Antoinette who offered a money back if not satisfied guarantee. Bowman went inside immediately, not because of any particular predilection for royalty or parsimony or both, but because just as Ferenc was entering the most distant booth he paused and looked round directly at Bowman and Ferenc's face was stamped with the unmistakably unpleasant characteristics of one whose suspicions could be instantly aroused. Bowman passed inside.

Marie-Antoinette was a white-haired old crone with eyes of polished mahogany and a gin-trap for a mouth. She gazed into a cloudy crystal ball that was cloudy principally because it hadn't been cleaned for months, spoke to Bowman encouragingly about the longevity, health, fame and happiness that could not fail to be his, took four francs from him and appeared to go into a coma, a sign Bowman took to indicate that the interview was over. He left. Cecile was standing just outside, swinging her handbag in what could have been regarded as an unnecessarily provocative fashion and looking at him with a degree of speculative amusement perhaps uncalled for in the circumstances.

'Still studying human nature?' she asked sweetly.

'I should never have gone in there.' Bowman took off his glasses and peered myopically around. The character running the shooting gallery across the parking lot, a short thick-set lad with the face of a boxer who had had a highly unspectacular career brought to an abrupt end, was regarding him with a degree of interest that verged on the impolite. Bowman put his spectacles back on and looked at Cecile.

'Your fortune?' she enquired solicitously. 'Bad news?'

'The worst. Marie-Antoinette says I will be married in two months. She must be wrong.'

'And you not the marrying kind,' she said sympathetically. She nodded at the next booth, which bore a legend above the entrance. 'I think you should ask Madame What's-her-name for a second opinion.'

Bowman studied Madame Zetterling's come-on, then looked again across the car-park. The gallery attendant appeared to be finding him as fascinating as ever. Bowman followed Cecile's advice and went inside.

Madame Zetterling looked like Marie-Antoinette's elder sister. Her technique was different inasmuch as the tools of her trade consisted of a pack of very greasy playing cards which she shuffled and dealt with a speed and dexterity that would have had her automatically blackballed in any casino in Europe, but the forecast for his future was exactly the same. So was the price.

Cecile was still waiting outside, still smiling. Ferenc was standing now by the archway in the hedge and had clearly taken over the eye-riveting stint from the shooting-stall attendant. Bowman polished his glasses some more.

'God help us,' Bowman said. 'This is nothing but a matrimonial agency. Extraordinary. Uncanny.' He replaced his glasses. Lot's wife had nothing on Ferenc. 'Quite incredible, in fact.'

'What is?'

'Your resemblance,' Bowman said solemnly, 'to the person I'm supposed to marry.'

'My, my!' She laughed, pleasantly and with genuine amusement. 'You *do* have an original mind, Mr Bowman.'

'Neil,' Bowman said, and without waiting for further advice entered the next booth. In the comparative obscurity of the entrance he looked round in time to see Ferenc shrug his shoulders and move off into the forecourt.

The third fortune-teller made up the cast for the three witches of *Macbeth*. She used tarot cards and ended up by telling Bowman that he would shortly be journeying across the seas where he would meet and marry a raven-haired beauty and when he said he was getting married to a blonde the following month she just smiled sadly and took his money.

Cecile, who now clearly regarded him as the best source of light entertainment around, had a look of frankly malicious amusement on her face.

'What shattering revelations this time?'

Bowman took his glasses off again and shook his head in perplexity: as far as he could see he was no longer the object of anyone's attention. 'I don't understand. She said: "Her father was a great seaman, as was his, as was his." Doesn't make any kind of sense to me.'

It did to Cecile. She touched a switch somewhere and the smile went out. She stared at Bowman, green eyes full of perplexed uncertainty.

'My father is an admiral,' she said slowly. 'So was my grandfather. And great-grandfather. You—you could have found this out.'

'Sure, sure. I carry a complete dossier on every girl I'm about to meet for the first time. Come up to my room and I'll show you my filing cabinets—I carry them about in a pantechnicon. And wait, there's more. I quote again: "She has a rose-shaped strawberry birthmark in a place where it can't be seen."'

'Good God!'

'I couldn't have put it better myself. Hang on. There may be worse yet to come.' Bowman made no excuse and gave no reason for entering the fourth booth, the only one that held any interest for him, nor was it necessary: the girl was so shaken by what she'd just been told that the oddity of Bowman's behaviour must have suddenly become of very secondary importance.

The booth was dimly lit, the illumination coming from an Anglepoise lamp with a very low wattage bulb that cast a pool of light on a green baize table and a pair of hands that lay lightly clasped on the table. Little of the person to whom the hands belonged could be seen as she sat in shadow with her head bent but enough to realize that she would never make it as one of the three witches of *Macbeth* or even as Lady Macbeth herself. This one was young, with flowing titian hair reaching below her shoulders and gave the vague impression, although her features were almost indistinguishable, that she must be quite beautiful: her hands certainly were.

Bowman sat on the chair opposite her and looked at the card on the table which bore the legend: 'Countess Marie le Hobenaut.'

'You really a countess, ma'am?' Bowman asked politely.

'You wish to have your hand read?' Her voice was low, gentle and soft. No Lady Macbeth: here was Cordelia.

'Of course.'

She took his hand in both of hers and bent over it, her head so low that the titian hair brushed the table. Bowman kept still—it wasn't easy but he kept still—as two warm tears fell on his hands. With his left hand he twisted the Anglepoise and she put a forearm up to protect her eyes but not before he had time to see that her face *was* beautiful and that the big brown eyes were sheened with tears.

'Why is Countess Marie crying?'

'You have a long lifeline—'

'Why are you crying?'

'Please.'

'All right. Why are you crying, please?'

'I'm sorry. I—I'm upset.'

'You mean I've only got to walk into a place—'

'My young brother is missing.'

'Your brother? I know someone's missing. Everyone knows. Alexandre. But your brother. They haven't found him?'

She shook her head, the titian hair brushing across the table.

'And that's your mother in the big green-and-white caravan?'

A nod this time. She didn't look up.

'But why all the tears? He's only been missing for a little while. He'll turn up, you'll see.'

Again she said nothing. She put her forearms on the table and her head on her forearms and cried silently, her shoulders shaking uncontrollably. Bowman, his face bitter, touched the young gypsy's shoulder, rose and left the booth. But when he emerged the expression on his face was one of dazed bewilderment. Cecile glanced at him in some trepidation.

'Four kids,' Bowman said quietly. He took her unresisting arm and led her through the archway towards the forecourt. Le Grand Duc, the blonde girl still with him, was talking to an impressively scar-faced and heavily built gypsy dressed in dark trousers and frilled off-white shirt. Bowman ignored Cecile's disapproving frown and halted a few convenient feet away.

'A thousand thanks, Mr Koscis, a thousand thanks,' Le Grand Duc was saying in his most gracious lord of the manor voice. 'Immensely interesting, immensely. Come, Lila, my dear, enough is enough. I think we have earned ourselves a drink and a little bite to eat.' Bowman watched them make their way towards the steps leading to the patio, then turned and looked consideringly at the green-and-white caravan.

Cecile said: 'Don't.'

Bowman looked at her in surprise.

'And what's wrong with wanting to help a sorrowing mother? Maybe I can comfort her, help in some way, perhaps even go looking for her missing boy. If more people would be more forthcoming in times of trouble, be more willing to risk a snub—'

'You really are a fearful hypocrite,' she said admiringly.

'Besides, there's a technique to this sort of thing. If Le Grand Duc can do it, I can. Still your apprehensions.'

Bowman left her there nibbling the tip of a thumb in what did appear to be a very apprehensive manner indeed and mounted the caravan steps.

At first sight the interior appeared to be deserted, then his eyes became accustomed to the gloom and he realized he was standing in an unlighted vestibule leading to the main living quarters beyond, identifiable by a crack of light from an imperfectly constructed doorway and the sound of voices, women's voices.

Bowman took a step through the outer doorway. A shadow detached itself from a wall, a shadow possessed of the most astonishing powers of acceleration and the most painful solidity. It struck Bowman on the breastbone with the top of a head that had the unforgiving consistency of a cement bollard: Bowman made it all the way to the ground without the benefit of even one of the caravan steps. Out of the corner of an eye he was dimly aware of Cecile stepping hurriedly and advisedly to one side then he landed on his back with a momentarily numbing impact that took care of any little air that the bullet-head had left in his lungs in the first place. His glasses went flying off into the middle distance and as he lay there whooping and gasping for the oxygen that wouldn't come the shadow came marching purposefully down the steps. He was short, thick-set, unfriendly, had a speech to make and was clearly determined on making it. He stooped, grabbed Bowman by the lapels and hauled him to his feet with an ease that boded ill for things to come.

'You will remember me, my friend.' His voice had the pleasant timbre of gravel being decanted from a metal hopper. 'You will remember that Hoval does not like trespassers. You will remember that next time Hoval will not use his fists.'

From this Bowman gathered that on this occasion Hoval did intend to use his fists and he did. Only one, but it was more than enough. Hoval hit him in the same place and, as far as Bowman could judge from the symptoms transmitted by a now nearly paralysed midriff, with approximately the same amount of force. He took half-a-dozen involuntary backward steps and then came heavily to earth again, this time in a seated position with his hands splayed out behind him. Hoval dusted off his hands in an unpleasant fashion and marched back up into the caravan again. Cecile looked around till she located Bowman's glasses, then came and offered him a helping hand which he wasn't too proud to accept.

'I think Le Grand Duc must use a different technique,' she said gravely.

'There's a lot of ingratitude in this world,' Bowman wheezed.

'Isn't there just? Through with studying human nature for the night?' Bowman nodded, it was easier than speaking. 'Then for goodness' sake let's get out of here. After that, I need a drink.'

'What do you think *I* require?' Bowman croaked.

She looked at him consideringly. 'Frankly, I think a nanny would be in order.' She took his arm and led him up the steps to the patio. Le Grand Duc, with a large bowl of fruit before him and Lila by his side, stopped munching a banana and regarded Bowman with a smile so studiously impersonal as to be positively insulting.

'That was a rousing set-to you had down there,' he observed.

'He hit me when I wasn't looking,' Bowman explained.

'Ah!' Le Grand Duc said non-committally, then added in a penetrating whisper when they'd moved on less than half-a-dozen feet: 'As I said, long past his prime.' Cecile squeezed Bowman's arm warningly but unnecessarily: he gave her the wan smile of one whose cup is overfull and led her to their table. A waiter brought drinks.

Bowman fortified himself and said: 'Well, now. Where shall we live? England or France?'

'What?'

'You heard what the fortune-teller said.'

'Oh, my God!'

Bowman lifted his glass. 'To David.'

'David?'

'Our eldest. I've just chosen his name.'

The green eyes regarding Bowman so steadily over the rim of a glass were neither amused nor exasperated, just very thoughtful. Bowman became very thoughtful himself. It could be that Cecile Dubois was, in that well-turned phrase, rather more than just a pretty face.

CHAPTER TWO

Certainly, two hours later, no one could have referred to Bowman's as a pretty face. It could be said in fairness that, owing to various troubles it had encountered from time to time, it didn't have very much going for it in the first place but the black stocking mask he'd pulled up almost to the level of his eyes gave it an even more discouraging look than it normally possessed.

He'd changed his grey gaberdine suit for a dark one and his white shirt for a navy roll-neck pullover. Now he put the spectacles he had worn for disguise away in his suitcase, switched off the overhead light and stepped out on to the terrace.

All the bedrooms on that floor opened on to the same terrace. Lights came from two of them. In the first, the curtains were drawn. Bowman moved to the door and its handle gave fractionally under his hand. Cecile's room, he knew: a trusting soul. He moved on to the next lit window, this one uncurtained, and peered stealthily round the edge. A commendable precaution, but superfluous: had he done an Apache war dance outside that window it was doubtful whether either of the two occupants would have noticed or, if they had, would have cared very much. Le Grand Duc and Lila, his black and her blonde head very close together, were seated side by side in front of a narrow table: Le Grand Duc, a tray of canapés beside him, appeared to be teaching the girl the rudiments of chess. One would have thought that the customary vis-à-vis position would have been more conducive to rapid learning: but then, Le Grand Duc had about him the look of a man who would always adopt his own strongly original attitude to all that he approached. Bowman moved on.

The moon still rode high but a heavy bar of black cloud was approaching from the far battlements of Les Baux. Bowman descended to the main terrace by the swimming pool but did not cross. The management, it seemed, kept the patio lights burning all night and anyone trying to cross the patio and descend the steps to the forecourt would have been bound to be seen by any gypsy still awake: and that there were gypsies who were just that Bowman did not doubt for a moment.

He took a sidepath to the left, circled the hotel to the rear and approached the forecourt uphill from the west. He moved very slowly and very quietly on rubber soles and kept to deep shadow. There was, of course, no positive reason why the gypsies should have any watcher posted: but as far as this particular lot were concerned, Bowman felt, there was no positive reason why they shouldn't. He waited till a cloud drifted over the moon and moved into the forecourt.

All but three of the caravans were in darkness. The nearest and biggest of the lit caravans was Czerda's: bright light came from both the half-opened door and a closed but uncurtained side window. Bowman went up to that window like a cat stalking a bird across a sunlit lawn and hitched an eye over the sill.

There were three gypsies seated round a table and Bowman recognized all three: Czerda, his son Ferenc and Koscis, the man whom Le Grand Duc had so effusively thanked for information received. They had a map spread on the table and Czerda, pencil in hand, was indicating something on it and clearly making an explanation of some kind. But the map was on so small a scale that Bowman was unable to make out what it was intended to represent, far less what Czerda was pointing out on it, nor, because of the muffling effect of the closed window, could he distinguish what Czerda was saying. The only reasonable assumption he could make from the scene before him was that whatever it was Czerda was planning it wouldn't be for the benefit of his fellow men. Bowman moved away as soundlessly as he had arrived.

The side window of the second illuminated caravan was open and the curtains only partially drawn. Closing in on this window Bowman could at first see no one in the central portion of the caravan. He moved close, bent forward and risked a quick glance to his right and there, at a small table near the door, two men were sitting playing cards. One of the men was unknown to Bowman but the other he immediately and feelingly recognized as Hoval, the gypsy who had so unceremoniously ejected him from the green-and-white caravan earlier in the night. Bowman wondered briefly why Hoval had transferred himself to the present one and what purpose he had been serving in the green-and-white caravan. From the ache Bowman could still feel in his midriff the answer to that one seemed fairly clear. But why?

Bowman glanced to his left. A small compartment lay beyond an open doorway in a transverse partition. From Bowman's angle of sight nothing was visible in the compartment. He moved along to the next window. The curtains on this one were drawn, but the window itself partly open from the top, no doubt for ventilation. Bowman moved the curtains very very gently and applied his eye to the crack he had made. The level of illumination inside was very low, the only light coming from the rear of the caravan. But there was enough light to see, at the very front of the compartment, a three-tiered bunk and here lay three men, apparently asleep. Two of them were lying with their faces turned towards Bowman but it was impossible to distinguish their features: their faces were no more than pale blurs in the gloom. Bowman eased the curtains again and headed for the caravan that really intrigued him—the green-and-white one.

The rear door at the top of the caravan steps was open but it was dark inside. By this time Bowman had developed a thing about the unlit vestibules of caravans and gave this one a wide berth. In any event it was the illuminated window half-way down the side of the caravan that held the more interest for him. The window was half-open, the curtains half-drawn. It seemed ideal for some more peeking.

The caravan's interior was brightly lit and comfortably furnished. There were four women there, two on a settee and two on chairs by a table. Bowman recognized the titian-haired Countess Marie with, beside her, the grey-haired woman who had been involved in the altercation with Czerda—Marie's mother and the mother of the missing Alexandre. The two other young women at the table, one auburn-haired and about thirty, the other a slight dark girl with most ungypsy-like cropped hair and scarcely out of her teens, Bowman had not seen before. Although it must have been long past their normal bed-times, they showed no signs of making any preparations for retiring. All four looked sad and forlorn to a degree: the mother and the dark young girl were in tears. The dark girl buried her face in her hands.

'Oh, God!' She sobbed so bitterly it was difficult to make the words out. 'When is it all going to end? *Where* is it all going to end?'

'We must hope, Tina,' Countess Marie said. Her voice was dull and totally devoid of hope. 'There is nothing else we can do.'

'There *is* no hope.' The dark girl shook her head despairingly. 'You know there's no hope. Oh, God, why did Alexandre have to do it?' She turned to the auburn-haired girl. 'Oh, Sara, Sara, your husband warned him only today—'

'He did, he did.' This was from the girl called Sara and she sounded no happier than the others. She put her arm round Tina. 'I'm so terribly sorry, my dear, so terribly sorry.' She paused. 'But Marie's right, you know. Where there's life there's hope.'

There was silence in the caravan. Bowman hoped, and fervently, that they would break it and break it soon. He had come for information but had so far come across nothing other than the mildly astonishing fact of four gypsies talking in German and not in Romany. But he wanted to learn more and learn it quickly for the prospect of hanging around that brightly illuminated window indefinitely lacked appeal of any kind: there was something in the brooding atmosphere of tragedy inside that caravan and menace outside calculated to instil a degree of something less than confidence in the bystander.

'There is no hope,' the grey-haired woman said heavily. She dabbed at her eyes with a handkerchief. 'A mother knows.'

Marie said: 'But, Mother—'

'There's no hope because there's no life,' her mother interrupted wearily. 'You'll never see your brother again, nor you your fiancé, Tina. I know my son is dead.'

There was silence again, which was just as well for Bowman for it was then that he heard the all but imperceptible sound of a fractionally disturbed piece of gravel, a sound which probably saved his life.

Bowman whirled round. He'd been right about one thing, anyway: there was menace abroad that night. Koscis and Hoval were frozen in a crouched position less than five feet away. Both men were smiling. Both held long curving knives in their hands and the lamplight gleamed dully off them in a very unpleasant fashion.

They'd been waiting for him, Bowman realized, or someone like him, they'd been keeping tabs on him ever since he'd entered the forecourt or maybe even long before that, they'd just wanted to give him enough rope to hang himself, to prove that he was up to what they would regard as no good—no good for themselves—and, when satisfied, eliminate the source of irritation: their actions, in turn, certainly proved to him that there was something sadly amiss with this caravan heading for Saintes-Maries.

The realization of what had happened was instantaneous and Bowman wasted no time on self-recriminations. There would be a time for those but the time was assuredly not when Koscis and Hoval were standing there taking very little trouble to conceal the immediacy of their homicidal intentions. Bowman lunged swiftly and completely unexpectedly—for a man with a knife does not usually anticipate that one without a knife will indulge in such suicidal practices—towards Koscis, who instinctively drew back, lifting his knife high in self-defence. Prudently enough, Bowman didn't complete his movement, but threw himself to his right and ran across the few intervening yards of forecourt leading to the patio steps.

He heard Koscis and Hoval pounding across the gravel in pursuit. They were saying things, to Bowman unintelligible things, but even in Romany the burden of their remarks was clear. Bowman reached the fourth step on his first bound, checked so abruptly that he almost but didn't quite lose his balance, wheeled round and swung his right foot all in one movement. Koscis it was who had the misfortune to be in the lead: he grunted in agony, the knife flying back from his hand, as he fell backwards on to the forecourt.

Hoval came up the steps as Koscis went down them, his right arm, knife pointing upwards, hooking viciously. Bowman felt the tip of the knife burning along his left forearm and then he'd hit Hoval with a great deal more force than Hoval had earlier hit him, which was understandable enough, for when Hoval had hit him he'd been concerned only with his personal satisfaction: Bowman was concerned with his life. Hoval, too, fell backwards, but he was luckier than Koscis: he fell on top of him.

Bowman pushed up his left sleeve. The wound on the forearm was about eight inches long but, although bleeding quite heavily, was little more than a superficial cut and would close up soon. In the meantime, he hoped it wouldn't incapacitate him too much.

He forgot about that trouble when he saw a new one approaching. Ferenc was running across the forecourt in the direction of the patio steps. Bowman turned, hurried across the patio to the steps leading to the upper terrace and stopped briefly to look back. Ferenc had both Koscis and Hoval on their feet and it was clear that it was only a matter of seconds before all three were on their way.

Three to one and the three with knives. Bowman carried no weapon of any kind and the immediate prospect was uninviting. Three determined men with knives will always hunt down an unarmed man, especially three men who appeared to regard the use of knives as second nature. A light still showed from Le Grand Duc's room. Bowman pulled down his black face mask and burst through the doorway: he felt he didn't have time to knock. Le Grand Duc and Lila were still playing chess but Bowman again felt that he didn't have time to worry about mildly surprising matters of that nature.

'For God's sake, help me, hide me!' The gasping, he thought, might have been slightly overdone but in the circumstances it came easily. 'They're after me!'

Le Grand Duc looked in no way perturbed, far less startled. He merely frowned in ducal annoyance and completed a move.

'Can't you see we're busy?' He turned to Lila who was staring at Bowman with parted lips and very large rounded eyes. 'Careful, my dear, careful. Your bishop is in great danger.' He spared Bowman a cursory glance, viewing him with distaste. 'Who are after you?'

'The gypsies, that's who. Look!' Bowman rolled up his left sleeves. 'They've knifed me!'

The expression of distaste deepened.

'You must have given them some cause for offence.'

'Well, I was down there—'

'Enough!' He held up a magisterial hand. 'Peeping Toms can expect no sympathy from me. Leave at once.'

'Leave at once? But they'll get me—'

'My dear.' Bowman didn't think Le Grand Duc was addressing him and he wasn't. He patted Lila's knee in a proprietorial fashion. 'Excuse me while I call the management. No cause for alarm, I assure you.'

Bowman ran out through the doorway, checked briefly to see if the terrace was still deserted. Le Grand Duc called: 'You might close that door after you.'

'But, Charles—' That was Lila.

'Checkmate,' said Le Grand Duc firmly, 'in two moves.'

There was the sound of footsteps, running footsteps, coming across the patio to the base of the terrace steps. Bowman moved quickly to the nearest port in the storm.

Cecile wasn't asleep either. She was sitting up in bed holding a magazine and attired in some fetching negligée that, in happier circumstances, might well have occasioned admiring comment. She opened her mouth, whether in astonishment or the beginning of a shout for help, then closed it again and listened with surprising calmness as Bowman stood there with his back to the closed door and told her his story.

'You're making all this up,' she said.

Bowman hoisted his left sleeve again, an action which by now he didn't much like doing as the coagulating blood was beginning to stick wound and material together.

'Including this?' Bowman asked.

She made a face. 'It *is* nasty. But why should they—'

'Ssh!' Bowman had caught the sound of voices outside, voices which rapidly became very loud. An altercation was taking place and Bowman had little doubt that it concerned him. He turned the handle of the door and peered out through a crack not much more than an inch in width.

Le Grand Duc, with Lila watching from the open doorway, was standing there with arms outspread like an overweight traffic policeman, barring the way of Ferenc, Koscis and Hoval. That they weren't immediately recognizable as those three was due to the fact that they'd obviously considered it prudent to take time out to wrap some dirty handkerchiefs or other pieces of cloth about their faces in primitive but effective forms of masks, which explained why Bowman had been given the very brief breathing space he had been.

'This is private property for guests only,' Le Grand Duc said sternly.

'Stand aside!' Ferenc ordered.

'Stand aside? I am the Duc de Croytor—'

'You'll be the dead Duc de—'

'How dare you, sir!' Le Grand Duc stepped forward with a speed and coordination surprising in a man of his bulk and caught the astonished and completely unprepared Ferenc with a round-house right to the chin. Ferenc staggered back into the arms of his companions who had momentarily to support him to prevent his collapse. There was some moments' hesitation, then they turned and ran from the terrace, Koscis and Hoval still having to support a very wobbly Ferenc.

'Charles.' Lila had her hands clasped in what is alleged to be the classic feminine gesture of admiration. 'How brave of you!'

'A bagatelle. Aristocracy versus ruffians—class always tells.' He gestured towards his doorway. 'Come, we have yet to finish both the chess and the canapés.'

'But—but how can you be so calm? I mean, aren't you going to phone? The management? Or the police?'

'What point? They were masked and will be far away by this time. After you.'

They went inside and closed their door. Bowman closed his.

'You heard?' She nodded. 'Good old duke. That's taken the heat off for the moment.' He reached for the door handle. 'Well, thanks for the sanctuary.'

'Where are you going?' She seemed troubled or disappointed or both.

'Over the hills and far away.'

'In your car?'

'I haven't got one.'

'You can take mine. Ours, I mean.'

'You mean that?'

'Of course, silly.'

'You're going to make me a very happy man one day. But for the car, some other time. Good night.'

Bowman closed her door behind him and was almost at his own room when he stopped. Three figures had emerged from the shadows.

'First you, my friend.' Ferenc's voice was no more than a whisper, maybe the idea of disturbing the Duke again didn't appeal to him. 'Then we attend to the little lady.'

Bowman was three paces from his own door and he had taken the first even before Ferenc had stopped talking—people generally assume that you will courteously hear them out—and had taken the third before they had moved, probably because the other two were waiting for the lead from Ferenc and Ferenc's reactions were temporarily out of kilter since his brief encounter with Le Grand Duc. In any event, Bowman had the door shut behind him before Ferenc's shoulder hit it and had the key turned before Ferenc could twist the door handle from his grip.

He spent no time on brow-mopping and self-congratulation but ran to the back of the apartment, opened the window and looked out. The branches of a sufficiently stout tree were less than six feet away. Bowman withdrew his head and listened. Someone was giving the door handle a good going over, then abruptly the sound ceased to be replaced by that of running footsteps. Bowman waited no longer: if there was one thing that had been learnt from dealing with those men it was that procrastination was uninsurable.

As a piece of arboreal trapeze work there was little enough to it. He just stood on the sill, half-leaned and half-fell outwards, caught a thick branch, swung into the bole of the tree and slid to the ground. He scrambled up the steep bank leading to the road that encircled the hotel from the rear. At the top he heard a low and excited call behind him and twisted round. The moon was out again and he could clearly see the three of them starting to climb up the bank: it was equally clear that the knives they held in their hands weren't impeding their progress at all.

Before Bowman lay the choice of running downhill or up. Downhill from the Baumanière lay open country, uphill lay Les Baux with its winding streets and back-alleys and labyrinth of shattered ruins. Bowman didn't hesitate. As one famous heavy-weight boxer said of his opponents—this was after he had lured the unfortunates into the ring—'they can run but they can't hide.' In Les Baux Bowman could both run and hide. He turned uphill.

He ran up the winding road towards the old village as quickly as the steepness, his wind and the state of his legs would permit. He hadn't indulged in this sort of thing in years. He spared a glance over his shoulder. Neither, apparently, had the three gypsies. They hadn't gained any that Bowman could see: but they hadn't lost any either. Maybe they were just pacing themselves for what they might consider to be a long run that lay ahead: if that were the case, Bowman thought, he might as well stop running now.

The straight stretch of road leading to the entrance to the village was lined with car parks on both sides but there were no cars there and so no place to hide. He passed on through the entrance.

After about another hundred yards of what had already become this gasping lung-heaving run Bowman came to a fork in the road. The fork on the right curved down to the battlemented walls of the village and had every appearance of leading to a cul-de-sac. The one to the left, narrow and winding and very steep, curved upwards out of sight and while he dreaded the prospect of any more of that uphill marathon it seemed to offer the better chance of safety so he took it. He looked behind again and saw that his momentary indecision had enabled his pursuers to make up quite a bit of ground on him. Still running in this same unnerving silence, the knives in their hands glinting rhythmically as their arms pumped to and fro, they were now less than thirty yards distant.

At the best speed he could, Bowman continued up this narrow winding road. He slowed down occasionally to peer briefly and rather desperately into various attractive dark openings on both sides, but mainly to the right, but he knew it was his labouring lungs and leaden legs that told him that those entrances were inviting, his reason told him that those attractions were almost certainly fatal illusions, leading to cul-de-sacs or some other form of trap from which there could be no escape.

And now, for the first time, Bowman could hear behind

him the hoarse and rasping breathing of the gypsies. They were clearly in as bad shape as he was himself but when he glanced over his shoulder he realized this was hardly cause for any wild rejoicing, he was hearing them now simply because they were that much closer than they had been: their mouths were open in gasping exertion, their faces contorted by effort and sheened in sweat and they stumbled occasionally as their weakening legs betrayed them on the unsure footing of the cobblestones. But now they were only fifteen yards away, the price Bowman had paid for his frequent examinations of possible places of refuge. But at least their nearness made one decision inevitable for him: there was no point in wasting any further time in searching for hiding-places on either side for wherever he went they were bound to see him go and follow. For him now the only hope of life lay among the shattered ruins of the ancient fortress of Les Baux itself.

Still pounding uphill he came to a set of iron railings that apparently completely blocked what had now turned from a narrow road into no more than a winding metalled path. I'll have to turn and fight, he thought, I'll have to turn and then it will be all over in five seconds, but he didn't have to turn for there was a narrow gap between the right-hand side of the railing and a desk in an inlet recess in the wall which was clearly the pay-box where you handed over your money to inspect the ruins. Even in that moment of overwhelming relief at spotting this gap, two thoughts occurred to Bowman: the first the incongruous one that that was a bloody stupid set-up for a pay-box where the more parsimoniously minded could slip through at will, the second that this was the place to stand and fight, for they could only squeeze through that narrow entrance one at a time and would have to turn sideways to do so, a circumstance which might well place a swinging foot on a par with a constricted knife arm: or it did seem like a good idea to him until it fortunately occurred that while he was busy trying to kick the knife from the hand of one man the other two would be busy throwing their knives at him through or over the bars of the railing and at a distance of two or three feet it didn't seem very likely that they would miss. And so he ran on, if the plodding, lumbering, stumbling progress that was now all he could raise could be called running.

A small cemetery lay to his right. Bowman thought of the macabre prospect of playing a lethal hide-and-seek among the tombstones and hastily put all thought of the cemetery out of his mind. He ran on another fifty yards, saw before him the open plateau of the Les Baux massif, where there was no place to hide and from which escape could be obtained only by jumping down the vertical precipices which completely enclosed the massif, turned sharply to his left, ran up a narrow path alongside what looked like a crumbling chapel and was soon among the craggy ruins of the Les Baux fortress itself. He looked downhill and saw that his pursuers had fallen back to a distance of about forty yards which was hardly surprising as his life was at stake and their lives weren't. He looked up, saw the moon riding high and serene in a new cloudless sky and swore bitterly to himself in a fashion that would have given great offence to uncounted poets both alive and dead. On a moonless night he could have eluded his pursuers with ease amidst that great pile of awesome ruins.

And that they were awesome was beyond dispute. The contemplation of large masses of collapsed masonry did not rank among Bowman's favourite pastimes but as he climbed, fell, scrambled and twisted among that particular mass of masonry and in circumstances markedly unconducive to any form of aesthetic appreciation there was inexorably borne in upon him a sense of the awful grandeur of the place. It was inconceivable that any ruins anywhere could match those in their wild, rugged yet somehow terrifyingly beautiful desolation. There were mounds of shattered building stones fifty feet high: there were great ruined pillars reaching a hundred feet into the night sky, pillars overlooking vertical cliff faces of which the pillars appeared to be a natural continuation and in some cases were: there were natural stairways in the shattered rock face, natural chimneys in the remnants of those man-made cliffs, there were hundreds of apertures, in the rock, some just large enough for a man to squeeze through, others large enough to accommodate a double-decker. There were strange paths let into the natural rock, some man-made, some not, some precipitous, some almost horizontal, some wide enough to bowl along in a coach and four, others narrow and winding enough to have daunted the most mentally retarded of mountain goats. And there were broken, ruined blocks of masonry everywhere, some big as a child's hand, others as large as a suburban house. And it was all white, eerie and dead and white: in that brilliantly cold pale moonlight it was the most chillingly awe-inspiring sight Bowman had ever encountered and not, he reflected, a place he would willingly have called home. But, here, tonight, he had to live or die.

Or they had to live or die, Ferenc and Koscis and Hoval. When it came to the consideration of this alternative there was no doubt at all in Bowman's mind as to what the proper choice must be and the choice was not based primarily on the instinct of self-preservation although Bowman would have been the last to deny that it was an important factor: those were evil men and they had but one immediate and all-consuming ambition in life and that was to kill him but that was not what ultimately mattered. There was no question of morality or legality involved, just the simple factor of logic. If they killed him now they would, he knew, go on to commit more and more heinous crimes: if he killed them, then they wouldn't. It was as simple as that. Some men deserve to die and the law cannot deal with them until it is too late and the law is not an ass in this respect, it's just because of inbuilt safeguards in every legal constitution designed to protect the rights of the individual that it is unable to cope in advance with those whose ultimate evil or murderous intent is beyond rational dispute but beyond legal proof. It was the old, old story of the greatest good of the greatest number and it was merely fortuitous, Bowman reflected wryly, that he happened to be one of the greatest number. If he had been scared he was no longer scared now, his mind was quite cold and detached. He had to get high. If he got to a certain height where they couldn't reach him it would be stalemate: if he went higher and they still tried to follow him the danger to the greatest good of the greatest number was going to be effectively reduced. He looked up at the towering shattered crags bathed in the white moonlight and started to climb.

Bowman had never had any pretensions towards being a

climber but he climbed well that night. With the devil himself behind him he would normally have made good speed: with three of them he made excellent time. Looking back from time to time, he could see that he was steadily outdistancing them but not to the extent that they ever lost sight of him for more than a few seconds at a time. And now they were clearly recognizable for whom they were for now they had completely removed their home-made masks. They had probably arrived, and rightly, at the safe conclusion that up in the wild desolation of those ruins in the middle of the night they no longer required them and even if they were seen on the way back it wouldn't matter, for the *corpus delicti* would have vanished for ever and no charge could be laid against them other than that of entering the fortress without paying the required admission fee of a franc per head, which they would probably have regarded as a reasonable exchange for a night's work well done.

Bowman stopped climbing. Through no fault of his own, because he was totally unfamiliar with the terrain, he had made a mistake. He had been aware that the walls of the narrow gully up which he was scrambling had been rapidly steepening on both sides, which hadn't worried him unduly because it had happened twice before, but now as he rounded a corner he found himself faced with a vertical wall of solid rock. It was a perfect cul-de-sac from which there was no escape except by climbing, and the vertical walls were wholly unclimbable. The blank wall facing Bowman was riddled by cracks and apertures but a quick glance at the only three or four that were accessible to him showed no moonlight at the far end, only uncompromising darkness.

He ran back to the corner, convinced he was wasting his time. He was. The three men had been in no doubt as to the direction in which he had disappeared. They were forty yards away, no more. They saw Bowman, stopped and came on again. But not so hurriedly now. The very fact that Bowman had turned back to check on their whereabouts would be indication enough that he was in serious trouble.

A man does not die before he has to. He ran back into the cul-de-sac and looked desperately at the apertures in the rock. Only two were large enough to allow a man to enter. If he could get inside one and turn around the darkness behind him would at least counter-balance the advantages of a man with a knife—and, of course, only one man could come at a time. For no reason at all he chose the right-hand aperture, scrambled up and wriggled inside.

The limestone tunnel started narrowing almost immediately. But he had to go on, he was not yet in total concealment. By the time he estimated that he was hidden the tunnel was no more than two feet wide and scarcely as high. It would be impossible for him to turn, all he could do was lie there and be hacked piecemeal at someone's leisure. And even that, he realized now, would not be necessary: all they would have to do would be to wall up the entrance and go home for a good night's sleep. Bowman inched ahead on hands and knees.

He saw a pale glow of light ahead. He was imagining it, he thought, he knew he must be imagining it, but when he suddenly realized that what lay ahead was a corner in the tunnel, he knew he wasn't. He reached the corner and wriggled round with difficulty. Before him he saw a patch of star-studded sky.

The tunnel had suddenly become a cave. A small cave, to be sure, a good deal less than head-high and its lip ending in nothingness less than six feet away: but a cave. He crawled to the lip and looked down. He at once wished he hadn't: the plain lay hundreds of sheerly vertical feet below, the rows of dusty olive trees so impossibly distant that they couldn't even be fairly described as toy bushes.

He leaned out another few vertiginous inches and twisted his head to look upwards. The top of the cliff lay no more than twenty feet above—twenty smoothly vertical feet with neither finger- nor toe-hold in sight.

He looked to the right and that was it. That was the path that even the moronic mountain goat would have balked at, a narrow broken ledge extending down at not too acute an angle to a point that passed, as he now saw, some four feet below the lip of the cave. The path, for want of a better word, went right to the top.

But even the moronic goat, which Bowman was not, will refuse suicidal chances acceptable to the sacrificial goat, which Bowman undoubtedly was, for death and suicide come to the same thing anyway. He didn't hesitate, for he knew with certainty that if he did he would elect to remain and fight it out in that tiny cave sooner than face that dreadful path. He swung out gingerly over the rim, lowered himself till he had located the ledge with his feet and started to edge his way upwards.

He shuffled along with his face to the wall, arms wide outstretched, palms in constant contact with the rock-face, not because of any purchase that could be gained, for there was none, but because he was no mountaineer, had no particular head for heights and knew very well that if he looked down he'd inevitably just lean out and go tumbling head over heels to the olive groves far below. A crack Alpinist, it was possible, would have regarded the climb as just a light Sunday afternoon workout but for Bowman it was the most terrifying experience of his life. Twice his foot slipped on loose stone, twice chunks of limestone disappeared into the abyss, but after a life-time that was all of two minutes long he made it and hauled himself over the brink and into safety, sweating like a man in a Turkish bath and trembling like a withered leaf in the last gale of autumn. He'd thought he wouldn't be scared again and he had been wrong: but now he was back on terra firma and it was on terra firma that he operated best.

He ventured a quick glance over the edge. There was no one in sight. He wondered briefly what had delayed them, maybe they'd thought he was lurking in the shadow in the cul-de-sac, maybe they'd picked the wrong aperture to start with, maybe anything. He'd no time to waste wondering, he had to find out, and immediately, whether there was any escape from the pinnacle he was perched on. He had to find out for three very good and urgent reasons. If there was no other escape route he knew in his heart that no power on earth would ever make him face that descent to the cave and that he'd just have to stay there till the buzzards bleached his bones—he doubted whether there were any buzzards in those parts but the principle of the thing was pretty well fixed in his mind. If there was an escape route, then he'd have to guard against the possibility of being cut off by the gypsies. Thirdly, if there was such a route and they regarded it as unassailable, they might just elect to leave him there and go off to deal with Cecile Dubois whom they clearly, if erroneously, suspected of being a party to his irritatingly interfering behaviour.

He crossed the no more than ten yards of the flat limestone summit, lowered himself flat and peered over the edge. His circumspection was needless. There *was* an escape route, a very steep scree-laden slope that debouched gradually into an area of massive limestone boulders which in turn gave on to Les Baux plateau massif itself. Uninviting but feasible.

He made his way back to the cliff-side and heard voices, at first indistinctly, then clearly.

'This is madness!' It was Hoval speaking and for the first time Bowman shared a point of view with him.

'For you, Hoval, for a mountaineer from the High Tatra?' Ferenc's voice. 'If he went this way, we can too. You know that if we do not kill this man everything will be lost.'

Bowman looked down. He could see Hoval quite clearly and the heads of Ferenc and Koscis.

Koscis, apparently trying to postpone a decision, said: 'I do not like killing, Ferenc.'

Ferenc said: 'Too late to be queasy now. My father's orders are that we do not return until this man lies dead.'

Hoval nodded reluctantly, reached down his feet, found the ledge and started to edge his way along. Bowman rose, looked around, located a limestone boulder that must have weighed at least fifty pounds, lifted it chest high and returned to the brink of the precipice.

Hoval was obviously a great deal more experienced than Bowman for he was making about twice the best speed that Bowman had been able to manage. Ferenc and Koscis, heads and shoulders clearly visible now, were glancing anxiously sideways, watching Hoval's progress and almost certainly far from relishing the prospect of having to emulate him. Bowman waited till Hoval was directly beneath him. Hoval had once already tried to murder and now was coming to try to murder again. Bowman felt no pity and opened his hands.

The boulder, with a curious absence of sound, struck head and shoulders: the whole brief sequence, indeed, was characterized by an eerie silence. Hoval made no sound at all on the long way down and may well have been dead before he started to fall: and no sound of what must have been an appalling impact came from either Hoval or the boulder that had killed him as they plunged into the olive groves so far away. They just disappeared soundlessly from sight, vanished in the darkness below.

Bowman looked at Ferenc and Koscis. For several seconds they crouched there, their faces stunned, for catastrophe rarely registers instantaneously, then Ferenc's face became savagely transformed. He reached inside his jacket, snatched out a gun, pointed it upwards and fired. He knew Bowman was up there but he could have had no idea where he was. It was no more than the uncontrollable expression of an access of blind fury but Bowman took a couple of rapid backward steps all the same.

The gun introduced a new dimension. Clearly, because of their predilection for knives, they had intended to dispose of Bowman as quietly and unobtrusively as possible, but Ferenc, Bowman felt sure, did not carry a gun unless he intended to use it in the last resort and that was plainly at hand: they were going to get him at no matter what risk to themselves. Bowman reflected briefly that whatever he had so nearly stumbled across must literally be a matter of life and death, then he turned and ran. Ferenc and Koscis would already be heading back through the tunnel on the assumption that there might be an escape route open to Bowman: in any event it would be pointless for them to remain where they were as any action they might try to take there would result only in their untimely end. Untimely, that is, from their point of view.

He ran down the steep slope of scree because he had no alternative but to run, taking increasingly huge bounding steps to maintain what was left of his balance. Three-quarters of the way down to the waiting jumble of limestone boulders his loss of balance passed the point of no return and he fell, rolling diagonally downhill, trying frantically and with a total lack of success to brake himself. The braking was done for him, violently and painfully, by the first of the boulders with which he came into contact and it was his right knee that took the major brunt of the impact.

He was sure he had smashed the knee-cap for when he tried to rise his leg just gave under him and he sat down again. A second time he tried it and this time with a little more success: the third time he made it and he knew the knee-cap had just been momentarily paralysed. Now it felt merely numb although he knew it must hurt badly later and would be severely bruised. He hobbled on his way through the thinning scattering of boulders at about half the best speed he could normally have made for the knee kept collapsing under him as if it had a will of its own.

A puff of white smoke flew off from a boulder just in front of him and the sound of the shot was almost simultaneous. Ferenc had anticipated too well. Bowman didn't try to take cover because Ferenc could see where he was and had Bowman tried to hide Ferenc would just have walked down to the place of concealment and put the pistol to his head to make quite sure that he didn't miss. Bowman made off down the slope, twisting and doubling among the rocks to throw Ferenc off aim, not even trying to locate where his pursuers were for the knowledge would have been useless to him anyway. Several shots came close, one kicking up a small cloud of soil at his right foot, but the combination of his swerving run and the fact that Ferenc had himself to dodge in and out among the rocks must have made him an almost impossible target. Besides, to shoot accurately downhill is notoriously difficult at the best of times. In between the shots Bowman could hear the sound of their pounding footsteps and he knew they were gaining on him: but still he didn't look round for if he were going to be shot through the back of the head he felt he'd just as soon not know about it in advance.

He was clear of the rocks now and running straight over the hard-packed earth towards the railed entrance to the village. Ferenc, closing up and also running straight, should have had his chance then but the firing had stopped and Bowman could only assume that he had run out of ammunition. He might well, Bowman realized, carry a spare magazine but if he did he would have been hard put to it to reload on the dead run.

Bowman's knee was hurting now but, contradictorily, it was bearing up much better. He glanced behind. His pursuers were still gaining, but more slowly. Bowman passed through the railed upper entrance to the village and ran down to the fork where he had hesitated on the way up. The two gypsies were not yet in sight but the sound of their running feet was clear. They would expect him, Bowman hoped, to continue out through the lower entrance to the village, so he turned left down the short road that led to the old battlements of the town. The road debouched into a small square, a cul-de-sac, but he was past caring about that. He registered the fact, without knowing why, that an ancient wrought-iron cross stood in the centre of the square. To the left was an equally ancient church, facing it was a low wall with apparently nothing beyond it and, between church and wall, a high face of vertical rocks with deep man-made apertures cut into it, for reasons that couldn't be guessed at.

He ran across to the low rock and peered over it. It was certainly no low rock on the other side: it dropped almost two hundred vertical feet to what looked like scrub trees at the foot.

Ferenc had been cleverer than Bowman thought he would have been. He was still peering over the wall when he heard the sound of running feet approaching the square, one set of feet: they'd split up to investigate both avenues of escape. Bowman straightened and hurried soundlessly across the square and hid in the shadows of one of the deep recesses cut in the natural rock.

Koscis it was. He slowed down on entering the square, his stertorous breathing carrying clearly in the night air, walked past the iron cross, glanced at the open doorway of the church, then, as if guided by some natural instinct, came heading straight towards the particular niche where Bowman stood as deeply pressed back in the shadow as he possibly could. There was a peculiar inevitability about the unhesitating manner of his approach. He held his knife, thumb on top of the handle, in what appeared to be his favourite waist-high level.

Bowman waited until the gypsy was fractionally away from the point which would make discovery certain, then hurled himself from the dark niche, managing to grab his knife wrist more by good luck than good judgment. Both men fell heavily to the ground, fighting for possession of the knife. Bowman tried to twist Koscis's right wrist but it seemed to be made of overlaid strands of wire hawser and

Bowman could feel the wrist slowly breaking free from his grasp. He anticipated the inevitable by suddenly letting go and rolling over twice, rising to his feet at the same instant as Koscis did. For a moment they looked at each other, immobile, then Bowman backed away slowly until his hands touched the low wall behind him. He had no place to run to any more and no place to hide.

Koscis advanced. His face, at first implacable, broke into a smile that was notably lacking in warmth. Koscis, the expert with a knife, was savouring the passing moment.

Bowman threw himself forward, then to the right, but Koscis had seen this one before. He flung himself forward to intercept the second stage of the movement, his knife arcing up from knee level, but what Koscis had forgotten was that Bowman knew he had seen this one before. Bowman checked with all the strength of his right leg, dropped to his left knee and as the knife hooked by inches over his head, his right shoulder and upper arm hit the gypsy's thighs. Bowman straightened up with a convulsive jerk and this, combined with the speed and accelerating momentum of Koscis's onrush lifted the gypsy high into the air and sent him, useless knife still in hand, sailing helplessly over the low wall into the darkness below. Bowman twisted round and watched him as he fell, a diminishing manikin tumbling over and over in almost incredibly slow motion, his passing marked only by a fading scream in the night. And then Bowman couldn't see him any more and the screaming stopped.

For a few seconds Bowman stood there, a man held in thrall, but only for a few seconds. If Ferenc hadn't been afflicted with a sudden and total deafness he was bound to have heard that eldritch fear-crazed scream and come to investigate and immediately.

Bowman ran from the square towards the main street: halfway up the narrow connecting lane he slid into a darkened alleyway for he'd heard Ferenc coming and for a brief moment saw him as he passed the end of the alleyway, pistol in one hand, knife in the other. Whether the pistol had been reloaded or not or whether Ferenc had balked at firing it so near the village was impossible to say. Even in what must have been that moment of intolerable stress Ferenc was still possessed of a sufficient instinct of self-preservation to keep exactly to the middle of the road where he couldn't be ambushed by an unarmed man. His lips were drawn back in an unconscious snarl compounded of rage and hate and fear and his face was the face of a madman.

CHAPTER THREE

It isn't every woman who, wakened in the middle of the night, can sit bolt upright in bed, sheets hauled up to the neck, hair dishevelled and eyes blurred with sleep and still look as attractive as if she were setting out for a ball, but Cecile Dubois must have been one of the few. She blinked, perhaps, rather more than a would-be dancer would have done, then gave Bowman what appeared to be a rather penetrating and critical look, possibly because as a result of all that climbing in the ruins and falling down scree-covered slopes Bowman's dark broadcloth had lost some of its showroom sheen: in fact, now that he could clearly see it for the first time, it was filthily dirty, stained and ripped beyond repair. He waited for her reaction, sarcastic, cynical or perhaps just plain annoyed, but she wasn't an obvious sort of girl.

She said: 'I thought you'd be in the next county by this time.'

'I was almost in another land altogether.' He took his hand from the light switch and eased the door until it was almost but not quite closed. 'But I came back. For the car. And for you.'

'For me?'

'Especially for you. Hurry up and get dressed. Your life's not worth a tinker's cuss if you stay here.'

'My life? But why should I—'

'Up, dress and pack. Now.' He crossed to the bed and looked at her, and although his appearance wasn't very encouraging it must have been convincing for she compressed her lips slightly, then nodded. Bowman returned to the door and looked out through the crack he had left. Very fetching though the dark-haired Miss Dubois might be, he reflected, it did not mean that she had to conform to the beautiful brunette pattern: she made decisions, quickly accepted what she regarded as being inevitable and the 'if you think I'm going to get dressed while you're standing there' routine apparently hadn't even crossed her mind. Not that he would have seriously objected but, for the moment, the imminent return of Ferenc held prior claim to his attentions. He wondered briefly what was holding Ferenc up, he should have posted hotfoot by that time to report to his old man that they had encountered some unexpected difficulties in the execution of their assignment. It could have been, of course, that even then Ferenc was prowling hopefully and stealthily through the back alleys of Les Baux with a gun in one hand, a knife in the other and murder in his heart.

'I'm ready,' Cecile said.

Bowman looked round in mild astonishment. She was, too, even to the extent of having combed her hair. A strapped suitcase lay on her bed. 'And packed?' Bowman asked.

'Last night.' She hesitated. 'Look, I can't just walk off without—'

'Lila? Leave her a note. Say you'll contact her Poste Restante, Saintes-Maries. Hurry. Back in a minute—I have to collect my stuff.'

He left her there, went quickly to his own room and paused briefly at the door. The south wind sighed through the trees and he could hear the splash of the fountain in the swimming pool but that was all he could hear. He went into his room, crammed clothes anyhow into a suitcase and was back in Cecile's room within the promised minute. She was still scribbling away industriously.

'Poste Restante, Saintes-Maries, that's all you've got to write,' Bowman said hastily. 'Your life story she probably knows about.'

She glanced up at him, briefly and expressionlessly over the rims of a pair of glasses that he was only mildly surprised to see that she was wearing, reduced him to the status of an insect on the wall, then got back to her writing. After another twenty seconds she signed her name with what seemed to Bowman to be a wholly unnecessary flourish considering the urgency of the moment, snapped the spectacles in the case and nodded to indicate that she was ready. He picked up her suitcase and they left, switching off the light and closing the door behind them. Bowman picked up his own suitcase, waited until the girl had slid the folded note under Lila's door, then both walked quickly and quietly along the terrace, then up the path to the road that skirted the back of the hotel. The girl followed closely and in silence behind Bowman and he was just beginning to congratulate himself on how quickly and well she was responding to his training methods when she caught his left arm firmly and hauled him to a stop. Bowman looked at her and frowned but it didn't seem to have any effect. Short-sighted, he thought charitably.

'We're safe here?' she asked.

'For the moment, yes.'

'Put those cases down.'

He put the cases down. He'd have to revise his training methods.

'So far and no farther,' she said matter-of-factly. 'I've been a good little girl and I've done what you asked because I thought there was possibly one chance in a hundred that you weren't mad. The other ninety-nine per cent of my way of thinking makes me want an explanation. Now.'

Her mother hadn't done much about training her either, Bowman thought. Not, at least, in the niceties of drawing-room conversation. But someone had done a very good job in other directions, for if she were upset or scared in any way it certainly didn't show.

'You're in trouble,' Bowman said. 'I got you into it. Now it's my responsibility to get you out of it.'

'*I'm* in trouble?'

'Both of us. Three characters from the gypsy caravan down there told me that they were going to do me in. Then you. But first me. So they chased me up to Les Baux and then through the village and the ruins.'

She looked at him speculatively, not at all worried or concerned as she ought to have been. 'But if they chased you—'

'I shook them off. The gypsy leader's son, a lovable little lad by the name of Ferenc, is possibly still up there looking for me. He has a gun in one hand, a knife in the other. When he doesn't find me he'll come back and tell Dad and then a few of them will troop up to our rooms. Yours and mine.'

'What on earth have *I* done?' she demanded.

'You've been seen with me all evening and you've been seen to give refuge, that's what you've done.'

'But—but this is ridiculous. I mean, taking to our heels like this.' She shook her head. 'I was wrong about that possible one per cent. You *are* mad.'

'Probably.' It was, Bowman thought, a justifiable point of view.

'I mean, you've only got to pick up the phone.'

'And?'

'The police, silly.'

'No police—because I'm not silly, Cecile. I'd be arrested for murder.'

She looked at him and slowly shook her head in disbelief or incomprehension or both.

'It wasn't so easy to shake them off tonight,' Bowman went on. 'There was an accident. Two accidents.'

'Fantasy.' She shook her head as she whispered the word again. 'Fantasy.'

'Of course.' He reached out and took her hand. 'Come, I'll show you the bodies.' He knew he could never locate Hoval in the darkness but Koscis's whereabouts would present no problem and as far as proving his case was concerned one corpse would be as good as two any time. And then he knew he didn't have to prove anything, not any more. In her face, very pale now but quite composed, something had changed. He didn't know what it was, he just registered the change. And then she came close to him and took his free hand in hers. She didn't start having the shakes, she didn't shrink away in horrified revulsion from a self-confessed killer, she just came close and took his other hand.

'Where do you want to go?' Her voice was low but there were no shakes in it either. 'Riviera? Switzerland?'

He could have hugged her but decided to wait for a more propitious moment. He said: 'Saintes-Maries.'

'Saintes-Maries!'

'That's where all the gypsies are going. So that's where I want to go.'

There was a silence, then she said without any particular inflection in her voice: 'To die in Saintes-Maries.'

'To live in Saintes-Maries, Cecile. To justify living, if you like. We idle layabouts have to, you know.' She looked at him steadily, but kept silent: he would have expected this by now, she was a person who would always know when to be silent. In the pale wash of moonlight the lovely face was grave to the point of sadness. 'I want to find out why a young gypsy is missing,' Bowman went on. 'I want to find out why a gypsy mother and three gypsy girls are terrified out of their lives. I want to find out why three other gypsies tried their damnedest to kill me tonight. And I want to find out why they're even prepared to go to the extraordinary lengths of killing you. Wouldn't you like to find those things out too, Cecile?'

She nodded and took her hands away. He picked up the suitcases and they walked down circumspectly past the main entrance to the hotel. There was no one around, no sound of any person moving around, no hue and cry, nothing but the soft quiet and peacefulness of the Elysian Fields or, perhaps, of any well-run cemetery or morgue. They carried on down the steeply winding road to where it joined the transverse road running north and south through the Valley of Hell and there they turned sharply right—a ninety-degree turn. Another thirty yards and Bowman gratefully set the cases down on the grassy verge.

'Where's your car parked?' he asked.

'At the inner end of the parking area.'

'That *is* handy. Means it has to be driven out through the parking lot and the forecourt. What make?'

'Peugeot 504. Blue.'

He held out his hand. 'The keys.'

'Why? Think I'm not capable of driving my own car out of—'

'Not out of, chérie. Over. Over anyone who tries to get in your way. Because they will.'

'But they'll be asleep—'

'Innocence, innocence. They'll be sitting around drinking slivovitz and waiting happily for the good news of my death. The keys.'

She gave him a very old-fashioned look, one compounded of an odd mixture of irritation and speculative amusement, dug in her handbag and brought out the keys. He took them and, as he moved off, she made to follow. He shook his head.

'Next time,' he said.

'I see.' She made a face. 'I don't think you and I are going to get along too well.'

'We'd better,' he said. 'For your sake, for my sake, we'd better. And it would be nice to get you to that altar unscarred. Stay here.'

Two minutes later, pressed deeply into shadow, he stood at the side of the entrance to the forecourt. Three caravans, the three he had examined earlier, still had their lights burning, but only one of them—Czerda's—showed any sign of human activity. It came as no surprise to him to discover that his guess as to what Czerda and his headmen would be doing had proved to be so remarkably accurate, except that he had no means of checking whether the alcohol they were putting away in such copious quantities was slivovitz or not. It was certainly alcohol. The two men sitting with Czerda on the caravan steps were cast in the same mould as Czerda himself, swarthy, lean, powerfully built, unmistakably Central European and unprepossessing to a degree. Bowman had never seen either before nor, looking at them, did he care very much whether he ever saw either of them again. From the desultory conversation, he gathered they were called Maca and Masaine: whatever their names it was clear that fate had not cast them on the side of the angels.

Almost directly between them and Bowman's place of concealment stood Czerda's jeep, parked so that it faced the entrance of the forecourt—the only vehicle there so positioned: in an emergency, clearly, it would be the first vehicle that would be pressed into service and it seemed to Bowman prudent to do something about that. Crouched low, moving slowly and silently across the forecourt and at all times keeping the jeep directly between him and the caravan steps, he arrived at the front end of the jeep, edged cautiously towards the near front tyre, unscrewed the valve cap and inserted the end of a match into the valve using a balled-up handkerchief to muffle the hiss of the escaping air. By and by the rim of the wheel settled down until it was biting into the inner carcass of the tread. Bowman hoped, fervently if belatedly, that Czerda and his friends weren't regarding the front near wing in any way closely for they could not have failed to be more than mildly astonished by the fact that it had sunk a clear three inches closer to the ground. But Czerda and his friends had, providentially, other and more immediate concerns to occupy their attention.

'Something is wrong,' Czerda said positively. 'Very far wrong. You know that I can always tell about those things.'

'Ferenc and Koscis and Hoval can look after themselves.' It was the man whose name Bowman thought to be Maca and he spoke confidently. 'If this Bowman ran, he could have run a very long way.'

'No.' Bowman risked a quick glance round the wing of the jeep and Czerda was now on his feet. 'They've been gone too long, far too long. Come. We must look for them.'

The other two gypsies rose reluctantly to their feet but remained there, as Czerda did, their heads cocked and slowly turning. Bowman had heard the sound as soon as they had, the sound of pounding feet from the patio by the pool. Ferenc appeared at the top of the steps, came down three at a time and ran across the forecourt to Czerda's caravan. It was the lurching stumbling run of a man very close to exhaustion and from his distressed breathing, sweating face and the fact that he made no attempt to conceal the gun in his hand it was clear that Ferenc was in a state of considerable agitation.

'They're dead, Father!' Ferenc's voice was a hoarse gasping wheeze. 'Hoval and Koscis. They're dead!'

'God's name, what are you saying?' Czerda demanded.

'Dead! Dead, I tell you! I found Koscis. His neck is broken, I think every bone in his body is broken. God knows where Hoval is.'

Czerda seized his son by the lapels and shook him violently. 'Talk sense! Killed?' His voice was almost a shout.

'This man Bowman. He killed them.'

'He killed—he killed—and Bowman?'

'Escaped.'

'Escaped! Escaped! You young fool, if this man escapes Gaiuse Strome will kill us all. Quickly! Bowman's room!'

'And the girl's.' Ferenc's wheezing had eased fractionally. 'And the girl's.'

'The girl?' Czerda asked. 'The dark one?'

Ferenc nodded violently. 'She gave him shelter.'

'And the girl's,' Czerda agreed viciously. 'Hurry.'

The four men ran off towards the patio steps. Bowman moved to the offside front tyre and because this time he didn't have to bother about muffing the escaping hiss of air he merely unscrewed the valve and threw it away. He rose and, still stooping, ran across the forecourt and through the sculptured arch in the hedge to the parking space beyond.

Here he ran into an unexpected difficulty. A blue Peugeot, Cecile had said. Fine. A blue Peugeot he could recognize any time—in broad daylight. But this wasn't daytime, it was night-time, and even although the moon was shining the thickly-woven wickerwork roofing cast an almost impenetrable shadow on the cars parked beneath it. Just as by night all cats are grey so by night all cars look infuriatingly the same. Easy enough, perhaps, to differentiate between a Rolls and a Mini, but in this age of mindless conformity the vast majority of cars are disturbingly alike in size and profile. Or so, dismayingly, Bowman found that night. He moved quickly from one car to the next, having to peer closely in each case for an infuriating length of time, only to discover that it was not the car he was seeking.

He heard the sound of low voices, but voices angry and anxious, and moved quickly to the archway. Close by Czerda's caravan, the four gypsies, who had clearly discovered that their birds had flown, were gesticulating and arguing heatedly, holding their council of war and obviously wondering what in hell to do next, a decision Bowman didn't envy their having to make for in their position he wouldn't have had the faintest idea himself.

Abruptly, the centre of his attention altered. Out of the corner of an eye he had caught sight of something which, even in that pale moonlight, definitely constituted a splash of colour. This brightly-hued apparition, located on the upper terrace, consisted of a pair of garishly-striped heliotrope pyjamas and inside the pyjamas was no other than Le Grand Duc, leaning on the balustrade and gazing down towards the forecourt with an expression of what might have been mild interest or benign indifference or, indeed, quite a variety of other expressions as it is difficult to be positive about those things when a large part of what can be seen of the subject's face consists of jaws champing regularly up and down while most of the remainder is concealed by a large red apple. But, clearly, however, he wasn't in the grip of any violent emotion.

Bowman left Le Grand Duc to his munching and resumed his search. The inner end of the parking lot, she had said. But her damned Peugeot wasn't at the inner end. He'd checked twice. He turned to the west side and the fourth one along was it. Or he thought it was. A Peugeot, anyway. He climbed inside and the key fitted the ignition. Women, he thought bitterly, but didn't pursue the subject with himself, there were things to be done.

The door he closed as softly as he could: it seemed unlikely that the faint click would have been heard in the forecourt even if the gypsies hadn't been conducting their heated council of war. He released the hand-brake, engaged first gear and kept the clutch depressed, reached for and turned on the ignition and headlamp switches simultaneously. Both engine and lamps came on precisely together and the Peugeot, throwing gravel from its rear wheels, jumped forward, Bowman spinning the wheel to the left to head for the archway in the hedge. At once he saw the four gypsies detach themselves from the rear of Czerda's caravan and run to cover what they accurately assumed would be the route he would take between the archway and the exit from the forecourt. Czerda appeared to be shouting and although his voice couldn't be heard above the accelerating roar of the engine his violent gesticulations clearly indicated that he was telling his men to stop the Peugeot although how he proposed to do this Bowman couldn't imagine. As he passed through the archway he could see in the blaze of the headlamps that Ferenc was the only one carrying a firearm and as he was pointing it directly at Bowman he didn't leave Bowman with very much option other than to point the car directly at him. The panic registering suddenly on Ferenc's face showed that he had lost all interest in using the gun and was now primarily concerned with saving himself. He dived frantically to his left and almost got clear but almost wasn't enough. The nearside wing of the Peugeot caught him in the thigh and suddenly he wasn't there any more, all Bowman could see was the metallic glint of his gun spinning in the air. On the left, Czerda and the two other gypsies had managed to fling themselves clear. Bowman twisted the wheel again, drove out of the forecourt and down towards the valley road. He wondered what Le Grand Duc had made of all that: probably, he thought, he hadn't missed as much as a munch.

The tyres squealed as the Peugeot rounded the right-angle turn at the foot of the road. Bowman drew up beside Cecile, stopped, got out but left the engine running. She ran to him and thrust out a suitcase.

'Hurry! Quickly!' Angrily, almost, she thrust the case at him.' Can't you hear them coming?'

'I can hear them,' Bowman said pacifically. 'I think we have time.'

They had time. They heard the whine of an engine in low gear, a whine diminishing in intensity as the jeep braked heavily for the corner. Abruptly it came into sight and clearly it was making a very poor job indeed of negotiating the right-hand bend. Czerda was hauling madly on the steering-wheel but the front wheels—or tyres, at least—appeared to have a mind of their own. Bowman watched with interest as the jeep carried straight on, careered across the opposite bank of the road, cut down a sapling and landed with a resounding crash.

'Tsk! Tsk!' Bowman said to Cecile. 'Did ever you see such careless driving?' He crossed over the road and looked into the field. The jeep, its wheels still spinning, lay on its side while the three gypsies, who had clearly parted company with their vehicle before it had come to rest, lay in a sprawled heap about fifteen feet away. As he watched they disentangled themselves and scrambled painfully to their feet. Ferenc, understandably, was not one of the three. Bowman became aware that he had been joined by Cecile.

'You did this,' she said accusingly. 'You sabotaged their jeep.'

'It was nothing,' he said deprecatingly. 'I just let a little air out of the tyres.'

'But—but you could have killed those men! The jeep could have landed on top of them and crushed them to death.'

'It's not always possible to arrange everything as one

would wish it,' Bowman said regretfully. She gave him the kind of look Dr Crippen must have got used to after he'd been hauled into court, so Bowman changed his tone. 'You don't look like a fool, Cecile, nor do you talk like one, so don't go and spoil the whole effect by behaving like one. If you think our three friends down there were just out to savour the delights of the night-time Provençal air, why don't you go and ask them how they are?'

She turned and walked back to the car without a word. He followed and they drove off in a one-sidedly huffy silence. Within a minute he slowed and pulled the car into a small cleared area on the right-hand side of the road. Through the windscreen they could see the vertical limestone bluffs with enormous man-made rectangular openings giving on the impenetrable darkness of the unseen caverns beyond.

'You're not stopping here?' Incredulity in her voice.

He switched off the engine and set the parking brake. 'I've stopped.'

'But they'll find us here!' She sounded a little desperate. 'They're bound to. Any moment now.'

'No. If they're capable of thinking at all after that little tumble they had, they'll be thinking that we're half-way to Avignon by this time. Besides, I think it's going to take them some time to recover their first fine enthusiasm for moonlight driving.'

They got out of the car and looked at the entrance to the caverns. Foreboding wasn't the word for it, nor was sinister: something stronger, much stronger. It was, quite literally, an appalling place and Bowman had no difficulty in understanding and sympathizing with the viewpoint of the policeman back at the hotel. But he didn't for a moment believe that you had to be born in Les Baux and grow up hand-in-hand with all the ancient superstitions in order to develop a night phobia about those caves: quite simply it was a place into which no man in his right mind would venture after the sun had gone down. He was, he hoped, in his right mind, and he didn't want to go in. But he had to.

He took a torch from his suitcase and said to Cecile: 'Wait here.'

'No! You're not going to leave me alone here.' She sounded pretty vehement about it.

'It'll probably be an awful lot worse inside.'

'I don't care.'

'Suit yourself.'

They set off together and passed through the largest of the openings to the left: if you could have put a three-storey house on wheels you could have trundled it through that opening without any trouble. Bowman traversed the walls with his torch, walls covered with the graffiti of countless generations, then opted for an archway to the right that led to an even larger cavern. Cecile, he noticed, even although wearing flat-heeled sandals, stumbled quite a bit, more than the occasional slight undulations in the limestone floor warranted: he was pretty well sure now that her vision was a good deal less than twenty-twenty which, he reflected, was maybe why she had consented to come with him in the first place.

The next cavern held nothing of interest for Bowman. True, its vaulted heights were lost in darkness, but as only a bat could have got up there anyway that was of no moment. Another archway loomed ahead.

'This is a dreadful place,' Cecile whispered.

'Well, I wouldn't like to live here all the time.'

Another few paces and she said: 'Mr Bowman.'

'Neil.'

'May I take your arm?' In these days he didn't think they asked.

'Help yourself,' he said agreeably. 'You're not the only person in need of reassurance round here.'

'It's not that. I'm not scared, really. It's just that you keep flashing that torch everywhere and I can't see and I keep tripping.'

'Ah!'

So she took his arm and she didn't trip any more, just shivered violently as if she were coming down with some form of malaria. By and by she said: 'What are you looking for?'

'You know damned well what I'm looking for.'

'Perhaps—well, they could have hidden him.'

'They could have hidden him. They couldn't have buried him, not unless they had brought along some dynamite with them, but they could have hidden him. Under a mound of limestone rock and stones. There's plenty around.'

'But we've passed by dozens of piles of limestone rocks. You didn't bother about them.'

'When we come to a freshly made mound you'll know the difference,' he said matter-of-factly. She shivered again, violently, and he went on: 'Why did you have to come in, Cecile? You were telling the truth when you said you weren't scared: you're just plain terrified.'

'I'd rather be plain terrified in here with you than plain terrified alone out there.' Any moment now and her teeth would start chattering.

'You may have a point there,' he admitted. They passed, slightly uphill this time, through another archway, into another immense cavern: after a few steps Bowman stopped abruptly.

'What is it?' she whispered. 'What's wrong?'

'I don't know.' He paused. 'Yes, I do know.' For the first time he shivered himself.

'You, too?' Again that whisper.

'Me, too. But it's not that. Some clod-hopping character has just walked over my grave.'

'Please?'

'This is it. This is the place. When you're old and sinful like me, you can smell it.'

'Death?' And now her voice was shaking. 'People can't smell death.'

'I can.'

He switched off the torch.

'Put it on, put it on!' Her voice was high-pitched, close to hysteria. 'For God's sake, put it on. *Please*.'

He detached her hand, put his arm round her and held her close. With a bit of luck, he thought, they might get some synchronization into their shivering, not as much perhaps as the ballroom champions on TV got in their dancing, but enough to be comfortable. When the vibrations had died down a little he said: 'Notice anything different about this cavern?'

'There's light! There's light coming from somewhere.'

'There is indeed.' They walked slowly forward till they came to a huge pile of rubble on the floor. The jumble of rocks stretched up and up until at the top they could see a large squarish patch of star-dusted sky. Down the centre of this rockfall, all the way from top to bottom, was a narrow patch of disturbed rubble, a pathway that seemed to have been newly made. Bowman switched on his torch and there was no doubt about it: it was newly made. He traversed the base of the rockfall with the beam of the torch and then the beam, almost of its own volition, stopped and looked on a mound of limestone rocks, perhaps eight feet in length by three high.

'With a freshly made mound of limestone,' Bowman said, 'you can see the difference.'

'You can see the difference,' she repeated mechanically.

'Please. Walk away a little.'

'No. It's funny, but I'm all right now.'

He believed her and he didn't think it was funny. Mankind is still close enough to the primeval jungles to find the greatest fear of all in the unknown: but here, now, they knew.

Bowman stooped over the mound and began to throw stones to one side. They hadn't bothered to cover the unfortunate Alexandre to any great depth for inside a moment Bowman came to the slashed remnants of a once white shirt, now saturated in blood. Lying in the encrusted blood and attached to a chain was a silver crucifix. He unclipped the chain and lifted both it and the crucifix away.

Bowman parked the Peugeot at the spot in the valley road where he had picked up Cecile and the cases. He got out.

'Stay here,' he said to Cecile. 'This time I mean it.' She didn't exactly nod her head obediently but she didn't argue either: maybe his training methods were beginning to improve. The jeep, he observed without any surprise, was where he'd last seen it: it was going to require a mobile crane to get it out of there.

The entrance to the Baumanière's forecourt seemed deserted but he'd developed the same sort of affectionate trust for Czerda and his merry band of followers as he would have for a colony of cobras or black widow spiders so he pressed deep into the shadows and advanced slowly into the forecourt. His foot struck something solid and there was a faint metallic clink. He became very still but he'd provoked no reaction that he could see or hear. He stooped and picked up the pistol that he'd inadvertently kicked against the base of a petrol pump. Young Ferenc's pistol, without a doubt. From what last Bowman had seen of Ferenc he didn't think he'd have missed it yet or would be wanting to use it for some time: but Bowman decided to return it to him all the same. He knew he wouldn't be disturbing anyone for lights from inside Czerda's caravan still shone through the windows and the half-open door. Every other caravan in the forecourt was in darkness. He crossed to Czerda's caravan, climbed the steps soundlessly and looked in through the doorway.

Czerda, with a bandaged left hand, bruised cheek and large strip of sticking-plaster on his forehead, wasn't looking quite his old self but he was in mint condition compared to Ferenc to whose injuries he was attending. Ferenc lay on a bunk, moaning and barely half-conscious, exclaiming in pain from time to time as his father removed a blood-soaked bandage from his forehead. When the bandage was at last jerked free to the accompaniment of a final yelp of pain, a pain that had the effect of restoring Ferenc to something pretty close to complete consciousness, Bowman could see that he had a very nasty cut indeed across his forehead, but a cut that faded into insignificance compared to the massive bruising of forehead and face: if he had sustained other bodily bruises of a comparable magnitude Ferenc had to be suffering very considerably and feeling in a very low state indeed. It was not a consideration that moved Bowman: if Ferenc had had his way he, Bowman, would be in a state in which he'd never feel anything again.

Ferenc sat shakily up on the bunk while his father secured a fresh bandage, then sat forward, put his elbows on his knees, his face in his hands and moaned.

'In God's name, what happened? My head—'

'You'll be all right,' Czerda said soothingly. 'A cut and a bruise. That's all.'

'But what *happened*? Why is my head—'

'The car. Remember?'

'The car. Of course. That devil Bowman!' Coming from Ferenc, Bowman thought, that was rather good. 'Did he —did he—'

'Damn his soul, yes. He got clear away—and he wrecked our jeep. See this?' Czerda pointed to his hand and forehead. Ferenc looked without interest and looked away. He had other things on his mind.

'My gun, Father! Where's my gun?'

'Here,' Bowman said. He pointed his gun at Ferenc and walked into the caravan: the blood-stained chain and crucifix dangled from his left hand. Ferenc stared at him: he looked as a man might look with his head on the block and the executioner starting the back swing on his axe, for executioner Ferenc would have been in Bowman's position. Czerda, whose back had been to the door, swung round and remained as immobile as his son. He didn't seem any more pleased to see Bowman than Ferenc did. Bowman walked forward, two paces, and placed the bloody crucifix on a small table.

'His mother might like to have that,' he said. 'I should wipe the blood off first, though.' He waited for some reaction but there was none so he went on: 'I'm going to kill you, Czerda. I'll have to, won't I, for no one can ever prove you killed young Alexandre. But I don't require proof, all I need is certainty. But not yet. I can't do it yet, can I? I mustn't cause innocent people to die, must I? But later. Later I kill you. Then I kill Gaiuse Strome. Tell him I said so, will you?'

'What do you know of Gaiuse Strome?' he whispered.

'Enough to hang him. And you.'

Czerda suddenly smiled but when he spoke it was still in the same whisper.

'You've just said you can't kill me yet.' He took a step forward.

Bowman said nothing. He altered the pistol fractionally until it was lined up on a spot between Ferenc's eyes. Czerda made no move to take a second step. Bowman looked at him and pointed to a stool close to the small table.

'Sit down,' he said, 'and face your son.'

Czerda did as he was told. Bowman took one step forward and it was apparent that Ferenc's reactions weren't yet back in working order for his suddenly horrified expession in what little was left of his face that was still capable of registering expressions and his mouth opening to shout a warning came far too late to be of any aid to

Czerda who crashed heavily to the floor as the barrel of Bowman's gun caught him behind the ear.

Ferenc bared his teeth and swore viciously at him. At least that was what Bowman assumed he was doing for Ferenc had reverted to his native Romany but he hadn't even started in on his descriptions when Bowman stepped forward wordlessly, his gun swinging again. Ferenc's reactions were even slower than Bowman had imagined: he toppled head-long across his father and lay still.

'What on earth—' The voice came from behind Bowman. He threw himself to one side, dropping to the floor, whirled round and brought the gun up: then, more slowly, he rose. Cecile stood in the doorway, her green eyes wide, her face stilled in shock.

'You fool,' Bowman said savagely. 'You almost died there. Don't you know that?' She nodded, the shock still in her face. 'Come inside. Shut the door. You *are* a fool. Why the hell didn't you do what I asked and stayed where you were?'

Almost as if in a trance she stepped inside and closed the door. She stared down at the two fallen men, then back at Bowman again.

'For God's sake, why did you knock those two men senseless? Two injured men?'

'Because it was inconvenient to kill them at present,' Bowman said coldly. He turned his back on her and began to search the place methodically and exhaustively. When one searches any place, be it gypsy caravan or baronial mansion, methodically and exhaustively, one has to wreck it completely in the process. So, in an orderly and systematic fashion, Bowman set about reducing Czerda's caravan to a total ruin. He ripped the beds to pieces, sliced open the mattresses with the aid of a knife he'd borrowed from the recumbent Czerda, scattering the flock stuffing far and wide to ensure that there was nothing hidden inside, and wrenched open cupboards, all locked, again with the aid of Czerda's knife. He moved into the kitchen recess, smashed all the items of crockery that were capable of holding anything, emptied the contents of a dozen food tins into the sink, smashed open preserving jars and a variety of wine bottles by the simple expedient of knocking them together two at a time and ended up by spilling the contents of the cutlery drawers on the floor to ensure that there was nothing hidden beneath the lining paper. There wasn't.

Cecile, who had been watching this performance still in the same kind of hypnotic trance, said: 'Who's Gaiuse Strome?'

'How long were you listening?'

'All the time. Who's Gaiuse Strome?'

'I don't know,' Bowman said frankly. 'Never heard of him until tonight.'

He turned his attention to the larger clothing drawers. He emptied the contents of each in turn on the floor and kicked them apart. There was nothing there for him, just clothes.

'Other people's property doesn't mean all that much to you, does it?' By this time Cecile's state of trance had altered to the dazed incomprehension of one trying to come to grips with reality.

'He'll have it insured,' Bowman said comfortingly. He began an assault on the last piece of furniture still intact, a beautifully carved mahogany bureau worth a small fortune in anybody's money, splintering open the locked drawers with the now invaluable aid of the point of Czerda's knife. He dumped the contents of the first two drawers on the floor and was about to open a third when something caught his eye. He stooped and retrieved a pair of heavy rolled-up woollen socks. Inside them was an elastic-bound package of brand-new crackling banknotes with consecutive serial numbers. It took him over half a minute to count them.

'Eighty thousand Swiss francs in one-thousand-franc notes,' Bowman observed. 'I wonder where friend Czerda got eighty thousand Swiss francs in one-thousand-franc notes? Ah, well.' He stuffed the notes into a hip pocket and resumed the search.

'But—but that's stealing!' It would be too much, perhaps, to say that Cecile looked horrified but there wasn't much in the way of admiration in those big green eyes: but Bowman was in no mood for moral disapprobation.

'Oh, shut up!' he said.

'But you've *got* money.'

'Maybe this is how I get it.'

He broke open another drawer, sifted through the contents with the toe of his shoe, then turned as he heard a sound to his left. Ferenc was struggling shakily to his feet, so Bowman took his arm, helped him to stand upright, hit him very hard indeed on the side of the jaw and lowered him to the floor again. The shock was back in Cecile's face, a shock mingled with the beginnings of revulsion, she was probably a gently nurtured girl who had been brought up to believe that the opera or the ballet or the theatre constituted the ideal of an evening's entertainment. Bowman started in on the next drawer.

'Don't tell me,' he said. 'Just an idle layabout laying about. Not funny?'

'No.' She had her lips compressed in a very schoolmarmish way.

'I'm pressed for time. Ah!'

'What is it?' In even the most puritanical of females repugnance doesn't stand a chance against curiosity.

'This.' He showed her a delicately fashioned rosewood lacquered box inlaid with ebony and mother-of-pearl. It was locked and so exquisitely made that it was quite impossible to insert the point of even Czerda's razor-sharp knife into the microscopic line between lid and box. Cecile seemed to derive a certain malicious satisfaction from this momentary problem for she waved a hand to indicate the indescribable wreckage that now littered almost every square inch of the caravan floor.

'Shall I look for the key?' she asked sweetly.

'No need.' He laid the rosewood box on the floor and jumped on it with both heels, reducing it at once to splintered matchwood. He removed a sealed envelope from the ruins, opened it and extracted a sheet of paper.

On it was a typewritten—in capitals—jumble of apparently meaningless letters and figures. There were a few words in plain language but their meaning in the context was completely obscure. Cecile peered over his shoulder. Her eyes were screwed up and he knew she was having difficulty in seeing.

'What is it?' she asked.

'Code, looks like. One or two words straight. There's "Monday", a date—May 24th—and a place-name—Grau du Roi.'

'Grau du Roi?'

'A fishing port and holiday resort down on the coast. Now, why should a gypsy be carrying a message in code?' He thought about this for a bit but it didn't do him any good: he was still awake and on his feet but his mind had turned in for the night. 'Stupid question. Up, up and away.'

'What? Still two lovely drawers left unsmashed?'

'Leave those for the vandals.' He took her arm so that she wouldn't trip too often on the way to the door and she peered questioningly at him.

'Meaning you can break codes?'

Bowman looked around him. 'Furniture, yes. Crockery, yes. Codes, no. Come, to our hotel.'

They left. Before closing the door Bowman had a last look at the two still unconscious and injured men lying amidst the irretrievably ruined shambles of what had once been a beautifully appointed caravan interior. He felt almost sorry for the caravan.

CHAPTER FOUR

When Bowman woke up the birds were singing, the sky was a cloudless translucent blue and the rays of the morning sun were streaming through the window. Not the window of an hotel but the window of the blue Peugeot which he'd pulled off the road in the early hours of the morning into the shelter of a thick clump of trees that had seemed, in the darkness, to offer almost total concealment from the road. Now, in daylight, he could see that it offered nothing of the kind and that they were quite visible to any passer-by who cared to cast a casual sideways glance in their direction and, as there were those not all that far distant whose casual sideways glances he'd much rather not be the object of, he deemed it time to move on.

He was reluctant to wake Cecile. She appeared to have passed a relatively comfortable night—or what had been left of the night—with her dark head on his shoulder, a fact that he dimly resented because he had passed a most uncomfortable night, partly because he'd been loath to move for fear of disturbing her but chiefly because his unaccustomedly violent exercise of the previous night had left him with numerous aches in a wide variety of muscles that hadn't been subjected to such inconsiderate treatment for a long time. He wound down the driver's window, sniffed the fresh cool morning air and lit a cigarette. The rasp of the cigarette lighter was enough to make her stir, straighten and peer rather blearily about her until she realized where she was.

She looked at him and said: 'Well, as hotels go, it was cheap enough.'

'That's what I like,' Bowman said. 'The pioneering spirit.'

'Do I *look* like a pioneer?'

'Frankly, no.'

'I want a bath.'

'And that you shall have and very soon. In the best hotel in Arles. Cross my heart.'

'You *are* an optimist. Every hotel room will have been taken weeks ago for the gypsy festival.'

'Indeed. Including the one *I* took. I booked my room two months ago.'

'I see.' She moved pointedly across to her own side of the seat which Bowman privately considered pretty ungrateful of her considering that she hadn't disdained the use of his shoulder as a pillow for the most of the night. 'You booked your room two months ago, Mr Bowman—'

'Neil.'

'I have been very patient, haven't I, Mr Bowman? I haven't asked questions?'

'That you haven't.' He looked at her admiringly. 'What a wife you're going to make. When I come home late from the office—'

'Please. What *is* it all about? Who are you?'

'A layabout on the run.'

'On the run? Following the gypsies that—'

'I'm a vengeful layabout.'

'I've helped you—'

'Yes, you have.'

'I've let you have my car. You've put me in danger—'

'I know. I'm sorry about that and I'd no right to do it. I'll put you in a taxi for Martignane airport and the first plane for England. You'll be safe there. Or take this car. I'll get a lift to Arles.'

'Blackmail!'

'Blackmail? I don't understand. I'm offering you a place of safety. Do you mean that you're prepared to come with me?'

She nodded. He looked at her consideringly.

'Such implicit trust in a man with so much and so very recently spilled blood on his hands?'

She nodded again.

'I still don't understand.' He gazed forward through the windscreen. 'Could it be that the fair Miss Dubois is in the process of falling in love?'

'Rest easy,' she said calmly. 'The fair Miss Dubois has no such romantic stirrings in mind.'

'Then why come along with me? Who knows, they may

be all lying in wait—the mugger up the dark alleyway, the waiter with the poison phial, the smiler with the knife beneath the cloak—any of Czerda's pals, in fact. So why?'

'I honestly don't know.'

He started up the Peugeot. 'I'm sure I don't know either.' But he did know. And she knew. But what she didn't know was that he knew that she knew. It was, Bowman thought, all very confusing at eight o'clock in the morning.

They'd just regained the main road when she said: 'Mr Bowman, you may be cleverer than you look.'

'That would be difficult?'

'I asked you a question a minute or two ago. Somehow or other you didn't get around to answering it.'

'Question? What question?'

'Never mind,' she said resignedly. 'I've forgotten what it was myself.'

Le Grand Duc, his heliotrope-striped pyjamas largely and mercifully obscured by a napkin, was having breakfast in bed. His breakfast tray was about the same width as the bed and had to be to accommodate the vast meal it held. He had just speared a particularly succulent piece of fish when the door opened and Lila entered without the benefit of knocking. Her blonde hair was uncombed. With one hand she held a wrap clutched round her while with the other she waved a piece of paper. Clearly, she was upset.

'Cecile's gone!' She waved the paper some more. 'She left this.'

'Gone?' Le Grand Duc transferred the forkful of fish to his mouth and savoured the passing moment. 'By heavens, this red mullet is superb. Gone where?'

'I don't know. She's taken all her clothes with her.'

'Let me see.' He stretched out his hand and took the note from Lila. '"Contact me Poste Restante Saintes-Maries." Rather less than informative, one might say. That ruffianly fellow who was with her last night—'

'Bowman? Neil Bowman?'

'That's the ruffianly fellow I meant. Check if he's still here. And your car.'

'I hadn't thought of that.'

'One has to have the mind for it,' Le Grand Duc said kindly. He picked up his knife and fork again, waited until

Lila had made her hurried exit from the room, laid down knife and fork, opened a bedside drawer and picked up the notebook which Lila had used the previous night while she was acting as his unpaid secretary when he had been interviewing the gypsies. He compared the handwriting in the notebook with that on the sheet of paper Lila had just handed him: it was indisputably the same handwriting. Le Grand Duc sighed, replaced the notebook, let the scrap of paper fall carelessly to the floor and resumed his attack on the red mullet. He had finished it and was just appreciatively lifting the cover of a dish of kidneys and bacon when Lila returned. She had exchanged her wrap for the blue minidress she had been wearing the previous evening and had combed her hair: but her state of agitation remained unchanged.

'He's gone, too. And the car. Oh, Charles, I *am* worried.'

'With Le Grand Duc by your side, worry is a wasted emotion. Saintes-Maries is the place, obviously.'

'I suppose so.' She was doubtful, hesitant. 'But how do I get there? My car—our car—'

'You will accompany me, chérie. Le Grand Duc always has some sort of transport or other.' He paused and listened briefly to a sudden babble of voices. 'Tsk! Tsk! Those gypsies can be a noisy lot. Take my tray, my dear.'

Not without some difficulty, Lila removed the tray. Le Grand Duc swung from the bed, enveloped himself in a violently-coloured Chinese dressing-gown and headed for the door. As it was clear that the source of the disturbance came from the direction of the forecourt the Duke marched across to the terrace balustrade and looked down. A large number of gypsies were gathered round the rear of Czerda's caravan, the one part of the caravan that was invisible from where Le Grand Duc was standing. Some of the gypsies were gesticulating, others shouting: all were clearly very angry about something.

'Ah!' Le Grand Duc clapped his hands together. 'This is fortunate indeed. It is rare that one is actually on the spot. This is the stuff that folklore is made of. Come.'

He turned and walked purposefully towards the steps leading down to the terrace. Lila caught his arm.

'But you can't go down there in your pyjamas!'

'Don't be ridiculous.' Le Grand Duc swept on his way,

descended the steps to the patio, ignored—or, more probably, was oblivious of—the stares of the early breakfasters on the patio and paused at the head of the forecourt steps to survey the scene. Already, he could see, the parking lot beyond the hedge was empty of caravans and two or three of those that had been in the forecourt had also disappeared while others were obviously making preparations for departure. But at least two dozen gypsies were still gathered round Czerda's caravan.

Like a psychedelic Caligula, with an apprehensive and highly embarrassed Lila following, Le Grand Duc made his imperious way down the steps and through the gypsies crowding round the caravan. He halted and looked at the spectacle in front of him. Battered, bruised, cut and heavily bandaged, Czerda and his son sat on their caravan's steps, both of them with their heads in their hands: both physically and mentally, their condition appeared to be very low. Behind them several gypsy women could be seen embarking on the gargantuan task of cleaning up the interior of the caravan which, in the daytime, looked to be an even more appalling mess than it had been by lamplight. An anarchist with an accurate line in bomb-throwing would have been proud to acknowledge that handiwork as his own.

'Tsk! Tsk! Tsk!' Le Grand Duc shook his head in a mixture of disappointment and disgust. 'A family squabble. Very quarrelsome, some of those Romany families, you know. Nothing here for the true folklorist. Come, my dear, I see that most of the gypsies are already on their way. It behoves us to do the same.' He led her up the steps and beckoned a passing porter. 'My car, and at once.'

'Your car's not here?' Lila asked.

'Of course it's not here. Good God, girl, you don't expect my employees to sleep in the same hotel as I do? Be here in ten minutes.'

'Ten minutes! I have to bath, breakfast, pack, pay my bill—'

'Ten minutes.'

She was ready in ten minutes. So was Le Grand Duc. He was wearing a grey double-breasted flannel suit over a maroon shirt and a panama straw hat with a maroon band, but for once Lila's attention was centred elsewhere. She was gazing rather dazedly down at the forecourt.

'Le Grand Duc,' she repeated mechanically, 'always has some sort of transport or other.'

The transport in this case was a magnificent and enormous handmade cabriolet Rolls-Royce in lime and dark green. Beside it, holding the rear door open, stood a chauffeuse dressed in a uniform of lime green, exactly the same shade as that of the car, piped in dark green, again exactly the same shade as the car. She was young, petite, auburn-haired and very pretty. She smiled as she ushered Le Grand Duc and Lila into the back seat, got behind the wheel and drove the car away in what, from inside the car, was a totally hushed silence.

Lila looked at Le Grand Duc who was lighting a large Havana with a lighter taken from a most impressively button-bestrewed console to his right.

'Do you mean to tell me,' she demanded, 'that you wouldn't let so deliciously pretty a creature stay in the same hotel as yourself?'

'Certainly not. Not that I lack concern for my employees.' He selected a button in the console and the dividing window slid silently down into the back of the driver's seat. 'And where did you spend the night, Carita, my dear?'

'Well, Monsieur le Duc, the hotels were full and—'

'Where did you spend the night?'

'In the car.'

'Tsk! Tsk!' The window slid up and he turned to Lila. 'But it is, as you can see, a very comfortable car.'

By the time the blue Peugeot arrived in Arles a coolness had developed between Bowman and Cecile. They had been having a discussion about matters sartorial and weren't quite seeing eye to eye. Bowman pulled up in a relatively quiet side-street opposite a large if somewhat dingy clothing emporium, stopped the engine and looked at the girl. She didn't look at him.

'Well?' he said.

'I'm sorry.' She was examining some point in the far distance. 'It's not on. I think you're quite mad.'

'Like enough,' he nodded. He kissed her on the cheek, got out, took his case from the rear seat and walked across the pavement, where he stopped to examine some exotic costumes in the drapery window. He could clearly see the reflection of the car and, almost equally clearly, that of Cecile. Her lips were compressed and she was distinctly angry. She appeared to hesitate, then left the car and crossed to where he was standing.

'I could hit you,' she announced.

'I wouldn't like that,' he said. 'You look a big strong girl to me.'

'Oh, for heaven's sake, shut up and put that case back in the car.'

So he shut up and put the case back in the car, took her arm and led her reluctantly into the faded emporium.

Twenty minutes later he looked at himself in a full-length mirror and shuddered. He was clad now in a black, high-buttoned and very tightly fitting suit which gave him some idea how the overweight and heroically corseted operatic diva must feel when she was reaching for a high C, a floppy white shirt, black string tie and wide-brimmed black hat. It was a relief when Cecile appeared from a dressing-room, accompanied by a plump, pleasant middle-aged woman dressed in black whom Bowman assumed to be the manageress. But he observed her only by courtesy of her peripheral vision, any man who didn't beam his entire ocular voltage directly at Cecile was either a psychiatric case or possessed of the visual acuity of a particularly myopic barnyard owl.

He had never thought of her as an eyesore but now he realized, for the first time but for keeps, that she was a stunningly lovely person. It wasn't because of the exquisite dress she wore, a beautiful, beautifully fitting, exotic and clearly very expensive gypsy costume that hadn't missed out on many of the colours of the rainbow, nor because of her white ruched mantilla head-dress affair, though he had heard tell that the awareness of wearing beautiful things gives women an inner glow that shows through. All he knew was that his heart did a couple of handsprings and it wasn't until he saw her sweet and ever so slightly amused smile that he called his heart to order and resumed what he hoped was his normally inscrutable expression. The manageress put his very thoughts in words.

'Madame,' she breathed, 'looks beautiful.'

'Madame,' he said, '*is* beautiful,' then reverted to his old self again. 'How much? In Swiss francs. You take Swiss francs?'

'Of course.' The manageress summoned an assistant who started adding figures while the manageress packed clothes.

'She's packing up *my* clothes.' Ceceile sounded dismayed. 'I can't go out in the street like this.'

'Of course you can.' Bowman had meant to be heartily reassuring but the words sounded mechanical, he still couldn't take his eyes off her. 'This is fiesta time.'

'Monsieur is quite correct,' the manageress said. 'Hundreds of young Arlésiennes dress like this at this time of year. A pleasant change and very good for them it is, too.'

'And it's not bad for business either.' Bowman looked at the bill the assistant had just handed him. 'Two thousand, four hundred Swiss francs.' He peeled three thousand-franc notes from Czerda's roll and handed them to the manageress. 'Keep the change.'

'But monsieur is too kind.' From her flabbergasted expression he took it that the citizens of Arles were not notably open-handed when it came to the question of gratuities.

'Easy come, easy go,' he said philosophically and led Cecile from the shop. They got into the Peugeot and he drove for a minute or two before pulling up in an almost deserted car-park. Cecile looked at him enquiringly.

'My cosmetic case,' he explained. He reached into his case in the back seat and brought out a small black zipped leather bag. 'Never travel without it.'

She looked at him rather peculiarly. 'A man doesn't carry a cosmetic case.'

'This one does. You'll see why.'

Twenty minutes later, when they stood before the reception desk of the grandest hotel in Arles, she understood why. They were clad as they had been when they had left the clothing emporium but were otherwise barely recognizable as the same people. Cecile's complexion was several shades darker, as was the colour of her neck, hands and wrists, she wore bright scarlet lipstick and far too much rouge, mascara and eye-shadow: Bowman's face was now the colour of well-seasoned mahogany, his newly acquired moustache dashing to a degree. The receptionist handed him back his passport.

'Your room is ready, Mr Parker,' he said. 'This is Mrs Parker?'

'Don't be silly,' Bowman said, took Cecile's suddenly stiff arm and followed the bell-boy to the lift. When the bedroom door closed behind them, she looked at Bowman with a noticeable lack of enthusiasm.

'Did you *have* to say that to the receptionist?'

'Look at your hands.'

'What's wrong with my hands—apart from the fact that that stuff of yours has made them filthy?'

'No rings.'

'Oh!'

'Well might you "Oh!" The experienced receptionist notices those things automatically—that's why he asked. And *he* may be asked questions—any suspicious couples checked in today, that sort of thing. As far as the criminal stakes are concerned a man with his lady-love in tow is automatically above suspicion—it is assumed that he has other things in mind.'

'There's no need to talk—'

'I'll tell you about the birds and bees later. Meantime, what matters is that the man trusts me. I'm going out for a bit. Have your bath. Don't wash that stuff off your arms, face and neck. There's little enough left.'

She looked into a mirror, lifted up her hands and studied both them and her face. 'But how in heaven's name am I going to have a bath without—'

'I'll give you a hand, if you like,' Bowman volunteered. She walked to the bathroom, closed and locked the door. Bowman went downstairs and paused for a moment outside a telephone kiosk in the lobby, rubbing his chin, a man deep in thought. The telephone had no dialling face which meant that outgoing calls were routed through the hotel switchboard. He walked out into the bright sunshine.

Even at that early hour the Boulevard des Lices was crowded with people. Not sightseers, not tourists, but local tradesmen setting up literally hundreds of stalls on the broad pavements of the boulevard. The street itself was as crowded as the pavements with scores of vehicles ranging from heavy trucks to handcarts unloading a variety of goods that ran the gamut from heavy agricultural machinery, through every type of food, furniture and clothes imaginable, down to the gaudiest of souvenir trinkets and endless bunches of flowers.

Bowman turned into a post office, located an empty telephone booth, raised the exchange and asked for a Whitehall number in London. While he was waiting for the call to come through he fished out the garbled message he had found in Czerda's caravan and smoothed it out before him.

At least a hundred gypsies knelt on the ground in the grassy clearing while the black-robed priest delivered a benediction. When he lowered his arm, turned, and walked towards a small black tent pitched near by, the gypsies rose and began to disperse, some wandering aimlessly around, others drifting back to their caravans which were parked just off the road a few miles north-east of Arles: behind the caravans loomed the majestic outline of the ancient Abbey de Montmajour.

Among the parked vehicles, three were instantly identifiable: the green-and-white caravan where Alexandre's mother and the three young gypsy girls lived, Czerda's caravan which was now being towed by a garishly yellow-painted breakdown truck and Le Grand Duc's imposing green Rolls. The cabriolet hood of the Rolls was down for the sky was cloudless and the morning already hot. The chauffeuse, her auburn hair uncovered to show that she was temporarily off-duty, stood with Lila by the side of the car: Le Grand Duc, reclining in the rear seat, refreshed himself with some indeterminate liquid from the open cocktail cabinet before him and surveyed the scene with interest.

Lila said: 'I never associated *this* with gypsies.'

'Understandable, understandable,' Le Grand Duc conceded graciously. 'But then, of course, you do not know your gypsies, my dear, while I am a European authority on them.' He paused, considered and corrected himself. '*The* European authority. Which means, of course, the world. The religious element can be very strong, and their sincerity and devotion never more apparent than when they travel to worship the relics of Sara, their patron saint. Every day, in the last period of their travel, a priest accompanies them to bless Sara and their—but enough! I must not bore you with my erudition.'

'Boring, Charles? It's all quite fascinating. What on earth is that black tent for?'

'A mobile confessional—little used, I fear. The gypsies have their own codes of right and wrong. Good God! There's Czerda going inside.' He glanced at his watch. 'Nine-fifteen. He should be out by lunch-time.'

'You don't like him?' Lila asked curiously. 'You think that he—'

'I know nothing about the fellow,' Le Grand Duc said. 'I would merely observe that a face such as his has not been fashioned by a lifetime of good works and pious thoughts.'

There was certainly little enough indicative of either as Czerda, his bruised face at once apprehensive and grim, closed and secured the tent flap behind him. The tent itself was small and circular, not more than ten feet in diameter. Its sole furnishing consisted of a cloth-screen cubicle which served as a confessional booth.

'You are welcome, my son.' The voice from the booth was deep and measured and authoritative.

'Open up, Searl,' Czerda said savagely. There was a fumbling motion and a dark linen curtain dropped to reveal a seated priest, with rimless eye-glasses and a thin ascetic face, the epitome of the man of God whose devotion is tinged with fanaticism. He regarded Czerda's battered face briefly, impassively.

'People may hear,' the priest said coldly. 'I'm Monsieur le Curé, or "Father".'

'You're "Searl" to me and always will be,' Czerda said contemptuously. 'Simon Searl, the unfrocked priest. Sounds like a nursery rhyme.'

'I'm not here on nursery business,' Searl said sombrely. 'I come from Gaiuse Strome.'

The belligerence slowly drained from Czerda's face: only the apprehension remained, deepening by the moment as he looked at the expressionless face of the priest.

'I think,' Searl said quietly, 'that an explanation of your unbelievably incompetent bungling is in order. I hope it's a very good explanation.'

'I must get out! I must get out!' Tina, the dark crop-haired young gypsy girl stared through the caravan window at the confessional tent, then swung round to face the other three gypsy women. Her eyes were red and swollen, her face very pale. 'I must walk! I must breathe the air! I—I can't stand it here any more.'

Marie le Hobenaut, her mother and Sara looked at one another. None of them looked very much happier than Tina. Their faces were still as sad and bitter as they had been when Bowman had watched them during the night, defeat and despair still hung as heavily in the air.

'You will be careful, Tina?' Marie's mother said anxiously. 'Your father—you must think of your father.'

'It's all right, Mother,' Marie said. 'Tina knows. She knows now.' She nodded to the dark girl who hurried through the doorway, and went on softly: 'She was so very much in love with Alexandre. You know.'

'I know,' her mother said heavily. 'It's a pity that Alexandre hadn't been more in love with her.'

Tina passed through the rear portion of the caravan. Seated on the steps there was a gypsy in his late thirties. Unlike most gypsies, Pierra Lacabro was squat to the point of deformity and extremely broad, and also unlike most gypsies who, in their aquiline fashion, are as aristocratically handsome as any people in Europe, he had a very broad, brutalized face with a thin cruel mouth, porcine eyes and a scar, which had obviously never been stitched, running from right eyebrow to right chin. He was, clearly, an extremely powerful person. He looked up as Tina approached and gave her a broken-toothed grin.

'And where are *you* going, my pretty maid?' He had a deep, rasping, gravelly and wholly unpleasant voice.

'For a walk.' She made no attempt to keep the revulsion from her face. 'I need air.'

'We have guards posted—and Maca and Masaine are on the watch. You know that?'

'Do you think I'd run away?'

He grinned again. 'You're too frightened to run away.'

With a momentary flash of spirit she said: 'I'm not frightened of Pierre Lacabro.'

'And why on earth should you be?' He lifted his hands, palms upwards. 'Beautiful young girls like you—why, I'm like a father to them.'

Tina shuddered and walked down the caravan steps.

Czerda's explanation to Simon Searl had not gone down well at all. Searl was at no pains to conceal his contempt and displeasure: Czerda had gone very much on the defensive.

'And what about me?' he demanded. '*I'm* the person who has suffered, not you, not Gaiuse Strome. I tell you, he destroyed everything in my caravan—and stole my eighty thousand francs.'

'Which you hadn't even earned yet. That was Gaiuse Strome's money, Czerda. He'll want it back: if he doesn't get it he'll have your life in place of it.'

'In God's name, Bowman's vanished! I don't know—'

'You will find him and then you will use this on him.' Searl reached into the folds of his robe and brought out a pistol with a screwed-on silencer. 'If you fail, I suggest you save us trouble and just use it on yourself.'

Czerda looked at him for a long moment. 'Who *is* this Gaiuse Strome?'

'I do not know.'

'We were friends once, Simon Searl—'

'Before God, I have never met him. His instructions come either by letter or telephone and even then through an intermediary.'

'Then do you know who this man is?' Czerda took Searl's arm and almost dragged him to the flap of the tent, a corner of which he eased back. Plainly in view was Le Grand Duc who had obviously replenished his glass. He was gazing directly at them and the expression on his face was very thoughtful. Czerda hastily lowered the flap. 'Well?'

'That man I have seen before,' Searl said. 'A wealthy nobleman, I believe.'

'A wealthy nobleman by the name of Gaiuse Strome?'

'I do not know. I do not wish to know.'

'This is the third time I have seen this man on the pilgrimage. It is also the third year I have been working for Gaiuse Strome. He asked questions last night. This morning he was down looking at the damage that had been done to our caravan. And now he's staring straight at us. I think—'

'Keep your thinking for Bowman,' Scarl advised. 'That apart, keep your own counsel. Our patron wishes to remain anonymous. He does not care to have his privacy invaded. You understand?'

Czerda nodded reluctantly, thrust the silenced pistol inside his shirt and left. As he did, Le Grand Duc peered thoughtfully at him over the rim of his glass.

'Good God!' he said mildly. 'Shriven already.'

Lila said politely: 'I beg your pardon, Charles.'

'Nothing, my dear, nothing.' He shifted his gaze and caught sight of Tina who was wandering disconsolately and apparently aimlessly across the grass. 'My word, there's a remarkably fine-looking filly. Downcast, perhaps, yes, definitely downcast. But beautiful.'

Lila said: 'Charles, I'm beginning to think that you're a connoisseur of pretty girls.'

'The aristocracy always have been. Carita, my dear, Arles and with all speed. I feel faint.'

'Charles!' Lila was instant concern. 'Are you unwell? The sun? If we put the hood up—'

'I'm hungry,' Le Grand Duc said simply.

Tina watched the whispering departure of the Rolls then looked casually around her. Lacabro had disappeared from the steps of the green-and-white caravan. Of Maca and Masaine there was no sign. Quite fortuitously, as it seemed, she found herself outside the entrance to the black confessional tent. Not daring to look round to make a final check to see whether she was under observation, she pushed the flap to one side and went in. She took a couple of hesitating steps towards the booth.

'Father! Father!' Her voice was a tremulous whisper. 'I must talk to you.'

Searl's deep grave voice came from inside the booth: 'That's what I'm here for, my child.'

'No, no!' Still the whisper. 'You don't understand. I have terrible things to tell you.'

'Nothing is too terrible for a man of God to hear. Your secrets are safe with me, my child.'

'But I don't *want* them to be safe with you! I want you to go to the police.'

The curtain dropped and Searl appeared. His lean ascetic

face was filled with compassion and concern. He put his arm round her shoulders.

'Whatever ails you, daughter, your troubles are over. What is your name, my dear?'

'Tina. Tina Daymel.'

'Put your trust in God, Tina, and tell me everything.'

In the green-and-white caravan Marie, her mother and Sara sat in gloomy silence. Now and again the mother gave a half sob and dabbed at her eyes with a handkerchief.

'Where *is* Tina?' she said at length. 'Where can she be? She takes so long.'

'Don't worry, Madame Zigair,' Sara said reassuringly. 'Tina's a sensible girl. She'll do nothing silly.'

'Sara's right, Mother,' Marie said. 'After last night—'

'I know. I know I'm being foolish. But Alexandre—'

'Please, Mother.'

Madame Zigair nodded and fell silent. Suddenly the caravan door was thrown open and Tina was thrown bodily into the room to fall heavily and face downwards on the caravan floor. Lacabro and Czerda stood framed in the entrance, the former grinning, the latter savage with a barely controlled anger. Tina lay where she had fallen, very still, clearly unconscious. Her clothes had been ripped from her back which was blood-stained and almost entirely covered with a mass of wicked-looking red and purplish weals: she had been viciously, mercilessly whipped.

'Now,' Czerda said softly. 'Now will you all learn?'

The door closed. The three women stared in horror at the cruelly mutilated girl, then fell to their knees to help her.

CHAPTER FIVE

Bowman's call to England came through quickly and he returned to his hotel within fifteen minutes of having left it. The corridor leading to his bedroom was thickly carpeted and his footfalls soundless. He was reaching for the handle of the door when he heard voices coming from inside the room. Not voices, he realized, just one—Cecile's—and it came only intermittently: the tone of her voice was readily recognizable but the muffling effect of the intervening door was too great to allow him to distinguish the words. He was about to lean his ear against the woodwork when a chambermaid carrying an armful of sheets came round a corner of the corridor. Bowman walked unconcernedly on his way and a couple of minutes later walked as unconcernedly back. There was only silence in the room. He knocked and went inside.

Cecile was standing by the window and she turned and smiled at him as he closed the door. Her gleaming dark hair had been combed or brushed or whatever she'd done with it and she looked more fetching than ever.

'Ravishing,' he said. 'How did you manage without me? My word, if our children only look—'

'Another thing,' she interrupted. The smile, he now noticed, lacked warmth. 'This Mr Parker business when you registered. You did show your passport, didn't you—Mr Bowman?'

'A friend lent it to me.'

'Of course. What else? Is your friend very important?'

'How's that?'

'What is your *job*, Mr Bowman?'

'I've told you—'

'Of course. I'd forgotten. A professional idler.' She sighed. 'And now—breakfast?'

'First, for me, a shave. It'll spoil my complexion but I can fix that. Then breakfast.'

He took the shaving kit from his case, went into the

bathroom, closed the door and set about shaving. He looked around him. She'd come in here, divested herself of all her cumbersome finery, had a very careful bath to ensure that she didn't touch the stain, dressed again, reapplied to the palms of her hands some of the stain he'd left her and all this inside fifteen minutes. Not to mention the hair brushing or combing or whatever. He didn't believe it, she had about her the fastidious look of a person who'd have used up most of that fifteen minutes just in brushing her teeth. He looked into the bath and it was indubitably still wet so she had at least turned on the tap. He picked up the crumpled bath-towel and it was as dry as the sands of the Sinai desert. She'd brushed her hair and that was all. Apart from making a phone call.

He shaved, re-applied some war-paint and took Cecile down to a table in a corner of the hotel's rather ornate and statuary-crowded patio. Despite the comparatively early hour it was already well patronized with late breakfasters and early coffee-takers. For the most part the patrons were clearly tourists, but there was a fair sprinkling of the more well-to-do Arlésiens among them, some dressed in the traditional fiesta costume of that part, some as gypsies.

As they took their seats their attention was caught and held by an enormous lime and dark green Rolls-Royce parked by the kerb: beside it stood the chauffeuse, her uniform matching the colours of the car. Cecile looked at the gleaming car in frank admiration.

'Gorgeous,' she said. 'Absolutely gorgeous.'

'Yes indeed,' Bowman agreed. 'You'd hardly think she could drive a great big car like that.' He ignored Cecile's old-fashioned look and leisurely surveyed the patio. 'Three guesses as to the underprivileged owner.'

Cecile followed his line of sight. The third table from where they sat was occupied by Le Grand Duc and Lila. A waiter appeared with a very heavy tray which he set before Le Grand Duc who picked up and drained a beaker of orange juice almost before the waiter had time to straighten what must have been his aching back.

'I thought that fellow would never come.' Le Grand Duc was loud and testy.

'Charles.' Lila shook her head. 'You've just *had* an *enormous* breakfast.'

'And now I'm having another one. Pass the rolls, ma chérie.'

'Good God!' At their table, Cecile laid a hand on Bowman's arm. 'The Duke—*and* Lila.'

'What's all the surprise about?' Bowman watched Le Grand Duc industriously ladling marmalade from a large jar while Lila poured him coffee. 'Naturally he'd be here—where the gypsies are, there the famous gypsy folklorist will be. And, of course, in the best hotel. There's the beginning of a beautiful friendship across there. Can she cook?'

'Can she—funnily enough, she can. A very good one, too. Cordon Bleu.'

'Good Lord! He'll kidnap her.'

'But what is she still doing with him?'

'Easy. You told her about Saintes-Maries. She'll want to go there. And she hasn't a car, not since we borrowed it. He'll definitely want to be going there. And he has a car—a pound to a penny that's his Rolls. And they seem on pretty good terms, though heaven knows what she sees in our large friend. Look at his hands—they work like a conveyor belt. Heaven grant I'm never aboard a lifeboat with him when they're sharing out the last of the rations.'

'I think he's good-looking. In his own way.'

'So's an orang-utan.'

'You don't like him, do you?' She seemed amused. 'Just because he said you were—'

'I don't trust him. He's a phoney. I'll bet he's not a gypsy folklorist, has never written a thing about them and never will. If he's so famous and important a man why has neither of us ever heard of him? And why does he come to this part three years running to study their customs? Once would be enough for even a folklore ignoramus like me.'

'Maybe he likes gypsies.'

'Maybe. And maybe he likes them for all the wrong reasons.'

Cecile looked at him, paused and said in a lowered voice: 'You think he's this Gaiuse Strome?'

'I didn't say anything of the kind. And don't mention that name in here—you still want to live, don't you?'

'I don't see—'

'How do you know there's not a real gypsy among all the ones wearing fancy dress on this patio?'

'I'm sorry. That was silly of me.'

'Yes.' He was looking at Le Grand Duc's table. Lila had risen and was speaking. Le Grand Duc waved a lordly hand and she walked towards the hotel entrance. His face thoughtful, Bowman's gaze followed her as she crossed the patio, mounted the steps, crossed the foyer and disappeared.

'She *is* beautiful, isn't she?' Cecile murmured.

'How's that?' Bowman looked at her. 'Yes, yes of course. Unfortunately I can't marry you both—there's a law against it.' Still thoughtful, he looked across at Le Grand Duc, then back at Cecile. 'Go talk to our well-built friend. Read his palm. Tell his fortune.'

'What?'

'The Duke there. Go—'

'I don't think that's funny.'

'Neither do I. Never occurred to me when your friend was there—she'd have recognized you. But the Duke won't—he hardly knows you. And certainly wouldn't in that disguise. Not that there's the slightest chance of him lifting his eyes from his plate anyway.'

'No!'

'Please, Cecile.'

'No!'

'Remember the caverns. I haven't a lead.'

'Oh, God, don't!'

'Well, then.'

'But *what* can I do?'

'Start off with the old mumbo-jumbo. Then say you see he has very important plans in the near future and if he is successful—then stop there. Refuse to read any more and come away. Give him the impression that he has no future. Observe his reactions.'

'Then you really do suspect—'

'I suspect nothing.'

Reluctantly she pushed back her chair and rose. 'Pray to Sara for me.'

'Sara?'

'She's the patron saint of the gypsies, isn't she?'

Bowman watched her as she moved away. She side-stepped politely to avoid bumping into another customer who had just entered, an ascetic and other-worldly looking priest: it was impossible to imagine Simon Searl as anything other than a selfless and dedicated man of God in whose hands one would willingly place one's life. They murmured apologies and Cecile carried on and stopped at the table of Le Grand Duc, who lowered his coffee cup and glanced up in properly ducal irritation.

'Well, what is it?'

'Good morning, sir.'

'Yes, yes, yes, good morning.' He picked up his coffee cup again. 'What is it?'

'Tell your fortune, sir?'

'Can't you see I'm busy? Go away.'

'Only ten francs, sir.'

'I haven't got ten francs.' He lowered his cup again and looked at her closely for the first time. 'But by Jove, though, if only you'd blonde hair—'

Cecile smiled, took advantage of the temporary moment of admiration and picked up his left hand.

'You have a long lifeline,' she announced.

'I'm as fit as a fiddle.'

'And you come of noble blood.'

'Any fool can see that.'

'You have a very kind disposition—'

'Not when I'm starving.' He snatched away his hand, used it to pick up a roll, then glanced upwards as Lila came back to the table. He pointed his roll at Cecile. 'Remove this young pest. She's upsetting me.'

'You don't *look* upset, Charles.'

'How can you see what's happening to my digestion?'

Lila turned to Cecile with a smile that was half-friendly, half-apologetic, a smile that momentarily faded as she realized who it was. Lila put her smile back in place and said: 'Perhaps you would like to read my hand?' The tone was perfectly done, conciliatory without being patronizing, a gently implied rebuke to Le Grand Duc's boorishness. Le Grand Duc remained wholly unaffected.

'At a distance, if you please,' he said firmly. 'At a distance.'

They moved off and Le Grand Duc watched them go

with an expression as thoughtful as possible for one whose jaws are moving with metronomic regularity. He looked away from the girls and across the table where Lila had been sitting. Bowman was looking directly at him but almost immediately looked away. Le Grand Duc tried to follow Bowman's altered line of sight and it seemed to him that Bowman was looking fixedly at a tall thin priest who sat with a cup of coffee before him, the same priest, Le Grand Duc realized, as he'd seen blessing the gypsies by the Abbey de Montmajour. And there was no dispute as to where the object of Simon Searl's interest lay: he was taking an inordinate interest in Le Grand Duc himself. Bowman watched as Lila and Cecile spoke together some little way off: at the moment Cecile was holding Lila's hand and appearing to speak persuasively while Lila smiled in some embarrassment. He saw Lila press something into Cecile's hand, then abruptly lost interest in both. From the corner of his eye he had caught sight of something of much more immediate importance: or he thought he had.

Beyond the patio was the gay and bustling fiesta scene in the Boulevard des Lices. Tradesmen were still setting up last-minute stalls but by this time they were far outnumbered by sightseers and shoppers. Together they made up a colourful and exotic spectacle. The rare person dressed in a sober business suit was strikingly out of place. Camera-behung tourists were there in their scores, for the most part dressed with that excruciatingly careless abandon that appears to afflict most tourists the moment they leave their own borders, but even they formed a relatively drab backcloth for the three widely differing types of people who caught and held the eye in the splendid finery of their clothes—the Arlésienne girls so exquisitely gowned in their traditional fiesta costumes, the hundreds of gypsies from a dozen different countries and the *guardians*, the cowboys of the Camargue.

Bowman leaned forward in his seat, his eyes intent. Again he saw what had attracted his attention in the first place—a flash of titian hair, but unmistakable. It was Marie le Hobenaut and she was walking very quickly. Bowman looked away as Cecile rejoined him and sat down.

'Sorry. Up again. A job. Left on the street—'

'But don't you want to hear—and my breakfast—'

'Those can wait. Gypsy girl, titian hair, green and black costume. Follow her. See where she's going—and she's going some place. She's in a tearing hurry. Now!'

'Yes, sir.' She looked at him quizzically, rose and left. He did not watch her go. Instead, he looked casually around the patio. Simon Searl, the priest, was the first to go and he did so almost immediately, leaving some coins by his coffee cup. Seconds later, Bowman was on his feet and following the priest out into the street. Le Grand Duc, with his face largely obscured by a huge coffee cup, watched the departure of both.

Among the colourful crowds, the very drabness of Searl's black robes made him an easy figure to follow. What made him even easier to follow was the fact that, as befitted a man of God, he appeared to have no suspicions of his fellow-men for he did not once look back over his shoulder. Bowman closed up till he was within ten feet of him. Now he could clearly see Cecile not much more than the same distance ahead of Searl and, occasionally, there was a brief glimpse of Marie le Hobenaut's titian hair. Bowman closed up even more on Searl and waited his opportunity.

It came almost at once. Hard by a group of fish-stalls half-a-dozen rather unprepossessing gypsies were trying to sell some horses that had seen better days. As Bowman, no more than five feet behind Searl now, approached the horses he bumped into a dark, swarthy young man with a handsome face and hairline moustache: he sported a black sombrero and rather flashy, tight-fitting dark clothes. Both men murmured apologies, side-stepped and passed on. The dark young man took only two steps, turned and looked after Bowman, who was now almost lost to sight, edging his way through the group of horses.

Ahead of him, Searl stopped as a restive horse whinnied, tossed its head and moved to block his progress. The horse reared, Searl stepped prudently backwards and as he did so Bowman kicked him behind the knee. Searl grunted in agony and fell to his sound knee. Bowman, concealed by horses on both sides of him, stooped solicitously over Searl and chopped the knuckles of his right hand into the base of the man's neck. Searl collapsed.

'Watch those damned horses!' Bowman shouted. At once several gypsies quieted the restive horses and pulled them apart to make a clear space round the fallen priest.

'What happened?' one of them demanded. 'What happened?'

'Selling that vicious brute?' Bowman asked. 'He ought to be destroyed. Kicked him right in the stomach. Don't just stand there. Get a doctor.'

One of the gypsies at once hurried away. The others stooped low over the prostrate man and while they did so Bowman made a discreet withdrawal. But it wasn't so discreet as to go unobserved by the same dark young man who had earlier bumped into Bowman: he was busy studying his fingernails.

Bowman was finishing off his breakfast when Cecile returned.

'I'm hot,' she announced. She looked it. '*And* I'm hungry.'

Bowman crooked a finger at a passing waiter.

'Well?'

'She went into a chemist's shop. She bought bandages—yards and yards—and a whole lot of cream and ointment and then she went back to the caravans—in a square not far from here—'

'The green-and-white caravan?'

'Yes. There were two women waiting for her at the caravan door and then all three went inside.'

'Two women?'

'One middle-aged, the other young with auburn hair.'

'Marie's mother and Sara. Poor Tina.'

'What do you mean?'

'Just rambling.' He glanced across the courtyard. 'The love-birds across there.'

Cecile followed his gaze to where Le Grand Duc, who was now sitting back with the relieved air of a man who has narrowly escaped death from starvation, smiled indulgently at Lila as she put her hand on his and talked animatedly.

Bowman said: 'Is your girl-friend simple-minded or anything like that?'

She gave him a long cool look. 'Not any more than I am.'

'Um. She knew you, of course. What did you tell her?'

'Nothing—except that you had to run for your life.'
'Didn't she wonder why *you* came?'
'Because I wanted to, I said.'
'Tell her I was suspicious of the Duke?'
'Well—'
'It doesn't matter. She have anything to tell you?'
'Not much. Just that they stopped by to watch a gypsy service this morning.'
'Service?'
'You know—religious.'
'Regular priest?'
'So Lila said.'
'Finish your breakfast.' He pushed back his chair. 'I won't be long.'
'But I thought—I thought you would want to know what the Duke said, his reactions. After all, that's why you sent me.'
'Was it?' Bowman seemed abstracted. 'Later.' He rose and entered the hotel: the girl watched him go with a puzzled expression on her face.

'Tall, you say, El Brocador. Thick-set. Very fast.' Czerda rubbed his own battered and bandaged face in painfully tender recollection, and looked at the four men seated at the table in his caravan—El Brocador, the swarthy young man Bowman had bumped into in the street, Ferenc, Pierre Lacabro and a still shaken and pale Simon Searl who was trying to rub the back of his neck and the back of his thigh simultaneously.
'His face was darker than you say,' El Brocador said. 'And a moustache.'
'Dark faces and a moustache you can buy in shops. He can't hide his stock in trade—violence.'
'I hope I meet this man soon,' Pierre Lacabro said. His tone was almost wistful.
'I wouldn't be in too much of a hurry,' Czerda said drily. 'You didn't see him at all, Searl?'
'I saw nothing. I just felt those two blows in the back—no, I didn't even feel the second blow.'
'Why in God's name did you have to go to that hotel patio anyway?'

'I wanted to get a close-up of this Duc de Croytor. It was *you*, Czerda, who made me curious about him. I wanted to hear his voice. Who he spoke to, see if he has any contacts, who—'

'He's with this English girl. He's harmless.'

'Clever men do things like that,' Searl said.

'Clever men don't do the things you do,' Czerda said grimly. 'Now Bowman knows who you are. He almost certainly knows now that someone in Madame Zigair's caravan has been badly hurt. If the Duc de Croytor is who you think he is then he must know now that you suspect him of being Gaiuse Strome—and, if he is, he's not going to like any of those three things at all.' The expression on Searl's face left no doubt but that he himself was of the same opinion. Czerda went on: 'Bowman. He's the only solution. This man must be silenced. Today. But carefully. Quietly. By accident. Who knows what friends this man may not have?'

'I have told you how this can be done,' El Brocador said.

'And a good way. We move on this afternoon. Lacabro, you're the only one of us he does not know. Go to his hotel. Keep watch. Follow him. We dare not lose him now.'

'That will be a pleasure.'

'No violence,' Czerda warned.

'Of course not.' He looked suddenly crestfallen. 'But I don't know what he looks like. Dark and thickset—there are hundreds of dark and thickset—'

'If he's the man El Brocador described and the man I remember seeing on the hotel patio,' Searl said, 'he'll be with a girl dressed as a gypsy. Young, dark, pretty, dressed mainly green and gold, four gold bangles on her left wrist.'

Cecile looked up from the remains of her breakfast as Bowman joined her at her table.

'You took your time,' she observed.

'I have not been idle. I've been out. Shopping.'

'I didn't see you go.'

'They have a back entrance.'

'And now?'

'Now I have urgent business to attend to.'

'Like this? Just sitting here?'

'Before I attend to the urgent thing I have to attend to I've something else urgent to attend to first. And that involves sitting here. Do you know they have some very nosey Chinese in the city of Arles?'

'What on earth are you talking about?'

'Couple sitting over by Romeo and Juliet there. Don't look. Man's big for a Chinese, forty, although it's always hard to say with them. Woman with him is younger, Eurasian, very good-looking. Both wearing lightly-tinted sun-glasses with those built-in reflectors so that you can't see through them from the outside.'

Cecile lifted a cup of coffee and looked idly round the patio. She said: 'I see them now.'

'Never trust people with reflecting sun-glasses. He seems to be displaying a very keen interest in Le Grand Duc.'

'It's his size.'

'Like enough.' Bowman looked thoughtfully at the Chinese couple, then at Le Grand Duc and Lila, then back at the Chinese again. Then he said: 'We can go now.'

She said: 'This urgent business—this first urgent business you had to attend to—'

'Attended to. I'll bring the car round to the front.'

Le Grand Duc watched his departure and announced to Lila: 'In about an hour we mingle with our subjects.'

'Subjects, Charles?'

'Gypsies, dear child. But first, I must compose another chapter of my book.'

'Shall I bring you pen and paper?'

'No need, my dear.'

'You mean—you mean you do it all in your head? It's not possible, Charles.'

He patted her hand and smiled indulgently.

'What you can get me is a litre of beer. It's becoming uncommonly warm. Find a waiter, will you?'

Lila moved obediently away and Le Grand Duc looked after her. There was nothing indulgent about the expression on his face when he saw her talk briefly and smilingly to the gypsy girl who had so recently read her fortune: there was nothing indulgent about it when he examined the Chinese couple at an adjacent table: even less so when he saw Cecile join Bowman in a white car in the street: and least of all when he observed another car move off within seconds of Bowman's.

Cecile gazed in perplexity round the interior of the white Simca. She said: 'What's all this about, then?'

'Such things as phones,' he explained. 'Fixed it while you were having breakfast. Fixed two of them in fact.'

'Two what?'

'Two hired cars. Never know when you're going to run short.'

'But—but in so short a time.'

'Garage is just down the street—they sent a man to check.' He took out Czerda's barely depleted wad of Swiss notes, crackled it briefly and returned it. 'Depends upon the deposit.'

'You really are quite amoral, aren't you?' She sounded almost admiring.

'How's that again?'

'The way you throw other people's money around.'

'Life is for the living, money for the spending,' Bowman said pontifically. 'No pockets in a shroud.'

'You're hopeless,' she said. 'Quite, quite hopeless. And why this car, anyway?'

'Why that get-up you're wearing?'

'Why—oh, I see. Of course the Peugeot's known. I hadn't thought of that.' She looked at him curiously as he turned the Simca in the direction of a sign-post saying 'Nimes'. 'Where do you think you're going?'

'I'm not quite sure. I'm looking for a place where I can talk undisturbed.'

'To me?'

'Still your apprehensions. I'll have all the rest of my life to talk to you. When we were on the patio a battered-looking gypsy in a battered-looking Renault sat and watched us for ten minutes. Both of them are about a hundred yards behind us now. I want to talk to the battered-looking gypsy.'

'Oh!'

'Well might you say "Oh!" How, one wonders, is it that Gaiuse Strome's henchmen are on to us so soon.' He gave her a sidelong glance. 'You're looking at me in a very peculiar manner, if I may say so.'

'I'm thinking.'

'Well?'

'If they're on to you, why did you bother switching cars?'

Bowman said patiently: 'When I hired the Simca I didn't know they were on to me.'

'And now you're taking me into danger again? Or what might be danger?'

'I hope not. If I am, I'm sorry. But if they're on to me, they're on to the charming gypsy girl who has been sitting by my side—don't forget that it was you that the priest was tailing when he met up with his unfortunate accident. Would you rather I'd left you behind to cope with them alone?'

'You don't offer very much in the way of choices,' she complained.

'I've got very little to offer.' Bowman looked in the mirror. The battered Renault was less than a hundred yards behind. Cecile looked over her shoulder.

'Why don't you stop here and talk to him? He'd never dare do anything here. There are far too many people around.'

'Far too many,' Bowman agreed. 'When I talk to him I don't want anyone within half a mile.'

She glanced at him, shivered and said nothing. Bowman took the Simca over the Rhône to Trinquetaille, turned left on to the Albaron road and then left again on to the road that ran south down the right bank of the river. Here he slowed and gently brought the car to a stop. The driver of the Renault, he observed, did the same thing at a discreet distance to the rear. Bowman drove the Simca on its way again: the Renault followed.

A mile farther on into the flat and featureless plains of the Camargue Bowman stopped again. So did the Renault. Bowman got out, went to the rear of the car, glanced briefly at the Renault parked about a hundred yards away, opened the boot, extracted an implement from the tool-kit, thrust it inside his jacket, closed the boot and returned to his seat. The implement he laid on the floor beside him.

'What's that?' Cecile looked and sounded apprehensive.

'A wheel-brace.'

'Something wrong with the wheels?'

'Wheel-braces can have other uses.'

He drove off. After a few minutes the road began to climb slightly, rounded an unexpectedly sharp left-hand corner and there suddenly, almost directly beneath them and less than twenty feet away, lay the murkily gleaming waters of the Grand Rhône. Bowman braked heavily, was out of the car even as it stopped and walked quickly back the way he had come. The Renault rounded the corner and its driver, caught completely unawares, slewed the car to a skidding stop less than ten yards from Bowman.

Bowman, one hand behind his back, approached the Renault and jerked the driver's door open. Pierre Lacabro glared out at him, his broad brutalized face set and savage.

'I'm beginning to think you're following me around,' Bowman said mildly.

Lacabro didn't reply. Instead, with one hand on the wheel and the other on the door frame to afford him maximum leverage he launched himself from the car with a speed surprising for a man of his bulk. Bowman had been prepared for nothing else. He stepped quickly to one side and as the driving Lacabro hurtled past him he brought the wheel-brace swinging down on Lacabro's left arm. The sound of the blow, the surprisingly loud crack of a breaking bone and Lacabro's shriek of pain were almost instantaneous.

'Who sent you?' Bowman asked.

Lacabro, writhing on the ground and clutching his damaged left forearm, snarled something incomprehensible in Romany.

'Please, please listen,' Bowman said. 'I'm dealing with murderers. I know I'm dealing with murderers. More important, I know how to deal with murderers. I've already broken one bone—I should think it's your forearm. I'm prepared to go right on breaking as many bones as I have to—assuming you stay conscious—until I find out why those four women in that green-and-white-painted caravan are terrified out of their lives. If you do become unconscious, I'll just sit around and smoke and wait till you're conscious again and break a few more bones.'

Cecile had left the Simca and was now only feet away. Her face was very pale. She stared at Bowman in horror.

'Mr Bowman, do you mean—'

'Shut up!' He returned his attention to Lacabro. 'Come now, tell me about those ladies.'

Lacabro mouthed what was almost certainly another obscenity, rolled over quickly and as he propped himself up on his right elbow Cecile screamed. Lacabro had a gun in his hand but shock or pain or both had slowed his reactions. He screamed again and his gun went flying in one direction while the wheel-brace went in another. He clutched the middle of his face with both hands: blood seeped through his fingers.

'And now your nose is gone, isn't it?' Bowman said. 'That dark girl, Tina, she's been hurt, hasn't she? How badly has she been hurt? Why was she hurt? Who hurt her?'

Lacabro took his hands away from his bleeding face. His nose wasn't broken, but it still wasn't a very pretty sight and wouldn't be for some time to come. He spat blood and a broken tooth, snarled again in Romany and stared at Bowman like a wild animal.

'*You* did it,' Bowman said with certainty. 'Yes, you did it. One of Czerda's hatchet-men, aren't you? Perhaps *the* hatchet-man. I wonder, my friend. I wonder. Was it *you* who killed Alexandre in the caverns?'

Lacabro, his face the face of a madman, pushed himself drunkenly to his feet and stood there, swaying just as drunkenly. He appeared to be on the verge of total collapse, his eyes turning up in his head. Bowman approached and, as he did so Lacabro, showing an incredible immunity to pain, an animal-like cunning and an equally animal-like power of recuperation, suddenly stepped forward and brought his right fist up in a tremendous blow which, probably due more to good fortune than calculation, struck Bowman on the side of the chin. Bowman staggered backwards, lost his balance and fell heavily on the short turf only a few feet away from the vertical drop into the Rhône. Lacabro had his priorities right. He turned and ran for the gun which had landed only a foot or two from where Cecile was standing, the shock in her face reflected in the immobility in her body.

Bowman pushed himself rather dizzily up on one arm. He could see it all happening in slow motion, the girl with the gun at her feet, Lacabro lurching towards it, the girl still stock-still. Maybe she couldn't even see the damn thing, he thought despairingly, but her eyes couldn't be all that bad, if she couldn't see a gun two feet away she'd no right to be out without a white stick. But her eyes weren't quite so bad as that. Suddenly she stooped, picked up the gun, threw it into the Rhône, then, with commendable foresight, dropped flat to the ground as Lacabro, his battered bleeding face masked in blood and hate, advanced to strike her down. But even in that moment of what must have been infuriating frustration and where his overriding instinct must have been savagely to maim the girl who had deprived him of his gun, Lacabro still had his priorities right. He ignored the girl, turned and headed for Bowman in a low crouching run.

But Cecile had bought Bowman all the time he needed. By the time Lacabro reached him he was on his feet again, still rather dazed and shaken but a going concern none the less. He avoided Lacabro's first bull-rush and wickedly swinging boot and caught the gypsy as he passed: it so chanced that he caught him by the left arm. Lacabro shouted in agony, dragged his arm free at whatever unknown cost to himself and came again. This time Bowman made no attempt to avoid him but advanced himself at equal speed. His clubbing right hand had no difficulty in reaching Lacabro's chin, for now Lacabro had no left guard left. He staggered backwards several involuntary paces, tottered briefly on the edge of the bluff, then toppled backwards into the Rhône. The splash caused by his impact on the muddied waters seemed quite extraordinarily loud.

Bowman looked gingerly over the crumbling edge of the bluff: there was no sign of Lacabro. If he'd been unconscious when he'd struck the water he'd have gone to the bottom and that was that: there could be no possibility of locating him in those dark waters. Not that Bowman relished the prospect of trying to rescue the gypsy: if he were not unconscious he would certainly express his gratitude by doing his best to drown his rescuer. Bowman did not feel sufficiently attached to Lacabro to take the risk.

He went to the Renault, searched it briefly, found what he expected to find—nothing—started up the engine, let in first gear, aimed it for the bank of the river and jumped out. The little car trundled to the edge of the bluff, cart-wheeled over the edge and fell into the river with a resounding crash that sent water rising to a height of thirty feet.

Much of this water rained down on Lacabro. He was half-sitting, half-lying on a narrow ledge of pebble and sand under the overhang of the bluff. His clothes were soaked, his right hand clutched his left wrist. On his dazed and uncomprehending face was a mixture of pain and bewilderment and disbelief. It was, by any reckoning, the face of a man who has had enough for one day.

Cecile was still sitting on the ground when Bowman approached her. He said: 'You're ruining that lovely gypsy costume sitting there.'

'Yes, I suppose I am.' Her voice was matter-of-fact, remarkably calm. She accepted his hand, got to her feet and looked around her. 'He's gone?'

'Let's say I can't find him.'

'That wasn't—that wasn't fair fighting.'

'That was the whole idea behind it, pet. Ideally, of course, he would have riddled me with bullets.'

'But—but can he swim?'

'How the hell should I know?' He led her back to the Simca and after they'd gone a mile in silence he looked at her curiously. Her hands were trembling, her face had gone white and when she spoke her voice was a muted whisper with a shake in it: clearly some sort of delayed shock had set in.

She said: 'Who *are* you?'

'Never mind.'

'I—I saved your life today.'

'Well, yes, thanks. But you should have used that gun to shoot him or hold him up.'

There was a long pause, then she sniffed loudly and said in almost a wail: 'I've never fired a gun in my life. I can't *see* to fire a gun.'

'I know. I'm sorry about that. I'm sorry about everything, Cecile. But I'm sorriest of all that I ever got you into this damnably ugly mess. God, I should have known better.'

'Why blame yourself?' Still the near-sob in her voice.

'You had to run some place last night and my room—' She broke off, peered at him and whispered: 'You're thinking of something else, aren't you?'

'Let's get back to Arles,' he said. She peered at him some more, looked away and tried to light a cigarette but her hand shook so much he did it for her. Her hand was still shaking when they got back to the hotel.

CHAPTER SIX

Bowman drew up outside the hotel entrance. Not five yards away Lila sat alone by a table just inside the patio entrance. It was difficult to say whether she looked primarily angry or disconsolate: she certainly did not look happy.

'Boy-friend's ditched her,' Bowman announced. 'Meet me in fifteen minutes. Alleyway at the back entrance of the hotel. Stay out of sight till you see a blue Citroën. I'll be inside. Stay off the patio. You'll be safe in the foyer.'

Cecile nodded to Lila. 'Can I talk to her?'

'Sure. Inside.'

'But if we're seen—'

'It won't matter. Going to tell her what a dreadful person I am?'

'No.' A shaky smile.

'Ah! Then you're going to announce our forthcoming nuptials.'

'Not that either.' Again the smile.

'You want to make your mind up.'

She put a hand on his arm. 'I think you might even be rather a kind person.'

'I doubt whether the lad in the Rhône would share your sentiments,' Bowman said drily.

The smile vanished. She got out, Bowman drove off, she watched him disappear with a small frown creasing her forehead, then went on to the patio. She looked at Lila, nodded towards the hotel foyer: they went in together, talking.

'You're sure?' Cecile asked. 'Charles recognizes Neil Bowman?'

Lila nodded.

'How? Why?'

'I don't know. He's very, very shrewd, you know.'

'Something more than a famous wine-grower or folklorist, you would say?'

'I would say.'

'And he doesn't trust Bowman?'

'That puts it very mildly indeed.'

'Stalemate. You know what Bowman thinks of the Duke. I'm afraid my money's on my man, Lila. He disposed of another of the bad men today—'

'He did *what*?'

'Threw him into the Rhône. I saw him do it. He says—'

'So that's why you looked like a ghost when I saw you just now.'

'I felt a bit like one, too. He says he's killed two others. I believe him. And I saw him lay out two more. Local colour is local colour but that would be ridiculous, you can't fake a dead man. He's on the side of the angels, Lila. Not, mind you, that I can see the angels liking it very much.'

'I'm no angel and I don't like any part of it,' Lila said. 'I'm out of my depth and I don't know how to cope. What *are* we to do?'

'You're no more lost than I am. Do? Do what we were told to do, I suppose?'

'I suppose so.' Lila sighed and resumed her earlier woebegone expression. Cecile peered at her.

'Where is Charles?'

'He's gone.' Her gloom deepened. 'He's just gone off with that little chauffeuse—that's what *he* calls her—and told me to wait here.'

'Lila!' Cecile stared at her friend. 'It's not possible—'

'Why? Why is it not? What's wrong with Charles?'

'Nothing, of course. Nothing at all.' Cecile rose. 'Two minutes for an appointment. Our Mr Bowman does not like to be kept waiting.'

'When I think of him with that little minx—'

'She looked a perfectly charming young girl to me.'

'That's what I thought, too,' Lila admitted. 'But that was an hour ago.'

Le Grand Duc was not, in fact, with the little minx, nor was he anywhere near her. In the square where the Rumanian and Hungarian caravans were pulled up, there were no signs of either Carita or the huge green Rolls and neither could have been said to be normally inconspicuous. Le Grand Duc, on the contrary, was very much in evidence: not far from the green-and-white caravan and with notebook in hand, he was talking with considerable animation to Simon Searl. Czerda, as befitted the leader of the gypsies and an already established acquaintance of Le Grand Duc, was close by but taking no part in the conversation: Searl, from what few signs of emotion that occasionally registered in his thin ascetic face, looked as if he wished he were taking no part in it either.

'Vastly obliged, Monsieur le Curé, vastly obliged.' Le Grand Duc was at his regally gracious best. 'I can't tell you how impressed I was by the service you held in the fields by the Abbey, this morning. Moving, most moving. By Jove, I'm adding to my store of knowledge every minute.' He peered more closely at Searl. 'Have you hurt your leg, my dear fellow?'

'A slight strain, no more.' The only obvious strain was in his face and voice.

'Ah, but you must look after those slight strains—can develop very serious complications, you know. Yes, indeed, very serious.' He removed his monocle, swinging it on the end of its thick black ribbon, the better to observe Searl. 'Haven't I seen you somewhere before—I don't mean at the Abbey. Yes, yes, of course—outside the hotel this morning. Odd, I don't recall you limping then. But then, I'm afraid my eyesight—' He replaced his monocle. 'My thanks again. And watch that strain. Do exercise the greatest care, Monsieur le Curé. For your own sake.'

Le Grand Duc tucked the notebook in an inner pocket and marched majestically away. Czerda looked at Searl, the unbandaged parts of his face registering no expression. Searl, for his part, licked dry lips, said nothing, turned and walked away.

To even a close observer who knew him, the man behind the wheel of the gleamingly blue Citroën parked in the alleyway behind the hotel must have been almost totally unrecognizable as Bowman. He was dressed in a white sombrero, dark glasses, an excruciating blue-and-white polka-dotted shirt, an unbuttoned, embroidered black waistcoat, a pair of moleskin trousers and high boots. The complexion was paler, the moustache larger. Beside him on the seat lay a small purse-stringed bag. The offside front door opened and Cecile peered in, blinking uncertainly.

'I don't bite,' Bowman said encouragingly.

'Good God!' She slid into her seat. 'What—what's this?'

'I'm a *guardian*, a cowboy in his Sunday best, one of many around. Told you I'd been shopping. Your turn, now.'

'What's in that bag?'

'My poncho, of course.'

She eyed him with the speculative look that had now become almost habitual with her as he drove her to the clothing emporium they'd visited earlier that morning. After a suitable lapse of time the same manageress fluttered around Cecile, making gushing, admiring remarks, talking with her arms as much as with her voice. Cecile was now attired in the fiesta costume of an Arlésienne, with a long sweeping darkly embroidered dress, a ruched lace white bodice and a wimpled hat of the same material. The hat was perched on a dark red wig.

'Madame looks—fantastic!' the manageress said ecstatically.

'Madame matches the price,' Bowman said resignedly. He peeled off some more banknotes and led Cecile to the Citroën where she sat and smoothed the rich material of her dress approvingly.

'Very nice, I must say. You like dressing girls up?'

'Only when I'm being bank-rolled by criminals. That's hardly the point. A certain dark gypsy girl has been seen with me. There's not an insurance company in Europe would look at that dark gypsy girl.'

'I see.' She smiled wanly. 'All this solicitude for your future wife?'

'Of course. What else?'

'The fact that, quite frankly, you can't afford to lose your assistant at the moment?'

'Never occurred to me.'

He drove the Citroën close to the point where the Hungarian and Rumanian caravans were parked in the square. He stopped the Citroën, lifted his purse-stringed bag, got out, straightened and turned. As he did so, he bumped into a large pedestrian who was sauntering slowly by. The pedestrian stopped and glared at him through a black-beribboned monocle: Le Grand Duc was not accustomed to being bumped into by anyone.

'Your pardon, m'sieur,' Bowman said.

Le Grand Duc favoured Bowman with a look of considerable distaste. 'Granted.'

Bowman smiled apologetically, took Cecile's arm and moved off. She said to him, *sotto voce* and accusingly: 'You did that on purpose.'

'So? If he doesn't recognize us, who will?' He took another couple of steps and halted. 'Well, now, what could this be?'

There was a sudden stir of interest as a plain black van turned into the square. The driver got out, made what was evidently an enquiry of the nearest gypsy who pointed across the square, entered the van again and drove it across to the vicinity of Czerda's caravan. Czerda himself was by the steps, talking to Ferenc: neither appeared to have made much progress in the recovery from their injuries.

The driver and an assistant jumped down, went to the rear of the van, opened the doors and, with considerable difficulty and not without willing help, they slid out a stretcher on which, left arm in sling and face heavily bandaged, lay the recumbent form of Pierre Lacabro. The malevolent gleam in the right eye—the left one was completely shut—showed clearly that Lacabro was very much alive. Czerda and Ferenc, consternation in their faces, moved quickly to help the stretcher-bearers. Inevitably, Le Grand Duc was one of the first on the immediate scene. He bent briefly over the battered Lacabro, then straightened.

'Tsk! Tsk! Tsk!' He shook his head sadly. 'Nobody's safe on the roads these days.' He turned to Czerda. 'Isn't this my poor friend Mr Koscis?'

'No.' Czerda spoke with considerable restraint.

'Ah! I'm glad to hear it. Sorry for this poor fellow of course. By the way, I wonder if you'd tell Mr Koscis that I'd like to have another word with him when he's here? At his convenience, of course.'

'I'll see if I can find him.' Czerda helped move the stretcher towards the steps of his own caravan and Le Grand Duc turned away, narrowly avoiding coming into collision with the Chinese couple who had earlier been on the patio of the hotel. He doffed his hat in gallant apology to the Eurasian woman.

Bowman had missed none of the by-play. He looked first at Czerda, whose face was registering a marked degree of mixed anger and apprehension, then at Le Grand Duc, then at the Chinese couple: he turned to Cecile.

'There now,' he whispered. 'I knew he could swim. Let's not show too keen a degree of interest in what's going on.' He led her away a few paces. 'You know what I want to do—it'll be safe, I promise.'

He watched her as she wandered casually past Czerda's caravan and stopped to adjust a shoe in the vicinity of the green-and-white caravan. The window at the side was curtained but the window itself slightly ajar.

Satisfied, Bowman moved off across the square to where a group of horses were tethered by some trees close by several other caravans. He looked aimlessly around to check that he was unobserved, saw Czerda's caravan door close as the stretcher was brought inside, dug into his bag and fetched out a fistful of coiled, brown-paper sheathed objects, each one fitted with an inch of blue touch-paper: they were, quite simply, old-fashioned fire-crackers . . .

In Czerda's caravan, Czerda himself, Ferenc, Simon Searl and El Brocador were gathered round Pierre Lacabro's still recumbent form. The expression on what little could be seen of Lacabro's face registered a degree of unhappiness that was not entirely attributable to his physical sufferings: he had about him the wounded appearance of one whose injuries are not being accorded their due meed of loving care and concerned sympathy.

'You fool, Lacabro!' Czerda's voice was almost a shout. 'You crazy idiot! No violence, I told you. *No* violence.'

'Maybe you should have told Bowman instead,' El Brocador suggested. 'Bowman knew. Bowman was watching. Bowman was waiting. Who is going to tell Gaiuse Strome?'

'Who but our unfrocked friend here,' Czerda said savagely. 'I do not envy you, Searl.'

From the look on Searl's face it was clear that he didn't envy himself either. He said unhappily: 'That may not be necessary. If Gaiuse Strome is who we now all think he is, then he knows already.'

'Knows?' Czerda demanded. 'What can he know? He doesn't know that Lacabro is one of my men and so one of his. He doesn't know that Lacabro didn't have a road accident. He doesn't know that Bowman is responsible. He doesn't know that once again we've managed to lose track of Bowman—while at the same time Bowman appears to know all our movements. If you think you have nothing to explain, Searl, you're out of your mind.' He turned to Ferenc. 'Round up the caravans. Now. We leave inside the half-hour. Tell them that tonight we camp by Vaccarès. What was that?'

There had come clearly and sharply the sound of a series of sharp reports. Men shouted, horses whinnied in fear, a policeman's whistle blew and still the series of flat staccato explosions continued. Czerda, followed by the three others, rushed to the door of his caravan and threw it open.

They were not alone in their anxiety and curiosity to discover the source of the disturbance. It would hardly be exaggeration to claim that within thirty seconds every pair of eyes in the square was trained on the north-eastern part of it where a group of gypsies and *guardians*, Bowman prominently active among them, were fighting to restrain a rearing, milling, whinnying and by now thoroughly fear-crazed group of horses.

One pair of eyes was otherwise engaged and those belonged to Cecile. She was pressed close in to the side of the green-and-white-painted caravan, standing on tiptoe and peering through a gap she had just made in the curtain.

It was dark inside the curtained caravan but the darkness was far from total and even Cecile's eyes quickly became accustomed to the gloom: when they did it was impossible for her to restrain her involuntary shocked gasp of horror. A girl with dark cropped hair was lying face down on a bunk—obviously the only way she could possibly lie. Her bare and savagely mutilated back had not been bandaged but had been liberally covered with salves of some kind. From her continuous restive movements and occasional moans it was clear that she was not sleeping.

Cecile lowered the curtain and moved off. Madame Zigair, Sara and Marie le Hobenaut were on the steps of the caravan, peering across the square, and Cecile walked by them as unconcernedly as she could, which was not easy when her legs felt shaky and she was sick inside. She crossed the square and rejoined Bowman who had just succeeded in calming down one of the panic-stricken horses. He released the horse, took her arm and led her towards where they'd left the Citroën parked. He looked at her, but didn't have to look closely.

'You didn't like what you saw, did you?' he said.

'Teach me how to use a gun and I'll use it. Even although I can't see. I'll get close enough.'

'As bad as that?'

'As bad as that. She's hardly more than a child, a little thin creature, and they've practically flayed the skin from her back. It was horrible. The poor child must be in agony.'

'So you don't feel so sorry for the man I threw in the Rhône?'

'I would. If I met him. With a gun in my hand.'

'No guns. I don't carry one myself. But I take your point.'

'And you seem to take my news very calmly.'

'I'm as mad as you are, Cecile, only I've been mad about it for a long time now and I can't keep showing it all the time. As for the beating the girl got, it had to be something like that. Like Alexandre, the poor kid got desperate and tried to pass on a message, some information, so they taught her what they thought would be a permanent lesson to herself and the other women, and it probably will.'

'What information?'

'If I knew that I'd have those four women out of that caravan and in safety in ten minutes.'

'If you don't want to tell, don't tell.'

'Look, Cecile—'

'It's all right. It doesn't matter.' She paused. 'You know that I wanted to run away this morning? Coming back from the Rhône?'

'I wouldn't have been surprised.'

'Not now. Not any more. You're stuck with me now.'

'I wouldn't want to be stuck with anyone else.'

She looked at him almost in surprise. 'You said that without smiling.'

'I said it without smiling,' he said.

They reached the Citroën, turned and looked back towards the square. The gypsies were milling around in a state of great activity. Ferenc, they could see, was going from one caravan to the next, speaking urgently to the owners, and as soon as he left them they began making preparations to hitch their towing units on to the caravans.

'Pulling out?' Cecile looked at Bowman in surprise. 'Why? Because of a few fire-crackers?'

'Because of our friend who's been in the Rhône. And because of me.'

'You?'

'They know now, since our friend returned from his bathe, that I'm on to them. They don't know how much I know. They don't know what I look like now but they know that I'll be looking different. They do know that they can't get me here in Arles because they can't have any idea where I am or where I might be staying. They know that to get me they'll have to isolate me and to do that they'll have to draw me out into the open. Tonight they'll camp in the middle of nowhere, somewhere deep in the Camargue. And there they'll hope to get me. For they know now that wherever their caravans are, there I'll be too.'

'You are good at making speeches, aren't you?' There was no malice in the green eyes.

'It's just practice.'

'And you haven't exactly a low opinion of yourself, have you?'

'No.' He regarded her speculatively. 'Do you think they have?'

'I'm sorry.' She touched the back of his hand in a gesture of contrition. 'I talk that way when I'm scared.'

'Me too. That's most of the time. We'll leave after you've picked your things up from the hotel and, in the best Pinkerton fashion, tail them from in front. Because if we follow them, they'll string out watchers at regular intervals to check every car that follows. And there won't be all that many cars moving south—tonight's the big fiesta night in Arles and most people won't be moving down to Saintes-Maries for another forty-eight hours.'

'They would recognize us? In those rigouts? Surely they can't—'

'They can't recognize us. They can't possibly be on to us yet. Not this time. I'm positive. They don't have to be. They'll be looking for a car with a couple in it. They'll be looking for a car with Arles number-plates, because it'll have to be a rented car. They'll be looking for a couple in disguise, because they'll have to be in disguise, and in those parts that means only gypsy or *guardian* fiesta costumes.

They'll be looking for a couple with by now certain well-known characteristics such as that you are slender, have high cheekbones and green eyes, while I'm far from slender and have certain scars on my face that only a dye can conceal. How many cars with how many couples going south to Vaccarès this afternoon will match up with all those qualifications?'

'One.' She shivered. 'You don't miss much, do you?'

'Neither will they. So we go ahead of them. If they don't catch up with us we can always turn back to find out where they've stopped. They won't suspect cars coming from the south. At least, I hope to God they don't. But keep those dark glasses on all the time: those green eyes are a dead giveaway.'

Bowman drove back to the hotel and stopped about fifty yards from the patio, the nearest parking place he could get. He said to Cecile: 'Get packed. Fifteen minutes. I'll join you in the hotel inside ten.'

'You, of course, have some little matter to attend to first?'

'I have.'

'Care to tell me what it is?'

'No.'

'That's funny. I thought you trusted me now.'

'Naturally. Any girl who is going to marry me—'

'I don't deserve that.'

'You don't. I trust you, Cecile. Implicitly.'

'Yes.' She nodded as if satisfied. 'I can see you mean that. What you don't trust is my ability not to talk under pressure.'

Bowman looked at her for several moments, then said: 'Did I suggest, sometime during the middle watches of the night, that you weren't—ah—quite as bright as you might be?'

'You called me a fool several times, if that's what you mean.'

'You can get around to forgiving me?'

'I'll work on it.' She smiled, got out of the car and walked away. Bowman waited till she had turned into the patio, left the car, walked back to the post office, picked up a telegram that was awaiting him in the Poste Restante, took it back to the car and opened it. The message was in English and uncoded. It read: MEANING UNCLEAR STOP QUOTE IT IS ESSENTIAL THAT CONTENTS BE DELIVERED AIGUES-MORTES OR GRAU DU ROI BY MONDAY MAY 24 INTACT AND REPEAT AND INCOGNITO STOP IF ONLY ONE POSSIBLE DO NOT DELIVER CONTENTS STOP IF POSSIBLE RELATIVE EXPENDITURE IMMATERIAL STOP NO SIGNATURE.

Bowman re-read the message twice and nodded to himself. The meaning was far from unclear to him: nothing, he thought, was unclear any more. He produced matches and burnt the telegram, piece by piece, in the front ashtray, grinding the charred paper into tiny fragments. He glanced around frequently to see if anyone was taking an unusual interest in his unusual occupation but no one was. In his rear mirror he could see Le Grand Duc's Rolls stopped at traffic lights some three hundred yards away. Even a Rolls, he reflected, had to stop at a red light: Le Grand Duc must find such annoying trifles a constant source of ducal irritation. He looked through the windscreen and could see the Chinese and his Eurasian lady leisurely sauntering towards the patio, approaching from the west.

Bowman wound down his window, tore his telegram envelope into tiny shreds and dropped them to the gutter: he hoped the citizens of Arles would forgive him his wanton litter-bugging. He left the car and passed into the hotel patio, meeting the Chinese couple on the way. They looked at Bowman impassively from behind their reflector glasses but Bowman did not as much as glance their way.

Le Grand Duc, stalled at the traffic lights, was, surprisingly enough, displaying no signs of irritation at all. He was absorbed in making notes in a book which, curiously, was not the one he habitually used when adding to his increasing store of gypsy folklore. Satisfied, apparently, with what he had written, he put the book away, lit a large Havana and pressed the button which controlled the dividing window. Carita looked at him enquiringly in the rear-view mirror.

'I need hardly ask you, my dear,' Le Grand Duc said, 'if you have carried out my instructions.'

'To the letter, Monsieur le Duc.'

'And the reply?'

'Ninety minutes, with luck. Without it, two and a half hours.'

'Where?'

'Replies in quadruplicate, Monsieur le Duc. Poste Restante, Arles, Saintes-Maries, Aigues-Mortes and Grau du Roi. That is satisfactory, I hope?'

'Eminently.' Le Grand Duc smiled in satisfaction. 'There are times, my dear Carita, when I hardly know what I'd do without you.' The window slid silently up, the Rolls whispered away on the green light and Le Grand Duc, cigar in hand, leaned back and surveyed the world with his customary patriarchal air. Abruptly, after a rather puzzled glance through the windscreen of the car, he bent forward all of two inches, an action which, in Le Grand Duc, indicated an extraordinarily high degree of interest. He pressed the dividing window button.

'There's a parking space behind that blue Citroën. Pull in there.'

The Rolls slowed to a stop and the Duke performed the almost unheard-of feat of opening the door and getting out all by himself. He strolled leisurely forward, halted and looked at the pieces of yellow telegram paper lying in the gutter, then at the Chinese who was slowly straightening with some of the pieces in his hand.

'You seem to have lost something,' Le Grand Duc said courteously. 'Can I be of help?'

'You are too kind.' The man's English was immaculate, Oxbridge at its most flawless. 'It is nothing. My wife has just lost one of her ear-rings. But it is not here.'

'I am sorry to hear it.' Le Grand Duc carried on, sauntered through the patio entrance, passed by the seated wife of the Chinese and nodded fractionally in gracious acknowledgement of her presence. She was, Le Grand Duc noted, unmistakably Eurasian and quite beautiful. Not blonde, of course, but beautiful. She was also wearing two ear-rings. Le Grand Duc paced with measured stride across the patio and joined Lila, who was just seating herself at a table. Le Grand Duc regarded her gravely.

'You are unhappy, my dear.'

'No, no.'

'Oh, yes, you are. I have an infallible instinct for such

things. For some extraordinary reasons you have some reservations about me. Me! Me, if I may say so, the Duc de Croytor!' He took her hand. 'Phone your father, my friend the Count Delafont, and phone him now. He will reassure you, you've my word for that. Me! The Duc de Croytor!'

'Please, Charles. Please.'

'That's better. Prepare to leave at once. A matter of urgency. The gypsies are leaving—at least the ones we're interested in are leaving—and where they go we must follow.' Lila made to rise but he put out a restraining hand. ' "Urgency" is a relative term. In about, say, an hour's time —we must have a quick snack before departing for the inhospitable wastes of the Camargue.'

CHAPTER SEVEN

To the newcomer the Camargue does indeed appear to be an inhospitable wasteland, an empty wasteland, a desolation of enormous skies and limitless horizons, a flat and arid nothingness, a land long abandoned by life and left to linger and wither and die all summer long under a pitiless sun suspended in the washed-out steel-blue dome above. But if the newcomer remains long enough, he will find that first impressions, as they almost invariably do, give a false and misleading impression. It is, it is true, a harsh land and a bleak land, but one that is neither hostile nor dead, a land that is possessed of none of the uniformly dreadful lifelessness of a tropical desert or a Siberian tundra. There is water here, and no land is dead where water is: there are large lakes and small lakes and lakes that are no lakes at all but marshes sometimes no more than fetlock deep to a horse, others deep enough to drown a house. There are colours here, the ever-changing blues and greys of the wind-rippled waters, the faded yellows of the beds of marshes that line the *étangs*, the near-blackness of smooth-crowned cypresses, the dark green of windbreak pines, the startlingly bright green of occasional lush grazing pastures, strikingly vivid against the brown and harsh aridity of the tough sparse vegetation and salt-flats hard-baked under the sun that occupy so much the larger part of the land area. And, above all, there is life here: birds in great number, very occasional small groups of black cattle and, even more rarely, white horses: there are farms, too, and ranches, but these are set so far back from roads or so well-concealed by windbreaks that the traveller rarely sees them. But one indisputable fact about the Camargue remains, one first impression that never changes, one that wholly justifies its time-and-again description as being an endless plain: the Camargue is as featurelessly smooth and flat as a sun-warmed summer sea.

For Cecile, as the blue Citroën moved south between

Arles and Saintes-Maries, the Camargue was nothing but an increasingly featureless desolation: her spirits became correspondingly increasingly depressed. Occasionally she glanced at Bowman but found no help there: he seemed relaxed, almost cheerful, and if the consideration of the recently spilled blood he had on his hands bore heavily on him he was concealing his feelings remarkably well. Probably, Cecile thought, he had forgotten all about it: the thought made her feel more depressed than ever. She surveyed the bleak landscape again and turned to Bowman.

'People *live* here?'

'They live here, they love here, they die here. Let's hope we don't today. Die here, I mean.'

'Oh, do be quiet. Where are all the cowboys I've heard of—the *guardians* as you call them?'

'In the pubs, I should imagine. This is fiesta day, remember—a holiday.' He smiled at her. 'I wish it was for us too.'

'But your life is one long holiday. You said so.'

'For us, I said.'

'A pretty compliment.' She looked at him consideringly. 'Can you tell me, offhand, when you last had a holiday?'

'Offhand, no.'

Cecile nodded, looked ahead again. Half a mile away, on the left-hand side of the road, was a fairly large group of buildings, some of them quite substantial.

'Life at last,' she said. 'What's that?'

'A *mas*. A farm, more of a ranch. Also a bit of a dude ranch—living accommodation, restaurant, riding school. Mas de Lavignolle, they call it.'

'You've been here before, then?'

'All those holidays,' Bowman said apologetically.

'What else?' She turned her attention to the scene ahead again, then suddenly leaned forward. Just beyond the farm was a windbreak of pines and just beyond that again there was coming into view a scene that showed that there could, indeed, be plenty of life in the Camargue. At least a score of caravans and perhaps a hundred cars were parked haphazardly on the hard-packed earth on the right-hand side of the road. On the left, in a field which was more dust than grass, there were lines of what appeared to be brightly coloured tents. Some of the tents were no more than striped awnings with, below them, trestle tables which, dependent on what was piled on them, acted as either bars or snack-bars. Other and smaller canvas-topped stalls were selling souvenirs or clothes or candy, while still others had been converted into shooting galleries, roulette stands and other games of chance. There were several hundred people milling around among the stalls, obviously enjoying and making the most of the amenities offered. Cecile turned to Bowman as he slowed to let people cross the road.

'What's all this, then?'

'Obvious, isn't it? A country fair. Arles isn't the only place in the Camargue—some of the people hereabouts don't even consider it as being part of the Camargue and act accordingly. Some communities prefer to provide their own diversions and amusements at fiesta time—the Mas de Lavignolle is one of them.'

'My, my, we are well-informed, aren't we?' She looked ahead again and pointed to a large oval-shaped arena with its sides made, apparently, of mud and wattles.

'What's that? A corral?'

'That,' Bowman said, 'is a genuine old-fashioned bull-ring where the main attraction of the afternoon will take place.'

She made a face. 'Drive on.'

He drove on. After less than fifteen minutes, at the end of a long straight stretch of dusty road he pulled the blue Citroën off the road and got out, Cecile looked at him enquiringly.

'Two straight miles of road,' he explained. 'Gypsy caravans travel at thirty miles an hour. So, four minutes' warning.'

'And a panic-stricken Bowman can be on his way in less than fifteen seconds?'

'Less. If I haven't finished off the champagne, longer. But enough. Come. Lunch.'

Ten miles to the north, on the same road, a long convoy of gypsy caravans were heading south, raising an immense cloud of dust in their passing. The caravans, normally far from inhibited in the brightness and diversity of their colours, seemed now, in their striking contrast to the bleakness of the landscape around them, more gay and exotic than ever.

The leading vehicles in the convoy, the yellow breakdown truck that had been pressed into the service of hauling Czerda's caravan, was the only one that was completely dust-free. Czerda himself was driving, with Searl and El Brocador seated beside him. Czerda was looking at El Brocador with an expression on his face that came as close to admiration as his presently rather battered features were capable of expressing.

He said: 'By heavens, El Brocador, I'd rather have you by my side than a dozen incompetent unfrocked priests.'

'I am not a man of action,' Searl protested. 'I never have claimed to be.'

'You're supposed to have brains,' Czerda said contemptuously. 'What happened to them?'

'We mustn't be too hard on Searl,' El Brocador said soothingly. 'We all know he's under great pressure, he's not, as he says, a man of action and he doesn't know Arles. I was born there, it is the back of my hand to me. I know every shop in Arles that sells gypsy costumes, fiesta costumes and *guardian* clothes. There are not so many as you might think. The men I picked to help me were all natives too. But I was the lucky one. First time, first shop—just the kind of shop Bowman would choose, a seedy old draper's in a side-street.'

'I hope, El Brocador, that you didn't have to use too much—ah—persuasion?' Czerda was almost arch about it and it didn't become him at all.

'If you mean violence, no. Those aren't my methods, you know that, and besides I'm far too well known in Arles to try anything of the sort. Anyway, I didn't have to, nobody would have had to. I know Madame Bouvier, everyone knows her, she'd throw her own mother in the Rhône for ten francs. I gave her fifty.' El Brocador grinned. 'She couldn't tell me enough fast enough.'

'A blue and white polka-dotted shirt, white sombrero and black embroidered waistcoat.' Czerda smiled in anticipation. 'It'll be easier than identifying a circus clown at a funeral.'

'True, true. But first we must catch our hare.'

'He'll be there,' Czerda said confidently. He jerked a thumb in the direction of the following caravans. 'As long as they are here, he'll be here. We all know that by this time. You just worry about your part, El Brocador.'

'No worry there.' El Brocador's confidence matched Czerda's own. 'Everyone knows what mad Englishmen are like. Just another crazy idiot who tried to show off before the crowd. And dozens of witnesses will have seen him tear free from us in spite of all we could do to stop him.'

'The bull will have specially sharpened horns? As we arranged?'

'I have seen to it myself.' El Brocador glanced at his watch. 'Can we not make better time? You know I have an appointment in twenty minutes.'

'Never fear,' Czerda said. 'We shall be in Mas de Lavignolle in ten minutes.'

At a discreet distance behind the settling dust the lime-green Rolls swept along in its customary majestic silence. The cabriolet hood was down, with Le Grand Duc sitting regally under the shade of a parasol which Lila held over him.

'You slept well?' she asked solicitously.

'Sleep? I never sleep in the afternoons. I merely had my eyes closed. I have many things, far too many things, on my mind and I think better that way.'

'Ah! I didn't understand.' The first quality one required in dealing with Le Grand Duc, she had learned, was diplomacy. She changed the subject rapidly. 'Why are we following so few caravans when we've left so many behind in Arles?'

'I told you, those are the ones I am interested in.'

'But why—'

'Hungarian and Rumanian gypsies are my special field.' There was a finality about the way he spoke that effectively sealed off that particular line of discussion.

'And Cecile. I'm worried about—'

'Your friend Miss Dubois has already left and unless I am much mistaken—' his tone left no room to doubt the impiety of any such thought—'she is also on this road and considerably ahead of us. She was, I must concede,' he added reflectively, 'attired in a very fetching Arlésienne fiesta dress.'

'A gypsy dress, Charles.'

'Arlésienne fiesta,' Le Grand Duc said firmly. 'I miss very little, my dear. Gypsy costume when you saw her, perhaps. But Arlésienne when she left.'

'But why should she—'

'How should I know?'

'You saw her go?'

'No.'

'Then how—'

'Our Carita here also misses very little. She left with, it seems, a shady-looking individual in *guardian* clothes. One wonders what happened to that other ruffian—Bowman, wasn't it? Your friend appears to possess a unique talent for picking up undesirables.'

'And me?' Lila was suddenly tight-lipped.

'Touché! I deserved that. Sorry, I did not intend to slight your friend.' He gestured with a hand ahead and to the left where a long narrow line of water gleamed like burnished steel under the early afternoon sun. 'And what is that, my dear?'

Lila glanced at it briefly. 'I don't know,' she said huffily.

'Le Grand Duc never apologizes twice.'

'The sea?'

'Journey's end, my dear. Journey's end for all the gypsies who have come hundreds, even thousands of miles from all over Europe. The Etang de Vaccarès.'

'Etang?'

'Lake. Lake Vaccarès. The most famous wildlife sanctuary in Western Europe.'

'You *do* know a lot, Charles.'

'Yes, I do,' Le Grand Duc conceded.

Bowman packed up the remains of lunch in a wicker basket, disposed of what was left of a bottle of champagne and closed the boot of the car.

'That was delightful,' Cecile said. 'And how very thoughtful of you.'

'Don't thank me, thank Czerda. He paid for it.' Bowman

looked north along the two-mile stretch of road. It was quite empty of traffic. 'Well, back to Mas de Lavignolle. The caravans must have stopped at the fair. Heigh-ho for the bull-fight.'

'But I hate bull-fights.'

'You won't hate this one.'

He reversed the Citroën and drove back to Mas de Lavignolle. There seemed to be many fewer people there than there had been when they had passed through even although the number of cars and caravans had almost doubled, a discrepancy easily and immediately accounted for as soon as the Citroën had stopped by the sound of laughter and shouting and cheering coming from the nearby bull-ring. For the moment Bowman ignored the bull-ring: remaining seated in the car, he looked carefully around him. He did not have to look for long.

'To nobody's surprise,' he announced, 'Czerda and his missionary pals have turned up in force. At least, their caravans have, so one assumes that Czerda and company have also.' He drummed his fingers thoughtfully on the steering wheel. 'To nobody's surprise, that is, except mine. Curious, curious. One wonders why?'

'Why what?' Cecile asked.

'Why they're here.'

'What do you mean? You expected to find them here. That's why you turned back, wasn't it?'

'I turned back because the time-factor, their delay in overtaking us, convinced me that they must have stopped somewhere and this seemed as likely a place as any. The point is that I would not have expected them to stop at all until they reached some of the lonely encampments on one of the *étangs* to the south where they could have the whole wide Camargue all to themselves. But instead they choose to stop here.'

He sat in silence and she said: 'So?'

'Remember I explained in some detail back in Arles just why I thought the gypsies were pulling out so quickly?'

'I remember some of it. It was a bit confusing.'

'Maybe I was confusing myself. Somewhere a flaw in the reasoning. My reasoning. But where?'

'I'm sorry. I don't understand.'

'I don't think I'm exaggerating my own importance,'

Bowman said slowly. 'Not, at least, as far as they are concerned. I'm convinced they're under pressure, under very heavy pressure, to kill me as quickly as humanly possible. When you're engaged on a job of great urgency you don't stop off and spend a peaceful summer's afternoon watching a bull-fight. You press on and with all speed. You entice Bowman to a lonely camp-site at the back of beyond where, because he's the only person who's not a member of your group, he can be detected and isolated with ease and disposed of at leisure. You do not stop at a fair-cum-bull-fight where he would be but one among a thousand people, thereby making isolation impossible.' Bowman paused. 'Not, that is, unless you knew something that he didn't know, and *knew* that you could isolate him even among that thousand. Do I make myself clear?'

'This time I'm not confused.' Her voice had dropped almost to a whisper. 'You make yourself very clear. You're as certain as can be that they'll get you here. There's only one thing you can do.'

'Only one thing,' Bowman agreed. He reached for the door handle. 'I've got to go and find out for sure.'

'Neil.' She gripped his right wrist with surprising strength.

'Well, at last. Couldn't keep on calling me Mr Bowman in front of the kids, could you? Victorian.'

'Neil.' There was pleading in the green eyes, something close to desperation, and he felt suddenly ashamed of his flippancy. 'Don't go. Please, please, don't go. Something dreadful is going to happen here. I know it.' She ran the tip of her tongue over dry lips. 'Drive away from here. Now. This moment. Please.'

'I'm sorry.' He forced himself to look away, her beseeching face would have weakened the resolution of an angel and he had no reason to regard himself as such. 'I have to stay and it may as well be here. It may as well be here for a showdown there has to be, it's inevitable, and I still think I stand a better chance here than I would on the shores of some lonely *étang* in the south.'

'You said, "I *have* to stay"?'

'Yes.' He continued to look ahead. 'There are four good reasons and they're all in that green-and-white caravan.' She made no reply and he went on: 'Or just Tina alone,

Tina and her flayed back. If anyone did that to you I'd kill him. I wouldn't think about it, I'd just naturally kill him. Do you believe that?'

'I think so.' Her voice was very low. 'No, I know you would.'

'It could just as easily have been you.' He altered his tone slightly and said: 'Tell me, now, would you marry a man who ran away and left Tina?'

'No, I would not.' She spoke very matter-of-factly.

'Ha!' He altered his tone some more. 'Am I to take it from that if I *don't* run away and leave Tina—' He broke off and looked at her. She was smiling at him but the green eyes were dim, she didn't know whether to laugh or cry and when she spoke it could have been a catch in her voice or the beginning of laughter.

'You're quite, quite hopeless,' she said.

'You're repeating yourself.' He opened the door. 'I won't be long.'

She opened her own door. '*We* won't be long,' she corrected him.

'You're not—'

'I am. Protecting the little woman is all very nice but not when carried to extremes. What's going to happen in the middle of a thousand people? Besides, you said yourself they can't possibly recognize us.'

'If they catch you with me—'

'If they catch you, I won't be there, because if they can't recognize you then their only way of getting you is when you are doing something you shouldn't be doing, like breaking into a caravan.'

'In broad daylight? You think I'm insane?'

'I'm not sure.' She took his arm firmly. 'One thing I *am* sure about. Remember what I said back in Arles? You're stuck with me, mate.'

'For life?'

'We'll see about that.'

Bowman blinked in surprise and peered at her closely. 'You make me a very happy man,' he said. 'When I was a little boy and I wanted something and my mother said "We'll see about that" I knew I'd always get it. All feminine minds work the same way, don't they?'

She smiled at him serenely, quite unperturbed. 'At the risk of repeating myself again, Neil Bowman, you're a lot cleverer than you look.'

'My mother used to say that too.'

They paid their admission money, climbed steps to the top of the arena. The terraces were comfortably full, colourfully crowded with hundreds of people, very few of whom could be accused of being drably dressed: *guardians* and gypsies were there in about equal proportions, there was a sprinkling of Arlésiens in their fiesta best but most of the spectators were either tourists or local people.

Between the spectators and the sanded ring itself was an area four feet wide, running the entire circumference of the ring and separated from it by a wooden barrier four feet high: it was into this area, the *callajon*, that the *razateur* leapt for safety when things were going too badly for him.

In the centre of the ring a small but uncommonly vicious-looking black Camargue bull appeared bent upon the imminent destruction of a white-costumed figure who pirouetted and swerved and twisted and turned and closely but easily avoided the rushes of the increasingly maddened bull. The crowd clapped and shouted their approval.

'Well!' Cecile, wide-eyed and fascinated, her fears in temporary abeyance, was almost enjoying herself. 'This is more like a bull-fight!'

'You'd rather see the colour of the man's blood than the bull's?'

'Certainly. Well, I don't know. He hasn't even got a sword.'

'Swords are for the Spanish *corridas* where the bull gets killed. This is the Provençal *cours libre* where nobody gets killed although the occasional *razateur*—the bull-fighter—does get bent a bit. See that red button tied between the horns? He's got to pull that off first. Then the two bits of string. Then the two white tassels tied near the tips of the horns.'

'Isn't it dangerous?'

'It's not a way of life I'd choose myself,' Bowman admitted. He lifted his eyes from the programme note he held in his hand and looked thoughtfully at the ring.

'Anything wrong?' Cecile asked.

Bowman didn't reply immediately. He was still looking at the ring where the white-clad *razateur*, moving in a tight circle with remarkable speed but with all the controlled grace of a ballet dancer, swerved to avoid the charging bull, leaned over at what appeared to be an impossible angle and deftly plucked away the red button secured between the bull's horns, one of which appeared almost to brush the *razateur*'s chest.

'Well, well,' Bowman murmured. 'So that's El Brocador.'

'El who?'

'Brocador. The lad in the ring there.'

'You know him?'

'We haven't been introduced. Good, isn't he?'

El Brocador was more than good, he was brilliant. Timing his evasive movements with ice-cold judgment and executing them with an almost contemptuous ease, he continued to avoid the bull's furious rushes with consummate skill: in four consecutive charges he plucked away the two strings that had supported the red button and the two white tassels that had been secured to the tips of the horns. After removing the last tassel and apparently unaware of the bull's existence, he bowed deeply and gravely to the crowd, ran lightly to the barrier and vaulted gracefully into the safety of the *callajon* as the bull, now only scant feet behind, charged full tilt into the barrier, splintering the top plank. The crowd clapped and roared its approval.

But not all of them. There were four men who were not only refraining from enthusiastic applause, they weren't even looking at the bull-ring. Bowman, who had himself spent very little time in watching the spectacle, had picked them out within two minutes of arriving on the terraces—Czerda, Ferenc, Searl and Masaine. They weren't watching the bull-ring because they were too busy watching the crowd. Bowman turned to Cecile.

'Disappointed?'

'What?'

'Very slow bull.'

'Don't be horrid. What on earth is this?'

Three clowns, dressed in their traditional baggy and garishly-coloured garments, with painted faces, large false noses and ridiculous pill-boxes perched on their heads, had appeared in the *callajon*. One carried an accordion which he started to play. His two companions, both managing to trip and fall flat on their faces in the process, climbed over the barrier into the ring and, when they had picked themselves up, proceeded to do a sailor's hornpipe.

As they danced, the *toril* gate opened and a fresh bull appeared. Like its predecessor, it was a small black Camargue bull but what it lacked in inches it more than made up for in sheer bad temper for it had no sooner caught sight of the two dancing clowns than it lowered its head and charged. It went for each clown in turn but they, without in any way breaking step or losing the rhythm of the dance, glided and pirouetted to safety as if unaware of the bull's existence: they were, obviously, *razateurs* of the highest order of experience.

Temporarily, the music stopped, but the bull didn't: it charged one of the clowns who turned and ran for his life, screaming for help. The crowd shouted with laughter. The clown, momentarily incensed, stopped abruptly, shook his fist at them, looked over his shoulder, screamed again, ran, mistimed his leap for the barrier and brought up heavily against it, the bull only feet away. It seemed inevitable that he must be either impaled or crushed. Neither happened, but he did not escape entirely unscathed for when he miraculously broke clear it could be seen that his baggy trousers were hooked on to one of the bull's horns. The clown, clad in white ankle-length underpants, continued his flight, still screaming for help, pursued by a now thoroughly infuriated bull who trailed the trousers along behind him. The crowd was convulsed.

The four gypsies weren't. As before, they ignored the action in the bull-ring. But now they were no longer still. They had begun to move slowly through the crowd, all moving in a clockwise fashion, closely scanning the faces of all whom they passed by. And as closely as they observed others, Bowman observed them.

Down in the *callajon* the accordionist began to play 'Tales from the Vienna Woods'. The two clowns came together and waltzed gravely in the centre of the ring. Inevitably, the bull charged the dancing couple. He was almost upon them when they waltzed apart from each other, each completing a single turn before joining up again immediately the bull's headlong rush had carried him beyond them.

The crowd went wild. Cecile laughed to the extent that she had to use a handkerchief to dab tears from her eyes. There was no trace of a smile on Bowman's face: with Czerda not twenty feet away and heading straight for him, he didn't feel like smiling.

'Isn't it marvellous?' Cecile said.

'Marvellous. Wait here.'

She was instantly serious, apprehensive. 'Where are you—'

'Trust me?'

'Trust you.'

'A white wedding. I won't be long.'

Bowman moved leisurely away. He had to pass within a few feet of Czerda who was still scrutinizing everyone he went by with a thoroughness that lifted eyebrows and brought frowns. A few feet further on, close to the exit, he passed behind the politely clapping Chinese couple that he'd seen before in Arles. They were, he thought, a remarkably distinguished looking couple. As it was extremely unlikely that they had come all the way from China, they obviously must be European residents. He wondered idly what manner of occupation such a man would pursue in Europe, then dismissed the thought from his mind: there were other and more urgent matters to occupy his attention.

He circled the arena at the back, walked about two hundred yards south down the road, crossed it and made his way back north coming up at the back of Czerda's caravans which were parked in two tight rows well back from the side of the road. The caravans appeared to be completely deserted. Certainly there was no apparent guard on Czerda's caravan or on the green-and-white caravan, but on that afternoon he was interested in neither. The caravan he *was* interested in, as he was now certain it would be, did have a guard. On a stool on the top of the steps the gypsy Maca was sitting, beer-bottle in hand.

Bowman sauntered leisurely towards the caravan: as he approached Maca lowered his beer-bottle, looked down at him and scowled warningly. Bowman ignored the scowl, approached even more closely, stopped and inspected both Maca and the caravan, taking his time about it. Maca made a contemptuous jerking movement with his thumb, unmistakably indicating that Bowman should be on his way. Bowman remained where he was.

'Clear off!' Maca ordered.

'Gypsy swine,' Bowman said pleasantly.

Maca, obviously doubting that he had heard aright, stared for a brief moment of incredulity, then his face contorted in rage as he shifted his grip to the neck of the bottle, rose and jumped down. But Bowman had moved even more quickly and he struck Maca very hard indeed even before the gypsy's feet had reached the ground. The combined effect of the blow and his own momentum had a devastating effect on Maca: eyes unfocused, he staggered back dazedly. Bowman struck him again with equal force, caught the now unconscious man before he could fall, dragged him round to one side of the caravan, dropped him and pushed him out of sight of any casual passer-by.

Bowman glanced quickly around him. If anyone had seen the brief fracas he was taking care not to publicize the fact. Twice Bowman circled the caravan but there was no lurking watcher in the shadows, no hint of danger to be seen. He climbed the steps and entered the caravan. The rear, smaller portion of the caravan was empty. The door leading to the forward compartment was secured by two heavy bolts. Bowman slid back the bolts and passed inside.

For a moment his eyes were unable to penetrate the gloom. The curtains were drawn and very heavy curtains they were, too. Bowman drew them back.

At the front of the caravan was the three-tiered bunk he had observed when he had peered in late the previous night: as before, three men lay on those bunks. Previously, that had been a matter of no significance: bunks are for sleeping in and one would have expected to find them occupied in the night-time: one would not have expected to find them occupied in the early afternoon. But Bowman had known that he would find them occupied.

All three men were awake. They propped themselves up on their elbows, eyes, accustomed to deep gloom, blinking in the harsh light of the Camargue. Bowman advanced wordlessly, reached over the man in the lowermost bunk and picked up his right hand. The wrist belonging to that hand was manacled to a ring-bolt let into the front wall of the caravan. Bowman let his wrist fall and examined the man in the middle bunk: he was similarly secured. Bowman didn't trouble to look at the wrist of the man on top. He stepped back and looked at them thoughtfully.

He said: 'Count le Hobenaut, husband of Marie le Hobenaut, Mr Tangevec, husband of Sara Tangevec and the third name I do not know. Who are you, sir?' This to the man in the bottom bunk, a middle-aged, greying and very distinguished looking person.

'Daymel.'

'You are Tina's father?'

'I am.' The expression on his face was that of a man receiving his executioner and not his saviour. 'Who in the name of God are you?'

'Bowman. Neil Bowman. I've come to take you three gentlemen away.'

'I don't know who you are.' This from the man in the middle bunk who didn't seem any happier to see Bowman than Daymel had been. 'I don't care who you are. For God's sake go away or you'll be the death of us all.'

'You are the Count le Hobenaut?' The man nodded. 'You heard about your brother-in-law? Alexandre?'

Le Hobenaut looked at him with an odd speculative desperation on his face, then said: 'What about my brother-in-law?'

'He's dead. Czerda murdered him.'

'What crazy talk is this? Alexandre? Dead? How can he be dead? Czerda promised us—'

'You believed him?'

'Of course. Czerda has everything to lose—'

'You two believe him?' Bowman asked. They nodded. 'A man who trusts a killer is a fool. You are fools—all three of you. Alexandre *is* dead. I found his body. If you think he's alive why don't you ask Czerda if you can see him? Or you, Daymel. Why don't you ask Czerda if you can see your daughter?'

'She's not—she's—'

'She's not dead. Just half dead. They flayed her back. Why did they flay her back? Why did they kill Alexandre? Because they were both trying to tell someone something. What was it that they were trying to tell, gentlemen?'

'I beg you, Bowman.' Le Hobenaut's distress was but one step removed from terror. 'Leave us!'

'Why are you so terrified for them? Why are they so terrified for you? And don't tell me again to go for I'm not going until I know the answers.'

'You'll never know the answers now,' Czerda said.

CHAPTER EIGHT

Bowman turned round slowly for there was nothing to be gained by haste now. Of the shock, of the inevitably profound chagrin, there was no sign in his face. But Czerda, standing in the doorway with a silenced gun in his hand and Masaine, beside him, with a knife in his, made no attempt to disguise their feelings. Both men were smiling and smiling broadly, although their smiles were noticeably lacking in warmth. At a nod from Czerda, Masaine advanced and tested the shackles securing the three men. He said: 'They have not been touched.'

'He was probably too busy explaining to them just how clever he was.' Czerda did not trouble to conceal the immense amount of satisfaction he was deriving from the moment. 'It was all too simple, Bowman. You really are a fool. Shopkeepers in Arles who receive a gratuity of six hundred Swiss francs are hardly likely to forget the person who gave it to them. I tell you, I could hardly keep a straight face when I was moving through the crowd there pretending to look for you. But we had to pretend, didn't we, to convince you that we hadn't recognized you or you'd never have come out into the open, would you? You fool, we had you identified before you entered the arena.'

'You might have told Maca,' Bowman murmured.

'We might, but Maca is no actor, I'm afraid,' Czerda said regretfully. 'He wouldn't have known how to make a fake fight look real. And if we'd left no guard at all you'd have been doubly suspicious.' He stretched out his left hand. 'Eighty thousand francs, Bowman.'

'I don't carry that sort of loose change with me.'

'*My* eighty thousand francs.'

Bowman looked at him with contempt. 'Where would a person like you get eighty thousand francs?'

Czerda smiled, stepped forward unexpectedly and drove

the silenced barrel of his gun into Bowman's solar plexus. Bowman doubled up, gasping in agony.

'I would have liked to strike you across the face, as you struck me.' He had removed his smile. 'But for the moment I prefer that you remain unmarked. The money, Bowman?'

Bowman straightened slowly. When he spoke, his voice came as a harsh croak.

'I lost it.'

'You *lost* it?'

'I had a hole in my pocket.'

Czerda's face twisted in anger, he lifted his gun to club Bowman, then smiled. 'You'll find it within the minute, you'll see.'

The green Rolls-Royce slowed as it approached the Mas de Lavignolle. Le Grand Duc, still with a parasol being held above his head, surveyed the scene thoughtfully.

'Czerda's caravans,' he observed. 'Surprising. One would not have expected the Mas de Lavignolle to be of any particular interest to our friend Czerda. But a man like that will always have a good reason for what he is doing. However, he will doubtless consider it a privilege to inform me of his reasons . . . What is it, my dear?'

'Look ahead.' Lila pointed. 'Just there.'

Le Grand Duc followed the direction of her arm. Cecile, flanked by El Brocador and Searl, the first all in white, the second all in black, mounted the steps of a caravan and disappeared inside. The door closed behind them.

Le Grand Duc pressed the dividing window button. 'Stop the car, if you please.' To Lila he said: 'You think that's your friend? Same dress, I admit, but all those Arlésienne fiesta dresses look the same to me, especially from the back.'

'That's Cecile.' Lila was positive.

'A *razateur* and a priest,' Le Grand Duc mused. 'You really must admit that your friend does have a marked propensity for striking up the most unusual acquaintanceships. You have your notebook?'

'I have what?'

'We must investigate this.'

'You're going to investigate—'

'Please. No Greek chorus. Everything is of interest to the true folklorist.'

'But you can't just barge in—'

'Nonsense. I am the Duc de Croytor. Besides, I never barge. I always make an entrance.'

The ache in his midriff, Bowman guessed, was as nothing compared to some of the aches that he was going to come by very shortly—if, that was, he would then be in a position to feel anything. There was a gleam in Czerda's eye, a barely-contained anticipation in the face that bespoke ill, Bowman thought, for the immediate future.

He looked round the caravan. The three shackled men had in their faces the uncomprehending and lacklustre despair of those to whom defeat is already an accepted reality. Czerda and Masaine had pleasantly anticipatory smiles on their faces, El Brocador was serious and thoughtful and watchful, Simon Searl had a peculiar look in his eyes which made his unfrocking a readily comprehensible matter, while Cecile just looked slightly dazed, a little frightened, a little angry but as far removed from hysteria as could be.

'You understand now,' Czerda said, 'why I said you'd find the money within the minute.'

'I understand now. You'll find it—'

'What money?' Cecile asked. 'What does that—that monster want?'

'His eighty thousand francs back again—minus certain small outlays I've been compelled to make—and who can blame him?'

'Don't tell him anything!'

'And don't you understand the kind of men you're dealing with? Ten seconds from now they'll have your arm twisted up behind your back till it's touching your ear, you'll be screaming in agony and if they happen to break your shoulder or tear a few ligaments, well, that's just too bad.'

'But—but I'll just faint—'

'Please.' Bowman looked at Czerda, carefully avoiding Cecile's gaze. 'It's in Arles. Safe-deposit in the station.'

'The key?'

'On a ring. In the car. Hidden. I'll show you.'

'Excellent,' Czerda said. 'A disappointment to friend Searl, I'm afraid, but inflicting pain on young ladies gives me no pleasure though I wouldn't hesitate if I had to. As you shall see.'

'I don't understand.'

'You will. You are a danger, you have been a great danger and you have to go, that's all. You will die this afternoon and within the hour so that no suspicion will ever attach to us.'

It was, Bowman thought, as laconic a death sentence as he'd ever heard of. There was something chilling in the man's casual certainty.

Czerda went on: 'You will understand now why I didn't injure your face, why I wanted you to go into that bull-ring unmarked.'

'Bull-ring?'

'Bull-ring, my friend.'

'You're mad. You can't make me go into a bull-ring.'

Czerda said nothing and there was no signal. Searl, eagerly assisted by a grinning Masaine, caught hold of Cecile, forced her face downwards on to a bunk and, while Masaine pinned her down, Searl gripped the collar of the Arlésienne costume and ripped it down to the waist. He turned and smiled at Bowman, reached into the folds of his clerical garb and brought out what appeared to be a version of a hunting stock, with a fifteen-inch interwoven leather handle attached to three long thin black thongs. Bowman looked at Czerda and Czerda wasn't watching anything of what was going on: he was watching Bowman and the gun pointing at Bowman was motionless.

Czerda said: 'I think perhaps you will go into that bull-ring?'

'Yes.' Bowman nodded. 'I think perhaps I will.'

Searl put his stock away. His face was twisted in the bitter disappointment of a spoilt child who has been deprived of a new toy. Masaine took his hands away from Cecile's shoulders. She pushed herself groggily to a sitting position and looked at Bowman. Her face was very pale but her eyes were mad. It had just occurred to Bowman that she was, as she'd said, quite capable of using a gun if shown how to use one when there came from outside the sound of a solid measured tread: the door opened and

Le Grand Duc entered with a plainly apprehensive Lila trailing uncertainly behind him. Le Grand Duc pushed the monocle more firmly into his eye.

'Ah, Czerda, my dear fellow. It's you.' He looked at the gun in the gypsy's hand and said sharply: 'Don't point that damned thing at me!' He indicated Bowman. 'Point it at that fellow there. Don't you know he's your man, you fool?'

Czerda uncertainly trained his gun back on Bowman and just as uncertainly looked at Le Grand Duc.

'What do you want?' Czerda tried to imbue his voice with sharp authority but Le Grand Duc wasn't the properly receptive type and it didn't come off. 'Why are you—'

'Be quiet!' Le Grand Duc was at his most intimidating, which was very intimidating indeed. '*I* am speaking. You are a bunch of incompetent and witless nincompoops. You have forced me to destroy the basic rule of my existence—to bring myself into the open. I have seen more intelligence exhibited in a cageful of retarded chimpanzees. You have lost me much time and cost me vast trouble and anxiety. I am seriously tempted to dispose of the services of you all—permanently. And that means you as well as your services. What are you doing here?'

'What are we doing here?' Czerda stared at him. 'But—but—but Searl here said that you—'

'I will deal with Searl later.' Le Grand Duc's promise was imbued with such menacing overtones that Searl at once looked acutely unhappy. Czerda looked nervous to a degree that was almost unthinkable for him, El Brocador looked puzzled and Masaine had clearly given up thinking of any kind. Lila simply looked stunned. Le Grand Duc went on: 'I did not mean, you cretin, what you are doing in Mas de Lavignolle. I meant what are you doing here, as of this present moment, in this caravan.'

'Bowman here stole the money you gave me,' Czerda said sullenly. 'We were—'

'He what?' Le Grand Duc's face was thunderous.

'He stole your money,' Czerda said unhappily. 'All of it.'

'All of it!'

'Eighty thousand francs. That's what we've been doing

—finding out where it is. He's about to show me the key to where the money is.'

'I trust for your sake that you find it.' He paused and turned as Maca came staggering into the caravan, both hands holding what was clearly a very painful face.

'Is this man drunk?' Le Grand Duc demanded. '*Are* you drunk, sir? Stand straight when you talk to me.'

'He did it!' Maca spoke to Czerda, he didn't appear to have noticed Le Grand Duc, for his eyes were for Bowman only. 'He came along—'

'Silence!' Le Grand Duc's voice would have intimidated a Bengal tiger. 'My God, Czerda, you surround yourself with the most useless and ineffectual bunch of lieutenants it's ever been my misfortune to encounter.' He looked round the caravan, ignoring the three manacled men, took two steps towards where Cecile was sitting and looked down at her. 'Ha! Bowman's accomplice, of course. Why is she here?'

Czerda shrugged. 'Bowman wouldn't cooperate—'

'A hostage? Very well. Here's another.' He caught Lila by the arm and shoved her roughly across the caravan. She stumbled, almost fell, then sat down heavily on the bunk beside Cecile. Her face, already horror-stricken, now looked stupefied.

'Charles!'

'Be quiet!'

'But Charles! My father—you said—'

'You are a feather-brained young idiot,' Le Grand Duc said with contempt. 'The real Duc de Croytor, to whom I fortunately bear a strong resemblance, is at present in the upper Amazon, probably being devoured by the savages in the Matto Grosso. I am *not* the Duc de Croytor.'

'We know that, Mr Strome.' Simon Searl was at his most obsequious.

Again displaying his quite remarkable speed, Le Grand Duc stepped forward and struck Searl heavily across the face. Searl cried out in pain and staggered heavily, to bring up against the wall of the caravan. There was silence for several seconds.

'I have no name,' Le Grand Duc said softly. 'There is no such person as you mentioned.'

'I'm sorry, sir.' Searl fingered his cheek. 'I—'

'Silence!' Le Grand Duc turned to Czerda. 'Bowman has something to show you? Give you?'

'Yes, sir. And there's another little matter I have to attend to.'

'Yes, yes, yes. Be quick about it.'

'Yes, sir.'

'I shall wait here. We must talk on your return, mustn't we, Czerda.'

Czerda nodded unhappily, told Masaine to watch the girls, put his jacket over his gun and left accompanied by Searl and El Brocador. Masaine, his knife still drawn, seated himself comfortably. Maca, tenderly rubbing his bruised face, muttered something and left, probably to attend to his injuries. Lila, her face woebegone, looked up at Le Grand Duc.

'Oh, Charles, how could you—'

'Ninny!'

She stared at him brokenly. Tears began to roll down her cheeks. Cecile put an arm round her and glared at Le Grand Duc. Le Grand Duc looked through her and remained totally unaffected.

'Stop here,' Czerda said.

They stopped, Bowman ahead of Czerda with a silencer prodding his back, El Brocador and Searl on either side of him, the Citroën ten feet away.

'Where's the key?' Czerda demanded.

'I'll get it.'

'You will not. You are perfectly capable of switching keys or even finding a hidden gun. Where is it?'

'On a key ring. It's taped under the driver's seat, back, left.'

'Searl?' Searl nodded, went to the car. Czerda said sourly: 'You don't trust many people, do you?'

'I should, you think?'

'What's the number of this deposit box?'

'Sixty-five.'

Searl returned. 'These are ignition keys.'

'The brass one's not,' Bowman said.

Czerda took the keys. 'The brass one's not.' He removed

it from the ring. 'Sixty-five. For once, the truth. How's the money wrapped?'

'Oilskin, brown paper, sealing-wax. My name's on it.'

'Good.' He looked round. Maca was sitting on the top of some caravan steps. Czerda beckoned him and he came to where they were, rubbing his chin and looked malevolently at Bowman. Czerda said: 'Young José has a motor-scooter, hasn't he?'

'You want a message done. I'll get him. He's in the arena.'

'No need.' Czerda gave him the key. 'That's for safe deposit sixty-five in Arles station. Tell him to open it and bring back the brown paper parcel inside. Tell him to be as careful with it as he would be with his own life. It's a very, very valuable parcel. Tell him to come back here as soon as possible and give it to me and if I'm not here someone will know where I've gone and he's to come after me. Is that clear?'

Maca nodded and left. Czerda said: 'I think it's time we paid a visit to the bull-ring ourselves.'

They crossed the road but went not directly to the arena but to one of several adjacent huts which were evidently used as changing rooms, for the one they entered was behung with *matadors'* and *razateurs'* uniforms and several outfits of clowns' attire. Czerda pointed to one of the last. 'Get into that.'

'That?' Bowman eyed the garish rigout. 'Why the hell should I?'

'Because my friend here asks you to.' Czerda waved his gun. 'Don't make my friend angry.'

Bowman did as he was told. When he was finished he was far from surprised to see El Brocador exchange his conspicuous white uniform for his dark suit, to see Searl pull on a long blue smock, then to see all three men put on paper masks and comic hats. They appeared to have a craving for anonymity, a not unusual predilection on the part of would-be murderers. Czerda draped a red flag over his gun and they left for the arena.

When they arrived at the entrance to the *callajon* Bowman was mildly astonished to discover that the comic act that had been in process when he'd left was still not finished: so much seemed to have happened since he'd left the arena that it was difficult to realize that so few minutes had elapsed. They arrived to find that one of the clowns, incredibly, was doing a handstand on the back of the bull, which just stood there in baffled fury, its head swinging from side to side. The crowd clapped ecstatically: had the circumstances been different, Bowman thought, he might even have clapped himself.

For their final brief act the clowns waltzed towards the side of the arena to the accompaniment of their companion's accordion. They stopped, faced the crowd side by side and bowed deeply, apparently unaware that their backs were towards the charging bull. The crowd screamed a warning: the clowns, still bent, pushed each other apart at the last moment and the bull hurtled wildly over the spot where they had been standing only a second previously and crashed into the barrier with an impact that momentarily stunned it. As the clowns vaulted into the *callajon* the crowd continued to whistle and shout their applause. It occurred to Bowman to wonder whether they would still be in such a happily carefree mood in a few minutes' time: it seemed unlikely.

The ring was empty now and Bowman and his three escorts had moved out into the *callajon*. The crowd stared with interest and in considerable amusement at Bowman's attire and he was, unquestionably, worth a second glance. He was clad in a most outlandish fashion. His right leg was enclosed in red, his left in white and the doublet was composed of red and white squares. The flexible green canvas shoes he wore were so ludicrously long that the toes were tied back to the shins. He wore a white conical pierrot's hat with a red pom-pom on top: for defence he was armed with a slender three-foot cane with a small tricolor at the end of it.

'I have the gun, I have the girl,' Czerda said softly. 'You will remember?'

'I'll try.'

'If you try to escape, the girl will not live. You believe me?'

Bowman believed him. He said: 'And if I die, the girl will not live either.'

'No. Without you, the girl is nothing, and Czerda does

not make war on women. I know who you are now, or think I do. It is no matter. I have discovered that you never met her until last night and it is unthinkable that a man like you would tell her anything of importance: professionals never explain more than they have to, do they, Mr Bowman? And young girls can be made to talk, Mr Bowman. She can do us no harm. When we've done what we intend to do, and that will be in two days, she is free to go.'

'She knows where Alexandre is buried.'

'Ah, so. Alexandre? Who is Alexandre?'

'Of course. Free to go?'

'You have my word.' Bowman didn't doubt him. 'In exchange, you will now put on a convincing struggle.' Bowman nodded. The three men grabbed him or tried to grab him and all four staggered about the *callajon*. The colourful crowd were by now in excellent humour, gay, chattering, relaxed: all evidently felt that they were having a splendid afternoon's entertainment and that this mock-fight that was taking place in the *callajon*—for mock-fight it surely was, there were no upraised arms, no blows being struck in anger—was but the prelude to another hilariously comic turn, it had to be, with the man trying to struggle free dressed in that ridiculous pierrot's costume. Eventually, to the accompaniment of considerable whistling, laughter and shouts of encouragement, Bowman broke free, ran a little way along the *callajon* and vaulted into the ring. Czerda ran after him, made to clamber over the barrier but was caught and restrained by Searl and El Brocador, who pointed excitedly to the north end of the ring. Czerda followed their direction.

They were not the only ones looking in that direction. The crowd had suddenly fallen silent, their laughter had ceased and the smiles vanished: puzzlement had replaced their humour, a puzzlement that rapidly shaded into anxiety and apprehension. Bowman's eyes followed the direction of those of the crowd: he could not only understand the apprehension of the crowd, he reflected, but shared it to the fullest extent.

The northern *toril* gate had been drawn and a bull stood at the entrance. But this was not the small light black bull of the Camargue that was used in the *cours libre*—the bloodless bull-fight of Provence: this was a huge Spanish fighting bull, one of the Andalusian monsters that fight to the death in the great *corridas* of Spain. It had enormous shoulders, an enormous head and a terrifying spread of horn. Its head was low but not as low as it would be when it launched itself into its charge: it pawed the ground, alternately dragging each front hoof backwards, gouging deep channels in the dark sand.

Members of the crowd were by this time looking at one another in uneasy and rather fearful wonder. For the most part they were *aficionados* of the sport and they knew that what they were seeing was quite unprecedented and this could be no better than sending a man, no matter how brave and skilful a *razateur* he might be, to his certain death.

The giant bull was now advancing slowly into the ring, at the same time still contriving to make those deep backwards scores in the sand. Its great head was lower than before.

Bowman stood stock-still. His lips were compressed, his eyes narrow and still and watchful. Some twelve hours previously, when inching up the ledge on the cliff-face in the ruined battlements of the ancient fortress he had known fear, and now he knew it again and admitted it to himself. It was no bad thing, he thought wryly. Fear it was that sent the adrenalin pumping, and adrenalin was the catalyst that triggered off the capacity for violent action and abnormally swift reaction: as matters stood now he was going to need all the adrenalin he could lay hands on. But he was coldly aware that if he survived at all it could only be for the briefest of periods: all the adrenalin in the world couldn't save him now.

From the safety of the *callajon* Czerda licked his lips, half in unconscious empathy with the man in the ring, half in anticipation of things to come. Suddenly he tensed and the whole crowd tensed with him. An eerie silence as of death enveloped the arena. The great bull was charging.

With unbelievable acceleration for a creature of its size it came at Bowman like an express train. Bowman, unblinking, his racing mind figuring out the correlation between the speed of the bull and the rapidly narrowing distance between them, stood as a man would who is frozen with fear. Trance-like, fearful, the spectators stared in horror, convinced in their minds that this mad pierrot's destruction was only a couple of heart-beats away. Bowman waited for one of those heart-beats to tick away and then, when the bull was less than twenty feet and a second away, he flung himself to his right. But the bull knew all about such tactics, for with remarkable speed in so massive an animal it veered instantly to its left to intercept: but Bowman had only feinted. He checked violently and threw himself to the left and the bull thundered harmlessly by, the huge right horn missing Bowman by a clear foot. The crowd, unbelieving, heaved a long collective sigh of relief, shook their heads at one another and murmured their relief. But the apprehension, the tension, still lay heavily in the air.

The Andalusian bull could brake as swiftly as it could accelerate. It pulled up in a shower of sand, whirled round and came at Bowman again without pause. Again Bowman judged his moment to a fraction of a second, again he repeated the same manœuvre, but this time in the reverse order. Again the bull missed, but this time only by inches. There came another murmur of admiration from the crowd, this time to the accompaniment of some sporadic hand-clapping: the tension in the air was beginning to ease, not much, but enough to be perceptible.

Again the bull turned but this time it stood still, less than thirty feet away. Quite without moving, it watched Bowman, just as Bowman, quite without moving, watched him. Bowman stared at the great horns: there could be no doubt about it, their tips had been filed to sharp points. It occurred to Bowman, with a curious sense of detachment, that he had rarely encountered a more superfluous refinement: whether the horns had been sharpened or filed to the diameter of a penny it wouldn't have made a ha'porth of difference: a swinging hook of one of those giant horns with all the power of those massive shoulder and neck muscles behind it would go straight through his body irrespective of the condition of the tip. Indeed, being gored by the sharpened horn might prove the easier and less agonizing way to die but it was a matter of academic importance anyway, the end result would be inevitable and the same.

The bull's red eyes never wavered. Did it think, Bowman wondered, was it thinking? Was it thinking what he was thinking, that this was but a game of Russian roulette in so far as the terms of probabilities went? Would he expect Bowman to execute the same manœuvre next time, refuse to be drawn, carry straight on and get him while Bowman had checked to fling himself the other way? Or would he think that Bowman's next evasive action might not be a feint but the real thing, swerve accordingly and still get him? Bluff and double-bluff, Bowman thought, and it was pointless to speculate: the laws of blind chance were at work here and sooner or later, sooner rather than later, for on every occasion he had only a fifty-fifty chance, one of those horns would tear the life out of him.

The thought of that fifty-fifty chance prompted Bowman to risk a quick glance at the barrier. It was only ten feet away. He turned and sprinted for it, three steps, aware that behind him the bull had broken into its charge, aware ahead of him, in the *callajon*, of the figure of Czerda with the red flag over his arm, but the gun beneath clearly hanging downwards. He knew, as Bowman knew he knew, that Bowman had no intention of leaving the ring.

Bowman spun, back to the barrier, to face the bull. Pirouetting like a spinning top, he moved swiftly away along the barrier as the onrushing enraged bull hooked viciously with his right horn, the sharpened point brushing Bowman's sleeve but not even tearing the material. The bull crashed into the barrier with tremendous force, splintered the top two planks, then reared up with his forefeet on top of the planks as he tried furiously to climb over. Some time elapsed before the bull realized that Bowman was still in the same ring though by this time a prudent distance away.

By now the crowd was clapping and shouting its approval. Smiles were reappearing and some were even beginning to enjoy what had originally appeared to be a ludicrously one-sided and suicidal contest.

The bull stood still for a full half minute, shaking its great head slowly from side to side as if dazed by the power of its head-on collision with the barrier, which it very probably was. When it moved this time, it had changed its tactics. It didn't charge Bowman, it stalked him. It walked forward as Bowman walked backward, slowly gaining on him, and when it abruptly lowered its head and charged it was so close that Bowman had no room left for manœuvre. He did the only thing open to him and leapt high in the air as the bull tried to toss him. He landed on the bull's shoulders, somersaulted and came to the ground on his feet: although hurt and badly winded he miraculously succeeded in retaining his balance.

The crowd roared and whistled its admiration. Laughing in delight, they clapped one another on the back. Here, below that pierrot's disguise, must be one of the great *razateurs* of the day. *The* great *razateur* of the day. Some of the spectators looked almost sheepish at having worried about the capacity for survival of so great a master as this.

The three manacled prisoners on their bunks, the two girls and Masaine watched in some trepidation as Le Grand Duc paced restlessly up and down the length of the caravan, glancing in mounting irritation at his watch.

'What in the devil's name is taking Czerda so long?' he demanded. He turned to Masaine. 'You, there. Where have they taken Bowman?'

'Why, I thought you knew.'

'Answer, you cretin!'

'For the key. For the money. You heard. And then to the bull-ring, of course.'

'The bull-ring? Why?'

'Why?' Masaine was genuinely puzzled. 'You wanted it done, didn't you?'

'Wanted what done?' Le Grand Duc was exercising massive restraint.

'Bowman. To get him out of the way.'

Le Grand Duc laid hands on Masaine's shoulders and shook him in a no longer to be contained exasperation.

'Why the bull-ring?'

'To fight a bull, of course. A huge black Spanish killer. Bare hands.' Masaine nodded at Cecile. 'If he doesn't, we're going to kill her. This way, Czerda says, no suspicion can fall on us. Bowman should be dead by now.' Masaine shook his head in admiration. 'Czerda's clever.'

'He's a raving maniac!' Le Grand Duc shouted. 'Kill Bowman? Now? Before we've made him talk? Before I know his contacts, how he broke our ring? Not to mention the eighty thousand francs we haven't got yet. At once, fellow! Stop Czerda! Get Bowman out of there before it's too late.'

Masaine shook his head stubbornly. 'My orders are to stay here and guard those women.'

'I shall attend to you later,' Le Grand Duc said chillingly. 'I cannot, must not be seen in public with Czerda again. Miss Dubois, run at once—'

Cecile jumped to her feet. Her Arlésienne costume was not the thing of beauty that it had been but Lila had effected running repairs sufficient to preserve the decencies. She made to move forward, but Masaine barred her way.

'She stays here,' he declared. 'My orders—'

'Great God in heaven!' Le Grand Duc thundered. 'Are you defying me?'

He advanced ponderously upon a plainly apprehensive Masaine. Before the gypsy could even begin to realize what was about to happen Le Grand Duc smashed down his heel, with all his massive weight behind it, on Masaine's instep. Masaine howled in agony, hobbled on one leg and stooped to clutch his injured foot with both hands. As he did so Le Grand Duc brought down his locked hands on the base of Masaine's neck, who collapsed heavily on the floor, unconscious before he struck it.

'Swiftly, Miss Dubois, swiftly!' Le Grand Duc said urgently. 'If not already gone, your friend may well be *in extremis*.'

And *in extremis* Bowman undoubtedly was. He was still on his feet—but it was only an exceptional will-power and instinct, though fast fading, for survival that kept him there. His face was streaked with sand and blood, twisted in pain and drawn in exhaustion. From time to time he held his left ribs which appeared to be the prime source of the pain he was suffering. His earlier pierrot finery was now bedraggled and dirtied and torn, two long rips on the right-hand side of his tunic were evidences of two extremely narrow escapes from the scything left horn of the bull. He had forgotten how many times now he'd been on the sanded floor of the arena but he hadn't forgotten the three occasions when his visits there had been entirely involuntary: twice the shoulder of the bull had hurled him to the ground, once the back-sweep of the left horn had caught him high on the left arm and sent him somersaulting. And now the bull was coming at him again.

Bowman side-stepped but his reactions had slowed, and slowed badly. Providentially, the bull guessed wrongly and hooked away from Bowman but his left shoulder struck him a glancing blow, though from something weighing about a ton and travelling at thirty miles an hour the word 'glancing' is a purely relative term. It sent Bowman tumbling head over heels to the ground. The bull pursued him, viciously trying to gore, but Bowman had still enough awareness and physical resources left to keep rolling over and over, desperately trying to avoid those lethal horns.

The crowd had suddenly become very quiet. This, they knew, was a great *razateur*, a master mime and actor, but surely no one would carry the interests of his art to the suicidal lengths where, every second now as he rolled over the sand, he escaped death by inches and sometimes less, for twice in as many seconds the bull's horns tore through the back of the doublet.

Both times Bowman felt the horn scoring across his back and it was this that galvanized him to what he knew must be his final effort. Half a dozen times he rolled away from the bull as quickly as he could, seized what was only half a chance and scrambled upright. He could do no more than just stand there, swaying drunkenly and staggering from side to side. Again, that eerie silence fell across the arena as the bull, infuriated beyond measure and too mad to be cunning any more, came charging in again, but just as it seemed inevitable that the bull must surely this time impale him, an uncontrollable drunken lurch by Bowman took him a bare inch clear of the scything horn: so incensed was the bull that he ran on for another twenty yards before realizing that Bowman was no longer in his way and coming to a halt.

The crowd appeared to go mad. In their relief, in their unbounded admiration for this demigod, they cheered, they clapped, they shouted, they wept tears of laughter. What an actor, what a performer, what a magnificent *razateur*! Such an exhibition, surely, had never been seen before.

Bowman leaned in total exhaustion against the barrier, a smiling Czerda only feet away from where he stood.

Bowman was finished and the desperation in his face showed it. He was finished not only physically, he had come to the end of his mental tether. He just wasn't prepared to run any more. The bull lowered its head in preparation for another charge: again, silence fell over the arena. What fresh wonder was this miracle man going to demonstrate now?

But the miracle man was through with demonstrations for the day. Even as the silence fell he heard something that made him spin round and stare at the crowd, incredulity in his face. Standing high at the back of the crowd and waving frantically at him was Cecile, oblivious of the fact that scores of people had turned to stare at her.

'Neil!' Her voice was close to a scream. 'Neil Bowman! Come on!'

Bowman came. The bull had started on its charge but the sight of Cecile and the realization that escape was at hand had given Bowman a fresh influx of strength, however brief it might prove to be. He scrambled into the safety of the *callajon* at least two seconds before the bull thundered into the barrier. Bowman removed the pierrot's hat which had been hanging by its elastic band down the back of his neck, impaled it on one of the sharpened horns, brushed unceremoniously by the flabbergasted Czerda and ran up the terraces as quickly as his leaden legs would permit, waving to the crowd who parted to make way for him: the crowd, nonplussed though it was by this remarkable turn of events, nevertheless gave him a tumultuous reception: so unprecedented had the entire act been that they no doubt considered that this was also part of it. Bowman neither knew nor cared what their reactions were: just so long as they opened up before him and closed again after he had passed it would give him what might prove to be vital extra seconds over the inevitable pursuers. He reached the top, caught Cecile by the arm.

'I just love your sense of timing,' he said. His voice, like his breathing, was hoarse and gasping and distressed. He turned and looked behind him. Czerda was ploughing his way up through the crowd and not leaving any newly made friends behind him: El Brocador was moving on a converging course: of Searl he could see no sign. Together they hurried down the broad steps outside the arena, skirting the bull pens, stables and changing rooms. Bowman slid a hand through one of the many rips in his tunic, located his car keys and brought them out. He tightened his grip on Cecile's arm as they reached the last of the changing rooms and peered cautiously round the corner. A second later he withdrew, his face bitter with chagrin.

'It's just not our day, Cecile. That gypsy I clobbered—Maca—is sitting on the bonnet of the Citroën. Worse, he's cleaning his nails with a knife. One of those knives.' He opened a door behind them, thrust Cecile into the changing room where he himself had robed before his performance, and handed her the car keys. 'Wait till the crowd comes out. Mingle with them. Take the car, meet me at the southern end—the seaward end—of the church at Saintes-Maries. For God's sake, don't leave the Citroën anywhere near by—drive it out to the caravan park east of the town and leave it there.'

'I see.' She was, Bowman thought, remarkably calm. 'And meantime you have things to attend to?'

'As always.' He peered through a crack in the door: for the moment there was no one in sight. 'Four bridesmaids,' he said, slipped out and closed the door behind him.

The three manacled men were lying in their bunks, quietly and seemingly uncaring, Lila was sniffing disconsolately and Le Grand Duc scowling thunderously when Searl came running up the steps. The apprehensive look was back on his face again and he was noticeably short of breath.

'I trust,' Le Grand Duc said ominously, 'that you are not the bearer of ill tidings.'

'I saw the girl,' Searl gasped. 'How did she—'

'By God, Searl, you and your nincompoop friend Czerda will pay for this. If Bowman is dead—' He broke off and stared over Searl's shoulder, then pushed him roughly to one side. 'Who in heaven's name is that?'

Searl turned to follow Le Grand Duc's pointing finger. A red-and-white-clad pierrot was making his way at a lurching, stumbling run across the improvised car park: it was evident that he was near total exhaustion.

'That's him,' Searl shouted. 'That's him.' As they watched, three gypsies appeared from behind some huts, Czerda unmistakably one of them, running in pursuit of Bowman and covering the ground a great deal faster than he was. Bowman looked over his shoulder, located his pursuers, swerved to seek cover among several caravans, checked again as he saw his way blocked by El Brocador and two other gypsies, turned at right-angles and headed for a group of horses tethered near by, white Camargue horses fitted with the heavy-pommelled and high-backed Camargue saddles which look more like ribbed and leather-upholstered armchairs than anything else. He ran for the nearest, unhitched it, got a foot into the peculiarly fenced stirrup and managed, not without considerable effort, to haul himself up.

'Quickly!' Le Grand Duc ordered. 'Get Czerda. Tell him if Bowman escapes neither he nor you shall. But I want him alive. If he dies, you die. I want him delivered to me within the hour at the Miramar Hotel in Saintes-Maries. I myself cannot afford to remain here another moment. Don't forget to catch that damned girl and bring her along also. Hurry, man, hurry!'

Searl hurried. As he made to cross the road he had to step quickly and advisedly to one side to avoid being run down by Bowman's horse. Bowman, Le Grand Duc could see, was swaying in the saddle to the extent that even although he had the reins in his hands he had to hold on to the pommel to remain in his seat. Beneath the artificial tan the face was pale, drawn in pain and exhaustion. Le Grand Duc became aware that Lila was standing by his side, that she too was watching Bowman.

'I've heard of it,' the girl said quietly. No tears now, just a quietness and a sadness and disbelief. 'And now I see it. Hounding a man to death.'

Le Grand Duc put a hand on her arm. 'I assure you, my dear girl—'

She struck his hand from her arm and said nothing. She didn't have to, the contempt and the loathing in her face said it all for her. Le Grand Duc nodded, turned away and watched the diminishing figure of Bowman disappearing round a bend in the road to the south.

Le Grand Duc was not the only one to take so keen an interest in Bowman's departure. Her face pressed against a small square window in the side of the changing room Cecile watched the galloping white horse and its rider till it vanished from sight. Sure knowledge of what would happen next kept her there nor did she have long to wait. Within thirty seconds five other horsemen came galloping by—Czerda, Ferenc, El Brocador, Searl and a fifth man whom she did not recognize. Dry-lipped, near tears and sick at heart, she turned away from the window and started searching among the racks of clothes.

Almost at once she found what she wanted—a clown's oufit consisting of the usual very wide trousers, red, with wide yellow braces as support, a red-and-yellow-striped football jersey and a voluminous dark jacket. She pulled on the trousers, stuffing in the long fiesta dress as best she could—the trousers were cut on so generous a scale that the additional bagginess was scarcely noticeable—pulled the red-and-yellow jersey over her head, shrugged into the big jacket, removed her red wig and stuck a flat green cap on her head. There was no mirror in the changing room: that, she thought dolefully, was probably as well.

She went back to the window. The afternoon show was clearly over and people were streaming down the steps and across the road to their cars. She moved towards the door. Dressed as she was in a dress so shriekingly conspicuous that it conferred a degree of anonymity on the wearer, with the men she most feared in pursuit of Bowman and with plenty of people outside with whom to mingle, this, she realized, would be the best opportunity she would be likely to have to make her way undetected to the Citroën.

And, as far as she could tell, no one remarked her presence as she crossed the road towards the car or, if they did, they made no song and dance about it which, as far as Cecile was then concerned, amounted to the same thing. She opened the car, glanced forwards and back to make sure she was unobserved, slid into the driver's seat, put the key in the ignition and cried out more in fright than in pain as a large and vice-like hand closed around her neck.

The grip eased and she turned slowly round. Maca was kneeling on the floor at the back. He was smiling in a not very encouraging fashion and he had a large knife in his right hand.

CHAPTER NINE

The hot afternoon sun beat down mercilessly on the baking plains beneath, on the *étangs*, on the marshes, on the salt-flats and the occasional contrasting patches of bright green vegetation. A shimmering haze characteristic of the Camargue rose off the plains and gave a curiously ethereal quality, a strange lack of definition to all the features of the landscape, an illusion enhanced by the fact that none of those features was possessed of any vertical element. All plains are flat, but none as flat as the Camargue.

Half-a-dozen horsemen on steaming horses galloped furiously across the plain. From the air, their method of progress must have seemed peculiar and puzzling in the extreme as the horses seldom galloped more than twenty yards in a straight line and were continuously swerving off course. But seen at ground level the mystery disappeared: the area was so covered with numerous marshes, ranging from tiny little patches to areas larger than a football field, that it made continuous progress in a direct line impossible.

Bowman was at a disadvantage and knew it. He was at a disadvantage on three counts: he was, as his strained face showed and the blood-stains and dirt-streaks could not conceal, as exhausted as ever—this full-stretch gallop, involving continuous twisting and turning, offered no possibility of recuperating any strength—and his mind was as far below its decision-making best as his body was of executing those decisions: his pursuers knew the terrain intimately whereas he was a complete stranger to it: and, fairly accomplished horseman though he considered himself to be, he knew he could not even begin to compare with the expertise his pursuers had developed and refined almost from the cradle.

Constantly he urged his now flagging horse on but made little or no attempt to guide it as the sure-footed animal, abetted by experience and generations of inborn instinct, knew far better than he did where the ground was firm and where it was not. Occasionally he lost precious seconds in trying to force his horse to go in certain directions when his horse balked and insisted on choosing his own path.

Bowman looked over his shoulder. It was hopeless, in his heart he knew it was hopeless. When he had left Mas de Lavignolle he had had a lead of several hundred yards over his pursuers: now it was down to just over fifty. The five men behind him were spread out in a shallow fan shape. In the middle was El Brocador who was clearly as superb a horseman as he was a *razateur*. It was equally clear that he had an intimate knowledge of the terrain as from time to time he shouted orders and gestured with an outflung arm to indicate the direction a certain rider should go. On El Brocador's left rode Czerda and Ferenc, still heroically bandaged: on his right rode Simon Searl, an incongruous sight indeed in his clerical garb, and a gypsy whom Bowman could not identify.

Bowman looked ahead again. He could see no sign of succour, no house, no farm, no lonely horseman, nothing: and by this time he had been driven, not, he was grimly aware, without good reason, so far to the west that the cars passing on the main Arles-Saintes-Maries road were no more than little black beetles crawling along the line of the horizon.

He looked over his shoulder again. Thirty yards now, not more. They were no longer riding in a fan shape but were almost in line ahead, bearing down on his left, forcing him now to alter his own line of flight to the right. He was aware that this was being done with some good purpose in mind but, looking ahead, he could see nothing to justify this move. The land ahead appeared as normally variegated as the terrain he had just crossed: there was, directly ahead, an unusually large patch of almost dazzlingly green turf, perhaps a hundred yards long by thirty wide, but, size apart, it was in no way different from scores of others he had passed in the last two or three miles.

His horse, Bowman realized, had run its heart out and was near the end. Sweat-stained, foam-flecked and breathing heavily, it was as exhausted as Bowman himself. Two hundred yards ahead lay that invitingly green stretch of turf and the incongruous thought occurred to Bowman of how pleasant it would be to lie there, shaded, on a peaceful summer's day. He wondered why he didn't give up, the end of this pursuit was as certain as death itself: he would have given up, only he did not know how to set about it.

He looked back again. The five horsemen behind had now adopted a deep crescent shape, the outriders not much more than ten yards behind him. He looked ahead again, saw the greensward not more than twenty yards away, then the thought occurred that Czerda was now within accurate shooting range and Bowman was certain that when the five men returned to the caravans he would not be returning with them. Again he looked backwards and was astonished to see all five men reining in their horses and reining them in strongly at that. He knew something was wrong, terribly wrong, but before he could even start to think about it his own horse stopped abruptly and in an unbelievably short distance, forelegs splayed and sliding on its haunches, at the very edge of the patch of greensward. The horse stopped but Bowman did not. Still looking over his shoulder, he had been taken totally unprepared. He left the saddle, sailed helplessly over the horse's head and landed on the stretch of green grass.

He should have been knocked out, at the worst broken his neck, at the best landed heavily and bruised badly, but none of those things happened because it was at once apparent that the greensward was not what it appeared to be. He did not fall heavily or bounce or roll: instead he landed with a soggy squelching splash on a soft, cushioning and impact-absorbing material. Into this he slowly started to sink.

The five horsemen walked their horses forward, stopped, leaned on their pommels and gazed impassively downwards. Bowman had assumed a vertical position now, although leaning slightly forward. Already, he was hip-deep in the deadly quicksand with the safety of firm land no more than four feet away. Desperately he flailed his arms in an endeavour to reach it but made no progress whatsoever. The watchers remained motionless on their horses: the impassiveness on their faces was frightening in its suggestion of a total implacability.

Bowman sank to the waist. He tried a gentle swimming motion for he realized that frantic struggling was only having the opposite effect to what was intended. It slowed up the sinking but did not stop it: the sucking effect of the quicksand was terrifying in its remorselessnes.

He looked at the five men. The total impassivity had disappeared. Czerda was smiling the pleased smile he reserved for occasions like this, Searl was slowly, obscenely licking his lips. All eyes were fixed on Bowman's face, but if he had any thoughts of shouting for help or begging for mercy no sign of it showed in his expressionless face. Nor were there any thoughts of it in his mind. Fear he had known on the battlements of Les Baux and in the bull-ring at Mas de Lavignolle: but here, now, there was no fear. On the other occasions there had been a chance, however slender, of survival, dependent upon his own resourcefulness, his coordination of hand and eye: but here all his hardly won knowledge and experiences and skill, his exceptional reflexes and physical attributes were useless: from a quicksand there can be no escape. It was the end, it was inevitable and he accepted it.

El Brocador looked at Bowman. The quicksand was now almost up to his armpits, only his shoulders, arms and head were now in view. El Brocador studied the impassive face, nodded to himself, turned and looked at Czerda and Searl in turn, distaste and contempt in his face. He unhooked a rope from his pommel.

'One does not do this to a man like this,' he said. 'I am ashamed for us all.' With a skilful flick of his wrist he sent the rope snaking out: it landed precisely midway between Bowman's out-stretched hands.

Even the most ardent publicist of the attractions of Saintes-Maries—if any such exists—would find it difficult to rhapsodize over the beauties of the main street of the town which runs from east to west along a sea-front totally invisible behind a high rock wall. It is, like the rest of the town, singularly devoid of scenic, artistic or architectural merit, although on that particular afternoon its drabness was perhaps slightly relieved by the crowds of outlandishly dressed tourists, gypsies, *guardians* and the inevitable fair-ground booths, shooting galleries, fortune-tellers' stands and souvenir shops that had been haphazardly set up for their benefit and edification.

It was not, one would have thought, a spectacle that would have brought a great deal of gratification to Le Grand Duc's aristocratic soul, yet, as he sat in the sidewalk café outside the Miramar hotel, surveying the scene before him, the expression on his face was mellow to the point of benevolence. Even more oddly in the light of his notoriously undemocratic principles, Carita, his chauffeuse, was seated beside him. Le Grand Duc picked up a litre carafe of red wine, poured a large amount in a large glass he had before him, a thimbleful into a small glass she had before her and smiled benevolently again, not at the passing scene but at a telegram form that he held in his hand. It was clear that Le Grand Duc's exceptional good humour was not because of Saintes-Maries and its inhabitants, but in spite of them. The source of his satisfaction lay in the paper he held in his hand.

'Excellent, my dear Carita, excellent. Exactly what we wished to know. By Jove, they have moved fast.' He contemplated the paper again and sighed. 'It's gratifying, most gratifying, when one's guesses turn out to be one hundred per cent accurate.'

'Yours always are, Monsieur le Duc.'

'Eh? What was that? Yes, yes, of course. Help yourself to some more wine.' Le Grand Duc had temporarily lost interest in both the telegram and Carita, and was gazing thoughtfully at a large black Mercedes that had just pulled up a few feet away. The Chinese couple whom Le Grand Duc had last seen on the hotel patio in Arles emerged and made for the hotel entrance. They passed by within a few feet of Le Grand Duc's table. The man nodded, his wife smiled faintly and Le Grand Duc, not to be outdone, bowed gravely. He watched them as they went inside, then turned to Carita.

'Czerda should be here soon with Bowman. I have decided that this is an inadvisable place for a rendezvous. Too public, too public by far. There's a big lay-by about one mile north of the town. Have Czerda stop there and wait for me while you come back here for me.'

She smiled and rose to leave but Le Grand Duc raised a hand.

'One last thing before you go. I have a very urgent phone

call to make and I wish it made in complete privacy. Tell the manager I wish to see him. At once.'

Le Hobenaut, Tangevec and Daymel were still in their bunks, still manacled to the caravan wall. Bowman, his pierrot suit now removed and his *guardian* clothes saturated and still dripping, lay on the floor with his hands bound behind his back. Cecile and Lila were seated on a bench under the watchful eyes of Ferenc and Masaine. Czerda, El Brocador and Searl were seated at a table: they weren't talking and they looked very unhappy. Their expression of unhappiness deepened as they listened to the measured tread of footsteps mounting the steps of the caravan. Le Grand Duc made his customary impressive entry. He surveyed the three seated men coldly.

'We have to move quickly.' His voice was brusque, authoritative and as cold as his face. 'I have received cabled information that the police are becoming suspicious and may well by this time be certain of us—thanks to you, Czerda, and that bungling fool Searl there. Are you mad, Czerda?'

'I do not understand, sir.'

'That's precisely it. You understand nothing. You were going to kill Bowman before he'd told us how he broke our ring, who his contacts are, where my eighty thousand francs are. Worst of all, you cretins, you were going to kill him publicly. Can't you see the enormous publicity that would have received? Secrecy, stealth, those are my watch-words.'

'We know where the eighty thousand francs are, sir.' Czerda tried to salvage something from the wreck.

'Do we? *Do* we? I suspect you have been fooled again, Czerda. But that can wait. Do you know what will happen to you all if the French police get you?' Silence. 'Do you know the rigorous penalties French courts impose on kidnappers?' Still silence. 'Not one of you here can hope to escape with less than ten years in prison. And if they can trace Alexandre's murder to you . . .'

Le Grand Duc looked at El Brocador and the four gypsies in turn. From the expressions on their faces it was quite clear that they knew what would happen if the murder could be traced to them.

'Very well, then. From this moment on your futures and your lives depend entirely on doing exactly what I order—it is not beyond my powers to rescue you from the consequences of your own folly. Exactly. Is that understood?'

All five men nodded. No one said anything.

'Very well. Unchain those men. Untie Bowman. If the police find them like that—well, it's all over. We use guns and knives to guard them from now on. Bring all their womenfolk in here—I want all our eggs in one basket. Go over our proposed plans, Searl. Go over them briefly and clearly so that even the most incompetent nincompoop, and that includes you, can understand what we have in mind. Bring me some beer, someone.'

Searl cleared his throat self-consciously and looked distinctly unhappy. The arrogance, the quietly cold competence with which he'd confronted Czerda in the confessional booth that morning had vanished as if it had never existed.

'Rendezvous any time between last night and Monday night. Fast motor-boat waiting—'

Le Grand Duc sighed in despair and held up a hand.

'Briefly and *clearly*, Searl. Clearly. Rendezvous where, you fool? With whom?'

'Sorry, sir.' The Adam's apple in the thin scraggy neck bobbed up and down as Searl swallowed nervously. 'Off Palavas in the Gulf of Aigues-Mortes. Freighter *Canton.*'

'Bound for?'

'Canton.'

'Precisely.'

'Recognition signals—'

'Never mind that. The motor-boat?'

'At Aigues-Mortes on the Canal du Rhône à Sète. I was going to have it moved down to Le Grau du Roi tomorrow—I didn't think—I—'

'You never have done,' Le Grand Duc said wearily. 'Why aren't those damned women here? And those manacles still fixed? Hurry.' For the first time he relaxed and smiled slightly. 'I'll wager our friend Bowman still doesn't know who our three other friends are. Eh, Searl?'

'I can tell him?' Searl asked eagerly. The prospect of climbing out of the hot seat and transferring the spotlight elsewhere was clearly an attractive one.

'Suit yourself.' Le Grand Duc drank deeply of his beer. 'Can it matter now?'

'Of course not.' Searl smiled widely. 'Let me introduce Count le Hobenaut, Henri Tangevec and Serge Daymel. The three leading rocket fuel experts on the other side of the Iron Curtain. The Chinese wanted them badly, they have been so far unable to develop a vehicle to carry their nuclear warheads. Those men could do it. But there wasn't a single land border between China and Russia that could be used, not a single neutral country that was friendly to both the great powers and wouldn't have looked too closely at irregular happenings. So Czerda brought them out. To the West. No one would ever dream that such men would defect to the West—the West has its own fuel experts. And, at the frontiers, no one ever asks questions of gypsies. Of course, if the three men had clever ideas, their wives would have been killed. If the women got clever ideas, the men would have been killed.'

'Or so the women were told,' Le Grand Duc said contemptuously. 'The last thing that we wanted was that any harm should come to those men. But women—they'll believe anything.' He permitted himself a small smile of satisfaction. 'The simplicity—if I may say so myself, the staggering simplicity of true genius. Ah, the women. Aigues-Mortes, and with speed. Tell your other caravans, Czerda, that you will rendezvous with them in the morning in Saintes-Maries. Come, Lila, my dear.'

'With you?' She stared at him in revulsion. 'You must be mad. Go with *you*?'

'Appearances must be maintained, now more than ever. What suspicion is going to attach to a man with so beautiful a young lady by his side? Besides, it's very hot and I require someone to hold my parasol.'

Just over an hour later, still fuming and tight-lipped, she lowered the parasol as the green Rolls-Royce drew up outside the frowning walls of Aigues-Mortes, the most perfectly preserved Crusader walled city in Europe. Le Grand Duc descended from the car and waited till Czerda had brought the breakdown truck towing the caravan to a halt.

'Wait here,' he ordered. 'I shall not be long.' He nodded

to the Rolls. 'Keep a sharp eye on Miss Delafont there. You apart, no others are on any account to show themselves.'

He glanced up the road towards Saintes-Maries. Momentarily, it was deserted. He marched quickly away and entered the bleak and forbidding town by the north gate, turned right into the car-park and took up position in the concealment of a barrel organ. The operator, a decrepit ancient who, in spite of the heat of the day, was wearing two overcoats and a felt hat, looked up from the stool where he had been drowsing and scowled. Le Grand Duc gave him ten francs. The operator stopped scowling, adjusted a switch and began to crank a handle: the screeching cacophonous result was an atonal travesty of a waltz that no composer alive or dead would ever have acknowledged as his. Le Grand Duc winced, but remained where he was.

Within two minutes a black Mercedes passed in through the archway, turned right and stopped. The Chinese couple got out, looked neither to left nor right, and walked hurriedly down the main street—indeed, Aigues-Mortes's only street—towards the tiny café-lined square near the centre of the town. More leisurely and at a discreet distance Le Grand Duc followed.

The Chinese couple reached the square and halted uncertainly on a corner by a souvenir shop, not far from the statue of St Louis. No sooner had they done so than four large men in plain dark clothes emerged from the shop, two from each door, and closed in on them. One of the men showed the Chinese man something cupped in the palm of his hand. The Chinese man gesticulated and appeared to protest violently but the four large men just shook their heads firmly and led the couple away to a pair of waiting black Citroëns.

Le Grand Duc nodded his head in what could not easily have been mistaken for anything other than satisfaction, turned and retraced his steps to the waiting car and caravan.

Less than sixty seconds' drive took them to a small jetty on the Canal du Rhône à Sète, a canal that links the Rhône to the Mediterranean at Le Grau du Roi and runs parallel to the western wall of Aigues-Mortes. At the end of the jetty was moored a thirty-five-foot power-boat with a large glassed-in cabin and an only slightly smaller cockpit aft. From the lines of the broad flaring bows it appeared to be a vessel capable of something unusual in terms of speed.

The Rolls and the caravan pulled clear off the road and halted so that the rear of the caravan was less than six feet from the head of the jetty. The transfer of the prisoners from the caravan to the boat was performed smoothly, expeditiously and in such a fashion that it could have aroused no suspicion in even the most inquisitive of bystanders: in point of fact the nearest person was a rod fisherman a hundred yards away and his entire attention was obviously concentrated on what was happening at the end of his line some feet below the surface of the canal. Ferenc and Searl, each with a barely concealed pistol, stood on the jetty near the top of a short gangway while Le Grand Duc and Czerda, similarly unostentatiously armed, stood on the poop of the boat while first the three scientists, then their womenfolk, then Bowman, Cecile and Lila filed aboard. Under the threat of the guns they took up position on the settees lining the side of the cabin.

Ferenc and Searl entered the cabin, Searl advancing to the helmsman's position. For a moment Le Grand Duc and Masaine remained in the cockpit, checking that they were quite unobserved then Le Grand Duc entered the cabin, pocketed his gun and rubbed his hands in satisfaction.

'Excellent, excellent, excellent.' He sounded positively cheerful. 'Everything, as always, under control. Start the engines, Searl!' He turned and poked his head through the cabin doorway. 'Cast off, Masaine!'

Searl pressed buttons and the twin engines started up with a deep powerful throb of sound, but a sound by no means loud enough to muffle a short sharp exclamation of pain: the sound emanated from Le Grand Duc, who was still looking aft through the doorway.

'Your own gun in your own kidney,' Bowman said. 'No one to move or you die.' He looked at Ferenc and Czerda and Searl and El Brocador. At least three of them, he knew, were armed. He said: 'Tell Searl to stop the engines.'

Searl stopped the engines without having to have the message relayed through Le Grand Duc.

'Tell Masaine to come here,' Bowman said. 'Tell him I've got a gun in your kidney.' He looked round the cabin: no one had moved. 'Tell him to come at once or I'll pull the trigger.'

'You wouldn't dare!'

'You'll be all right,' Bowman said soothingly. 'Most people can get by on one kidney.'

He jabbed the gun again and Le Grand Duc gasped in pain. He said hoarsely: 'Masaine! Come here at once. Put your gun away. Bowman has his gun on me.'

There was a few seconds' silence, then Masaine appeared in the doorway. No profound thinker at the best of times, he was obviously uncertain as to what to do: the sight of Czerda, Ferenc, Searl and El Brocador busy doing nothing convinced him that nothing was, for the moment, the wise and prudent course of action. He moved into the cabin.

'Now we come up against the question of the delicate balances of power,' Bowman said conversationally. He was still pale and haggard, he felt unutterably tired and stiff and sore all over: but he felt a prince compared to the condition he'd been in two hours previously. 'A question of checks and balances. How much influence and authority can I exert on you standing here with this gun in my hand? How much of my will can I impose? So much—but only so much.'

He pulled Le Grand Duc back by the shoulder, stepped to one side and watched Le Grand Duc collapse heavily on a settee, a well-made settee which didn't break. Le Grand Duc glared at Bowman, the aristocratic voltage in the blue eyes turned up to maximum power: Bowman remained unshrivelled.

'It's difficult to believe just looking at you,' Bowman went on to Le Grand Duc, 'but you're almost certainly the most intelligent of your band of ruffians. Not, of course, that that would call for any great intelligence. I have a gun here and it is in my hand. There are four others here who also have guns and although they're not in their hands at the present moment it wouldn't take very long for the guns to get there. If it came to a fight, I think it extremely unlikely that I could get all four before one of you—more probably two—got me. I am not a Wild Bill Hickock.

Moreover, there are eight innocent people here—nine, if you count me—and a gun-fight in this enclosed space would almost certainly result in some of them being hurt, even killed. I wouldn't like that any more than I would like being shot myself.'

'Get to the point,' Le Grand Duc growled.

'It's obvious, surely. What demands can I make upon you that wouldn't be too great to precipitate this gun-fight that I'm sure we all want to avoid? If I told you to hand over your guns, would you, quietly and tamely, with the knowledge that long prison sentences and probably indictments for murder awaited you all? I doubt it. If I said I'll let you go but take the scientists and their women, would you go along with that? Again, I doubt it, for they would be living evidence of your crimes, with the result that if you set foot anywhere in Western Europe you'd finish in prison and if you set foot in Eastern Europe you'd be lucky to end up in a Siberian prison camp as the Communists aren't too keen on people who kidnap their top scientists. In fact, there'd be no place left for you in any part of Europe. You'd just have to go on the *Canton* and sail all the way home with her and I don't think you'd find life in China all it's cracked up to be—by the Chinese, of course.

'On the other hand, I doubt whether you'd be prepared to fight to the death to prevent the departure of the two young ladies and myself. They're only ciphers, a couple of romantically minded and rather empty-headed young holidaymakers who thought it rather fun to get mixed up in these dark goings on.' Bowman carefully avoided looking at the two girls. 'I admit that it is possible for me to start trouble, but I don't see I would get very far: it would be only my word against yours, there wouldn't be a shred of evidence I could offer and there's no way I can think of how you could be tied up with the murder in the cave. The only evidence lies in the scientists and their wives and they would be half-way to China before I could do anything. Well?'

'I accept your reasoning,' Le Grand Duc said heavily. 'Try to make us give ourselves or the scientists up—or their wives—and you'd never leave this boat alive. You and those two young fools there are, as you say, another matter. You can arouse suspicion, but that's all you can do: better that than have two or three of my men die uselessly.'

'It might even be you,' Bowman said.

'The possibility had not escaped me.'

'You're my number one choice of hostage and safe conduct,' Bowman said.

'I rather thought I might be.' Le Grand Duc rose with obvious reluctance to his feet.

'I don't like this,' Czerda said. 'What if—'

'You want to be the first to die?' Le Grand Duc asked wearily. 'Leave the thinking to me, Czerda.'

Czerda, obviously ill at ease, said no more. At a gesture from Bowman the two girls left the cabin and climbed the gangway. Bowman, walking backwards with his gun a few inches from Le Grand Duc's midriff, followed. At the top of the gangway Bowman said to the girls: 'Get back and out of sight.'

He waited ten seconds then said to Le Grand Duc: 'Turn round.' Le Grand Duc turned. Bowman gave him a hefty shove that set him stumbling, almost falling, down the gangway. Bowman threw himself flat: there was always the off-chance of someone or ones down there changing their minds. But no shots were fired, there was no sound of footsteps on the gangway. Bowman raised a cautious head. The engines had started up again.

The power-boat was already twenty yards away and accelerating. Bowman rose quickly and, followed by Cecile and Lila, ran to the Rolls. Carita gazed at him in astonishment.

'Out!' Bowman said.

Carita opened her mouth to protest but Bowman was in no mood for protests. He jerked open the door and practically lifted her on to the road. Immediately afterwards he was behind the wheel himself.

'Wait!' Cecile said. 'Wait! We're coming with—'

'Not this time.' He leaned down and plucked Cecile's handbag from her. She stared at him, slightly open-mouthed, but said nothing. He went on: 'Go into the town. Phone the police in Saintes-Maries, tell them there's a sick girl in a green-and-white caravan in a lay-by a kilometre and a half north of the town and that they're to get her to a hospital at once. Don't tell them who you are, don't tell them a single thing more than that. Just hang up.' He nodded at Lila and Carita. 'Those two will do for a start.'

'Do for what?' She was, understandably, bemused.

'Bridesmaids.'

The road between Aigues-Mortes and Le Grau du Roi is only a few kilometres long and, for the most part, it parallels the canal at a distance of a few feet: the only boundary line between them, if such it can be called, is a thin line of tall reeds. It was through those reeds, less than a minute after starting up the Rolls, that Bowman caught his first glimpse of the power-boat, fewer than a hundred yards ahead. It was already travelling at an illegally high speed, its stern dug deep into the water, spray flying high and wide from the deflectors on the bows: the wash set up by the wake of its passing was sending waves high up both sides of the canal banks.

Searl was at the wheel, Masaine, El Brocador and Ferenc were seated but keeping a watchful eye on the passengers, while Le Grand Duc and Czerda were conversing near the after door of the cabin. Czerda still looked most unhappy.

He said: 'But how can you be *sure* that he can bring no harm to us?'

'I'm sure.' The passage of time had restored Le Grand Duc to his old confident self.

'But he'll go to the police. He's bound to.'

'So? You heard what he said himself. His solitary word against all of ours? With all his evidence half-way to China? They'll think he's mad. Even if they don't, there's nothing in the world they can prove.'

'I still don't like it,' Czerda said stubbornly. 'I think—'

'Leave the thinking to me,' Le Grand Duc said curtly. 'Good God!'

There was a splintering of glass, the sound of a shot and a harsh cry of pain from Searl, who abandoned the wheel in favour of clutching his left shoulder. The boat swerved violently and headed straight for the left bank: it would unquestionably have struck it had not Czerda, although older than any of his companions and the farthest from the wheel, reacted with astonishing speed, hurled himself forward and spun the wheel hard to starboard. He succeeded in preventing the power-boat from burying—and probably crushing—its bows in the bank, but wasn't in time to prevent the wildly slewing boat from crashing its port side heavily against the bank with an impact that threw all who were standing, except Czerda, and quite a few who were seated, to the deck. It was at that instant that Czerda glanced through a side window and saw Bowman, at the wheel of the Rolls-Royce and less than five yards distant on the paralleling road, taking careful aim with Le Grand Duc's pistol through an opened window.

'Down!' shouted Czerda. He was the first down himself. 'Flat on the floor.'

Again there came the sound of smashing glass, again the simultaneous report from the pistol, but no one was hurt. Czerda rose to a crouch, eased the throttle, handed the wheel over to Masaine, and joined Le Grand Duc and Ferenc who had already edged out, on all fours, to the poop-deck. All three men peered cautiously over the gunwale, then stood upright, thoughtfully holding their guns behind their backs.

The Rolls had dropped thirty yards back. Bowman was being blocked by a farm tractor towing a large four-wheeled trailer, and balked from overtaking by several cars approaching from the south.

'Faster,' Czerda said to Masaine. 'Not too fast—keep just ahead of that tractor. That's it. That's it.' He watched the last of the north-bound cars go by on the other side of the road. 'Here he comes now.'

The long green nose of the Rolls appeared in sight beyond the tractor. The three men in the cockpit levelled their guns and the tractor-driver, seeing them, braked and swerved so violently that he came to a rest with the right front wheel of his tractor overhanging the bank of the canal. Its abrupt braking and swerve brought the entire length of the car completely and suddenly in sight. Bowman, gun cocked in hand and ready to use, saw what was about to happen, dropped the gun and threw himself below the level of the door sills. He winced as bullet after bullet thudded into the bodywork of the Rolls. The windscreen suddenly starred and became completely opaque. Bowman thrust his fist through the bottom of the glass, kicked the accelerator down beyond the detente and accelerated swiftly away. It was obvious that, with the element of surprise gone, he stood no chance whatsoever against the three armed men in the poop. He wondered vaguely how Le Grand Duc felt about the sudden drop in the resale market value of his Rolls.

He drove at high speed past the arena on his left into the town of Grau du Roi, skidding the car to a halt at the approaches to the swing bridge that crossed the canal and connected the two sides of the town. He opened Cecile's bag, peeled money from the roll of Swiss francs he had taken from Czerda's caravan, put the roll back in the bag, thrust the bag into a cubby-hole, hoped to heaven the citizens of Grau du Roi were honest, left the car and ran down the quayside.

He slowed down to a walk as he approached the craft moored along the left bank, just below the bridge. It was a wide-beamed, high-prowed fishing boat, of wooden and clearly very solid construction, that had seen its best days some years ago. Bowman approached a grey-jerseyed fisherman of middle age who was sitting on a bollard and lethargically mending a net.

'That's a fine boat you've got there,' Bowman said in his best admiring tourist fashion. 'Is it for rent?'

The fisherman was taken aback by the directness of the approach. Matters involving finance were customarily approached with a great deal more finesse.

'Fourteen knots and built like a tank,' the owner said proudly. 'The finest wooden-hulled fishing boat in the south of France. Twin Perkins diesels. Like lightning! And so strong. But only for charter, m'sieur. And even then only when the fishing is bad.'

'Too bad, too bad.' Bowman took out some Swiss francs and fingered them. 'Not even for an hour? I have urgent reasons, believe me.' He had, too. In the distance he could hear the rising note of Le Grand Duc's power-boat.

The fisherman screwed up his eyes as if in thought: it is not easy to ascertain the denomination of foreign banknotes at a distance of four feet. But sailors' eyes are traditionally keen. He stood and slapped his thigh.

'I will make an exception,' he announced, then added cunningly: 'But I will have to come with you, of course.'

'Of course. I would have expected nothing else.' Bowman

handed over two one-thousand Swiss franc notes. There was a legerdemain flick of the wrist and the notes disappeared from sight.

'When does m'sieur wish to leave?'

'Now.' He could have had the boat anyway, Bowman knew, but he preferred Czerda's banknotes to the waving of a gun as a means of persuasion: that he would eventually have to wave his gun around he did not doubt.

They cast off, went aboard and the fisherman started the engines while Bowman peered casually aft. The sound of the power-boat's engines was very close now. Bowman turned and watched the fisherman push the throttles forward as he gave the wheel a turn to starboard. The fishing boat began to move slowly away from the quayside.

'It doesn't seem too difficult,' Bowman observed. 'To handle it, I mean.'

'To you, no. But it takes a lifetime of knowledge to handle such a vessel.'

'Could I try now?'

'No, no. Impossible. Perhaps when we get to the sea—'

'I'm afraid it will have to be now. Please.'

'In five minutes—'

'I'm sorry. I really am.' Bowman produced his pistol, pointed with it to the starboard for'ard corner of the wheel-house. 'Please sit down there.'

The fisherman stared at him, relinquished the wheel and moved across to the corner of the wheel-house. He said quietly, as Bowman took over the wheel: 'I knew I was a fool. I like money too much, I think.'

'Don't we all.' Bowman glanced over his shoulder. The power-boat was less than a hundred yards from the bridge. He opened the throttles wide and the fishing boat began to surge forward. Bowman dug into his pocket, came up with the last three thousand francs of Czerda's money that he had on him and threw it across to the man. 'This will make you even more foolish.'

The fisherman stared at the notes, made no attempt to pick them up. He whispered: 'When I am dead, you will take it away. Pierre des Jardins is not a fool.'

'When you are dead?'

'When you kill me. With that pistol.' He smiled sadly. 'It is a wonderful thing to have a pistol, no?'

'Yes.' Bowman reversed hold on his pistol, caught it by the barrel and threw it gently across to the fisherman. 'Do you feel wonderful too, now?'

The man stared at the pistol, picked it up, pointed it experimentally at Bowman, laid it down, picked up and pocketed the money, picked up the pistol a second time, rose, crossed to the wheel and replaced the pistol in Bowman's pocket. He said: 'I'm afraid I am not very good at firing those things, m'sieur.'

'Neither am I. Look behind you. Do you see a power-boat coming up?'

Pierre looked. The power-boat was no more than a hundred yards behind. He said: 'I see it. I know it. My friend Jean—'

'Sorry. Later about your friend.' Bowman pointed ahead to where a freighter was riding out in the gulf. 'That's the freighter *Canton*. A communist vessel bound for China. Behind us, in the power-boat, are evil men who wish to put aboard that vessel people who do not wish to go there. It is my wish to stop them.'

'Why?'

'If you have to ask why I'll take this pistol from my pocket and make you sit down again.' Bowman looked quickly behind him: the power-boat was barely more than fifty yards behind.

'You are British, of course?'

'Yes.'

'You are an agent of your government?'

'Yes.'

'What we call your Secret Service?'

'Yes.'

'You are known to our government?'

'I am to your Deuxième Bureau. Their boss is my boss.'

'Boss?'

'Chief. *Chef*.'

Pierre sighed. 'It has to be true. And you wish to stop this boat coming up?' Bowman nodded. 'Then please move over. This is a job for an expert.'

Bowman nodded again, took the gun from his pocket, moved to the starboard side of the wheel-house and wound down the window. The power-boat was less than ten feet astern, not more than twenty feet away on a parallel course and coming up fast. Czerda was at the wheel now, with Le Grand Duc by his side. Bowman raised his pistol, then lowered it again as the fishing boat leaned over sharply and arrowed in on the power-boat. Three seconds later the heavy oaken bows of the fishing-boat smashed heavily into the port quarter of the other vessel.

'That was, perhaps, more or less what you had in mind, m'sieur,' Pierre asked.

'More or less,' Bowman admitted. 'Now please listen. There is something you should know.'

The two boats moved apart on parallel courses. The power-boat, being the faster, pulled ahead. Inside its cabin there was considerable confusion.

'Who was that madman?' Le Grand Duc demanded.

'Bowman!' Czerda spoke with certainty.

'Guns out!' Le Grand Duc shouted. 'Guns out! Get him!'

'No.'

'No? No? You dare countermand—'

'I smell petrol. In the air. One shot—poof. Ferenc, go and check the port tank.' Frenc departed and returned within ten seconds.

'Well?'

'The tank is ruptured. At the bottom. The fuel is nearly gone.' Even as he spoke the port engine faltered, spluttered and stopped. Czerda and Le Grand Duc looked at each other: nothing was said.

Both boats had by now cleared the harbour and were out in the open sea of the Gulf of Aigues-Mortes. The power-boat, on one engine now, had dropped back until it was almost parallel with the fishing boat. Bowman nodded to Pierre, who nodded in turn. He spun the wheel rapidly, their vessel angled in sharply, they made violent contact again in exactly the same place as previously, then sheered off.

'God damn it all!' Aboard the power-boat Le Grand Duc was almost livid with fury and making no attempt to conceal it. 'He's holed us! He's holed us! Can't you avoid him?'

'With one engine, it is very difficult to steer.' Under the circumstances, Czerda's restraint was commendable. He was in no way exaggerating. The combination of a dead port engine and a holed port quarter made the maintenance of a straight course virtually impossible: Czerda was no seaman and even with his best efforts the power-boat was now pursuing a very erratic course indeed.

'Look!' Le Grand Duc said sharply. 'What's that?'

Abut three miles away, not more than half-way towards Palavas, a large and very old-fashioned freighter, almost stopped in the water, was sending a message by signalling lamp.

'It's the *Canton*!' Searl said excitedly. He so far forgot himself as to stop rubbing the now padded flesh wound on top of his shoulder. 'The *Canton*! We must send a recognition signal. Three long, three short.'

'No!' Le Grand Duc was emphatic. 'Are you mad? We mustn't get them involved in this. The international repercussions—look out!'

The fishing boat was veering again. Le Grand Duc and Ferenc rushed to the cockpit and loosed off several shots. The windows in the wheel-house of the fishing boat starred and broke, but Bowman and Pierre had already dropped to the deck which Le Grand Duc and Ferenc had to do at almost exactly the same moment as the heavy oaken stem of the fishing boat crashed into the port quarter at precisely the spot where they were standing.

Five times inside the next two minutes the manœuvre was repeated, five times the power-boat shuddered under the crushing assaults. By now, at Le Grand Duc's orders, all firing had ceased: ammunition was almost exhausted.

'We must keep the last bullets for when and where they will do the most good.' Le Grand Duc had become very calm. 'Next time—'

'The *Canton* is leaving!' Searl shouted. 'Look, she has turned away.'

They looked. The *Canton* was indeed turning away, beginning to move with increasing speed through the water.

'What else did you expect?' Le Grand Duc asked. 'Never fear, we shall see her again.'

'What do you mean?' Czerda demanded.

'Later. As I was saying—'

'We're sinking!' Searl's voice was almost a scream. 'We're

sinking!' He was in no way exaggerating: the power-boat was now deep in the water, the sea pouring in through gaps torn in the hull by the bows of the fishing boat.

'I am aware of that,' Le Grand Duc said. He turned to Czerda. 'They're coming again. Hard a starboard—to your right, quickly. Ferenc, Searl, El Brocador, come with me.'

'My shoulder,' Searl wailed.

'Never mind your shoulder. Come with me.'

The four men stood just inside the doorway of the cabin as the fishing boat came at them again. But this time the power-boat, though sluggish and far from responsive because of its depth in the water, had succeeded in turning away enough to reduce the impact to the extent that the two boats merely grazed each other. As the wheel-house of the fishing boat passed by the cabin of the power-boat, Le Grand Duc and his three men rushed out into the cockpit. Le Grand Duc waited his moment then, with that speed and agility so surprising in a man of his bulk, stood on the gunwale and flung himself on to the poop of the fishing boat. Within two seconds the others had followed.

Ten seconds after that Bowman turned round sharply as the port door of the wheel-house opened abruptly and Ferenc and Searl stood framed there, both with guns in their hands.

'No.' Bowman spun again to locate the voice behind him. He hadn't far to look. The guns of Le Grand Duc and El Brocador were less than a foot from his face. Le Grand Duc said: 'Enough is enough?'

Bowman nodded. 'Enough is enough.'

CHAPTER TEN

Fifteen minutes later, with the first shades of evening beginning to fall, the fishing boat, a curiously unperturbed Pierre des Jardins at the wheel, moved placidly up the Canal du Rhône à Sète. The three scientists and their womenfolk, the last of whom had been hauled aboard only seconds before the power-boat had sunk, were seated on the foredeck under the concealed guns of the gypsies, for all the world like vacation trippers enjoying a leisurely cruise in the warm summer evening. All the glass had been knocked out from the broken windows and the few bullet holes in the woodwork of the wheel-house were discreetly camouflaged by El Brocador and Masaine, who were leaning negligently against the starboard side of the structure. Pierre apart, the only two other occupants of the wheel-house were Bowman and Le Grand Duc, the latter with a gun in his hand.

A few kilometres up the canal they passed by the tractor and trailer that had so abruptly left the road when the shooting contest between the Rolls and the power-boat had begun. The tractor was as it had been, a front wheel still over-hanging the canal: clearly and understandably, the driver had deemed it wiser to wait for assistance rather than risk a watery grave for his tractor by trying to extricate it under its own power. The driver, oddly enough, was still there, pacing up and down with a legitimately thunderous look on his face.

Czerda joined the three men in the wheel-house. He said worriedly: 'I do not like it, I do not like it at all. It is much too quiet. Perhaps we are going to some kind of trap. Surely some person—'

'Does that make you feel happier?' Le Grand Duc pointed in the direction of Aigues-Mortes: two black police cars, sirens wailing and blue lights flashing, were approaching at high speed. 'Something tells me that our friend the tractor driver has been complaining to someone.'

Le Grand Duc's guess proved to be correct. The police cars swept by and almost at once started slowing as the tractor driver stood in the middle of the road and frantically waved his arms. They stopped and uniformed figures jumped out of the car and surrounded the gesticulating tractor driver who was obviously retelling his story with a great deal of verve and gusto.

'Well, if the police are bothering somebody else, they can't very well be bothering us at the same time,' Le Grand Duc observed philosophically. 'Happier now, Czerda?'

'No,' Czerda said and looked as if he meant it. 'Two things. Dozens of people, hundreds for all I know, must have seen what was happening out in the gulf. Why did no one stop us on the way in? Why did no one report what was happening to the police?'

'Quite frankly, I don't know,' Le Grand Duc said thoughtfully. 'I can guess, though. Same thing happens time and again—when large numbers of people see something happening they invariably leave it to someone else to do something about it. Why, there have been cases of pedestrians watching a man being beaten to death in the street and not lifting a hand to help. Mankind is curiously apathetic about that sort of thing. Maybe it's a natural reluctance to step into the limelight. I do not profess to know. All that matters is that we came up the harbour without causing an eyebrow to be lifted. Your other question? You had two?'

'Yes.' Czerda was grim. 'What in God's name are we going to do now?'

'That is no problem.' Le Grand Duc smiled. 'Did I not tell you that we would see the good ship *Canton* again?'

'Yes, but how—'

'How long will it take us to drive to Port le Bouc?'

'Port le Bouc?' Czerda furrowed his brow. 'With the caravan and truck?'

'How else?'

'Two and a half hours. Not more than three. Why?'

'Because that's where the *Canton* has instructions to await us if any difficulty arose at the Palavas rendezvous. It will remain there until noon tomorrow—and we will be there tonight. Don't you know by now, Czerda, that I always have another string to my bow? Many strings, in fact. And there, tonight, the scientists and their women will be taken aboard. So will Bowman. And so, to eliminate any possibility of risk whatsoever, will the two young ladies and, I'm afraid, this unfortunate fisherman here.' Pierre des Jardins glanced at Le Grand Duc, lifted an eyebrow, then concentrated on his task again: it was a minuscule reaction for a man listening to what was virtually a death sentence. 'And then, Czerda, you and your men will be as free as the air for when Bowman and his three friends arrive in China they will simply disappear and never be heard of again. The only witnesses against you will be gone for ever and no breath of suspicion will ever attach itself to you or your men on either side of the Iron Curtain.'

'If I have ever questioned you in the past, I apologize.' Czerda spoke slowly, almost reverently. 'This is genius.' He looked as a man might look after the Forth Bridge had been lifted off his back.

'Elementary, elementary.' Le Grand Duc waved a disparaging hand. 'Now, then. We shall be in sight of the jetty shortly and we don't want to give the young ladies any shocks to their delicate nervous systems, the kind of shock, for instance, that might prompt them to drive away at speed with the truck and caravan before we even reach the jetty. Everybody into the fish-hold now and to keep out of sight till the word is given. You and I will remain here —seated, of course—while Bowman takes the vessel alongside. Understood?'

'Understood.' Czerda looked at him admiringly. 'You think of everything!'

'I try,' Le Grand Duc said modestly. 'I try.'

The three girls with a youngster seated on a scooter were at the head of the jetty as Bowman, apparently alone, brought the boat alongside. They ran down, secured the ropes he threw them and jumped aboard. Cecile and Lila were half-smiling, half-apprehensive, wondering what news he bore: Carita remained in the background, aloof and rather remote.

'Well?' Cecile demanded. 'Well, tell us. What happened?'

'I'm sorry,' Bowman said. 'Things have gone wrong.'

'Not for us,' Le Grand Duc said jovially. He stood up, gun in hand, accompanied by Czerda, similarly equipped, and beamed at the girls. 'Not really, I must say. How nice to see you again, my dear Carita. Had a pleasant time with the two young ladies?'

'No,' Carita said shortly. 'They wouldn't speak to me.'

'Prejudice, sheer prejudice. Right, Czerda, everyone on deck and in the caravan inside a minute.' He looked towards the head of the jetty. 'And who is that youth with the scooter?'

'That's José!' Czerda was as near a mood of excited anticipation as it would ever be possible for him to achieve. 'The boy I sent to get the money that Bowman stole from me—from us, I mean.' He stepped out on deck and waved an arm. 'José! José!'

José swung his leg over the scooter, came down the jetty and jumped aboard. He was a tall thin youth with an enormous shock of black hair, beady eyes and a prematurely knowing expression.

'The money?' Czerda asked. 'You have the money?'

'What money?'

'Of course, of course. To you, only a brown paper parcel.' Czerda smiled indulgently. 'But it was the right key?'

'I don't know.' José's mental processes quite evidently knew nothing about the intelligent expression on his face.

'What do you mean, you don't know?'

'I don't know whether it was the right key or the wrong key,' José explained patiently. 'All I know is that there are no safe-deposit boxes in the railway station in Arles.'

There was a fairly lengthy silence during which a number of thoughts, none of them particularly pleasant, passed through the minds of several of those present, then Bowman cleared his throat and said apologetically: 'I'm afraid this is all rather my fault. That was the key to my suitcase.'

There was another silence, more or less of the same length, then Le Grand Duc said with immense restraint: 'The key to your suitcase. I would have expected nothing else. Where are the eighty thousand francs, Mr Bowman?'

'Seventy thousand. I'm afraid I had to deduct a little of it. Current expenses, you know.' He nodded to Cecile. 'That dress alone cost me—'

'Where are they?' Le Grand Duc shouted. He was through with restraint for the day. 'The seventy thousand francs?'

'Ah yes. Well, now.' Bowman shook his head. 'There's so much happened since last night—'

'Czerda!' Le Grand Duc was back on balance again but it was a close thing. 'Put your pistol to Miss Dubois's head. I shall count three.'

'Don't bother,' Bowman said. 'I left it in the Les Baux caves. By Alexandre.'

'*By* Alexandre?'

'I'm not an idiot,' Bowman said tiredly. 'I knew the police might be there this morning. Rather, would be there and might find Alexandre. But it's close by.'

Le Grand Duc gave him a long, thoughtful stare then turned to Czerda. 'This would be only a minor detour on our way to Port le Bouc?'

'Another twenty minutes. No more.' He nodded towards Bowman. 'The canal here is deep. Do we need him along, sir?'

'Only,' Le Grand Duc said ominously, 'until we discover whether he's telling the truth or not.'

Night had fallen when Czerda pulled up in the lay-by at the head of the Valley of Hell. Le Grand Duc, who, along with El Brocador, had been Czerda's passenger in the front of the towing truck, got out, stretched himself and said: 'The ladies we will leave here. Masaine will stay behind to guard them. All the others will come with us.'

Czerda looked his puzzlement. 'We require so many?'

'I have my purpose.' Le Grand Duc was at his most enigmatic. 'Do you question my judgment?'

'Now? Never!'

'Very well, then.'

Moments later a large group of people were moving through the terrifying vastness of the tomb-like caverns. There were eleven of them in all—Czerda, Ferenc, Searl, El Brocador, the three scientists, the two girls, Bowman and Le Grand Duc. Several carried torches, their beams reflecting weirdly, whitely, off the great limestone walls. Czerda led the way, briskly, confidently, until he came to a cavern where a broken landfall led up to the vague outline of a starlit sky above. He advanced to the jumbled base of the landfall and stopped.

'This is the place,' he said.

Le Grand Duc probed with his torch. 'You are sure?'

'I am certain.' Czerda directed his torch towards a mound of stones and rubble. 'Incredible, is it not? Those idiots of police haven't even found him yet!'

Le Grand Duc directed his own torch at the mound. 'You mean—'

'Alexandre. This is where we buried him.'

'Alexandre is of no concern any more.' Le Grand Duc turned to Bowman. 'The money, if you please.'

'Ah, yes. The money.' Bowman shrugged and smiled. This is the end of the road, I'm afraid. There is no money.'

'What!' Le Grand Duc advanced and thrust the barrel of his gun into Bowman's ribs. 'No money?'

'It's there, all right. In a bank. In Arles.'

'You fooled us?' Czerda said incredulously. 'You brought us all this way—'

'Yes.'

'You bought your life for two hours?'

'For a man under sentence of death two hours can be a very long time.' Bowman smiled, looked at Cecile, then turned back to Czerda. 'But also a very short time.'

'You bought your life for two hours!' Czerda seemed more astonished at this fact than he was concerned by the loss of the money.

'Put it that way.'

Czerda brought up his gun. Le Grand Duc stepped forward, seized Czerda's wrist and pressed his gun-hand down. He said in a low, harsh, bitter voice: 'My privilege.'

'Sir.'

Le Grand Duc pointed his gun at Bowman, then jerked it to the right. For a moment Bowman seemed to hesitate, then shrugged. They moved away together, Le Grand Duc's gun close to Bowman's back, round a right-angled corner into another cavern. After a few moments the sound of a shot reverberated through the caverns, its echoes followed by the thud as of a falling body. The scientists looked stunned, a complete and final despair written in their faces. Czerda and his three companions looked at one another in grim satisfaction. Cecile and Lila clung to each other, both, in the reflected wash of torchlight, ashen-faced and in tears. Then all heard the measured tread of returning footsteps and stared at the right-angled corner where the two men had disappeared.

Le Grand Duc and Bowman came into view at the same instant. Both of them carried guns, rock-steady in their hands.

'Don't,' Bowman said.

Le Grand Duc nodded. 'As my friend observes, please, please, don't.'

But after a moment of total disbelief, Ferenc and Searl did. There were two sharp reports, two screams and the sound, sharply metallic, of two guns striking the limestone floor. Ferenc and Searl stood in stupefied agony, clutching shattered shoulders. The second time, Bowman reflected, that Searl had been wounded in that shoulder but he could bring himself to feel no pity for he knew now that it had been Searl who had used the whip to flay the skin from Tina's back.

Bowman said: 'Some people take a long time to learn.'

'Incorrect, Neil. Some people never learn.' Le Grand Duc looked at Czerda, the expression on his face indicating that he would have preferred to be looking elsewhere. 'We had nothing against you, from a judicial point of view, that is. Not a shred of proof, not a shred of evidence. Not until you, personally and alone, led us to Alexandre's grave and admitted to the fact that you had buried him. In front of all those witnesses. Now you know why Mr Bowman bought his life for two hours.' He turned to Bowman. 'Incidentally, where is the money, Neil?'

'In Cecile's handbag. I just kind of put it there.'

The two girls advanced, slowly, uncertainly. There were no longer any signs of tears but they were totally uncomprehending. Bowman pocketed his gun, went to them and put his arms round the shoulders of both.

'It's all right, now,' he said. 'It's all over, it really is.' He lifted his hand from Lila's shoulders, pressed her cheek with his fingertips till she turned to look at him in dazed enquiry. He smiled. 'The Duc de Croytor is indeed the Duc de Croytor. My boss, these many years.'

EPILOGUE

Beneath the frowning cliffs of Les Baux, the Baumanière slept peacefully in the light of a yellow moon. Bowman, sitting on a chair and sipping a drink, lifted an eyebrow as Cecile emerged from a room, tripped and almost fell over an extension cord. She recovered herself and sat beside him.

'Twenty-four hours,' she said. 'Only twenty-four hours. I just can't believe it.'

'You want to get yourself a pair of spectacles,' Bowman observed.

'I have a pair of spectacles, thank you.'

'Then you want to wear them.' Bowman put a kindly hand on hers. 'After all, you've got your man now.'

'Oh, do be quiet.' She made no attempt to remove her hand. 'How's that young girl?'

'Tina's in hospital, in Arles. She'll be around in a couple of days. Her father and Madame Zigair are there with her now. The Hobenauts and Tangevecs are having dinner inside. Not a very festive occasion, I should imagine, but I would say they must be experiencing a certain sense of relief, wouldn't you? And Pierre des Jardins, by this time, must be home in Le Grau du Roi.'

'I can't believe it.' Bowman peered at her, then realized that she had been only half listening to him and was now on another topic altogether. 'He—he's your boss?'

'Charles? He is indeed. Nobody believes anything about Charles. I'm ex-Army Intelligence, ex-military attaché in Paris. I've got another job now.'

'I'll bet you have,' she said feelingly.

'The only other person who knows anything about this is Pierre, the fishing-boat skipper. That's why he maintained such a marvellous sang-froid. He's sworn to secrecy. So are you.'

'I don't know if I like that.'

'You'll do what you're told. Charles, I can assure you, is much higher up the pecking order than I am. We've been together for eight years. For the last two years we've known that Iron Curtain gypsies have been smuggling things across the frontier. What, we didn't know. This time, of all people, the Russians tipped us off—but even they didn't know what was really happening.'

'But this Gaiuse Strome—'

'Our Chinese pal in Arles and elsewhere? Temporarily held by the French police. He was getting too close to things and Charles had him copped on a technicality. They'll have to let him go. Diplomatic immunity. He arranged it all—he's the Chinese military attaché in Tirhana.'

'Tirhana?'

'Albania.'

She reached into her handbag, brought out her glasses, looked at him closely and said: 'But we were told—'

'We?'

'Lila and myself, we're secretaries in the Admiralty. To keep an eye on you. We were told that one of you was under suspicion—'

'I'm sorry. Charles and I arranged that. There we were, a goodie and a baddie. We could never be seen together. We had to have a channel of communication. Girl-friends chatter. Girls get on the phone to their bosses back home. We had the channel.'

'You fixed all this?' She withdrew her hand. 'You knew—'

'I'm sorry. We had to do it.'

'You mean—'

'Yes.'

'Strawberry birthmark—'

'Sorry again.' Bowman shook his head admiringly. 'But I must say it was the most complete dossier I've ever seen.'

'I despise you! I detest you! You're the most utterly contemptible—'

'Yes, I know, and I'm not worried. What does worry me is that so far we've only managed to fix up two bridesmaids and I said—'

'Two,' she said firmly, 'will be quite enough.'

Bowman smiled, rose, offered her his hand and together they walked arm in arm to the balustrade and looked down. Almost directly beneath them were the Duc de Croytor and

Lila, seated at, inevitably, a loaded table. It was apparen that Le Grand Duc was under a very considerable emotiona strain for despite the fact that he held a paper-sheathed le of lamb in his hand he was not eating.

'Good God!' he was saying. 'Good God!' He peered a his blonde companion's lovely face from a distance of abou six inches. 'I turn pale at the very thought. I might hav lost you for ever. I never knew!'

'Charles!'

'You *are* a Cordon Bleu cook?'

'Yes, Charles.'

'Brochettes de queues de langoustines au beurre blanc?'

'Yes, Charles.'

'Poulet de la ferme au champagne?'

'Yes, Charles.'

'Filets de sole Retival?'

'But of course.'

'Pintadeau aux morilles?'

'My speciality.'

'Lila. I love you. Marry me!'

'Oh, Charles!'

They embraced in front of the astonished eyes of th other guests. Symbolically, perhaps, Le Grand Duc's le of lamb fell to the floor.

Still arm in arm, Bowman led Cecile down to the patio Bowman said: 'Don't be fooled by Romeo down there. H doesn't give a damn about the cuisine. Not where you friend is concerned.'

'The big bold baron is a little shy boy inside?'

Bowman nodded. 'The making of old-fashioned proposal is not exactly his forte.'

'Whereas it is yours?'

Bowman ushered her to a table and ordered drinks. ' don't quite understand.'

'A girl likes to be asked to marry,' she said.

'Ah! Cecile Dubois, will you marry me?'

'I may as well, I suppose.'

'Touché!' He lifted his glass. 'To Cecile.'

'Thank you, kind sir.'

'Not you. Our second-born.'

They smiled at each other, then turned to look at th

couple at the next table. Le Grand Duc and Lila were still gazing rapturously into each other's eyes, but Le Grand Duc, nevertheless, was back on balance again. Imperiously, he clapped his hands together.

'Encore!' said Le Grand Duc.

Alistair MacLean

His first book, *HMS Ulysses*, published in 1955, was outstandingly successful. It led the way to a string of best-selling novels which have established Alistair MacLean as the most popular thriller writer of our time.

Caravan to Vaccarès *30p*

Puppet on a Chain *30p*

Force 10 from Navarone *30p*

The Guns of Navarone *30p*

Where Eagles Dare *30p*

South by Java Head *30p*

Ice Station Zebra *30p*

Fear is the Key *30p*

The Satan Bug *30p*

The Golden Rendezvous *30p*

When Eight Bells Toll *30p*

HMS Ulysses *30p*

The Last Frontier *30p*

The Dark Crusader *30p*

Fontana Books

James Jones

The Ice-Cream Headache *30p*
A collection of thirteen powerful stories by this best-selling author. 'Each story is perfectly constructed and rich in overtones.' *Times Educational Supplement*

Go to the Widow-Maker *60p*
A superb novel which dramatises a breed of men of action who are slowly being killed by twenty years of peace. In Jones's world of dangerous living, love is for men—women are for sex. 'Jones is the Hemingway of our time . . . There is savage poetry in his descriptions of spear-fishing and treasure-hunting.' *Spectator*

The Thin Red Line *40p*
His novel of the Marines on Guadalcanal—a gory, appallingly accurate description of men at war. 'Raw, violent, powerful and terrible, the most convincing account of battle experience I have ever read.' *Richard Lister, Evening Standard*

From Here to Eternity *60p*
The world famous novel of the men of the U.S. Army stationed at Pearl Harbour in the months immediately before America's entry into World War II. 'One reads every page persuaded that it is a remarkable, a *very* remarkable book indeed.' *Listener*

Fontana Books

Fontana Books

Fontana is best known as one of the leading paperback publishers of popular fiction and non-fiction. It also includes an outstanding, and expanding section of books on history, natural history, religion and social sciences.

Most of the fiction authors need no introduction. They include Agatha Christie, Hammond Innes, Alistair MacLean, Catherine Gaskin, Victoria Holt and Lucy Walker. Desmond Bagley and Maureen Peters are among the relative newcomers.

The non-fiction list features a superb collection of animal books by such favourites as Gerald Durrell and Joy Adamson.

All Fontana books are available at your bookshop or newsagent; or can be ordered direct. Just fill in the form below and list the titles you want.

FONTANA BOOKS, Cash Sales Department, P.O. Box 4, Godalming, Surrey. Please send purchase price plus 5p postage per book by cheque, postal or money order. No currency.

NAME (Block letters) ______________________

ADDRESS ______________________

____

____

While every effort is made to keep prices low, it is sometimes necessary to increase prices at short notice. Fontana Books reserve the right to show new retail prices on covers which may differ from those previously advertised in the text or elsewhere.